# SONGS OF LOVE ON A DECEMBER NIGHT

## ALSO BY DAVID ADAMS RICHARDS

FICTION

*The Coming of Winter*

*Blood Ties*

*Dancers at Night: Stories*

*Lives of Short Duration*

*Road to the Stilt House*

*Nights Below Station Street*

*Evening Snow Will Bring Such Peace*

*For Those Who Hunt the Wounded Down*

*Hope in the Desperate Hour*

*The Bay of Love and Sorrows*

*Mercy Among the Children*

*River of the Brokenhearted*

*The Christmas Tree: Two Tales for the Holidays*

*The Friends of Meager Fortune*

*The Lost Highway*

*Incidents in the Life of Markus Paul*

*Crimes Against My Brother*

*Principles to Live By*

*Mary Cyr*

*Darkness*

*The Tragedy of Eva Mott*

NONFICTION

*Hockey Dreams*

*Lines on the Water*

*Lord Beaverbrook*

*God Is.*

*Facing the Hunter*

*A Lad from Bradford & Other Essays*

*Murder and Other Essays*

POETRY

*Wild Green Light* (with Margo Wheaton)

*Small Heroics*

*A Fierce and Tumultuous Joy*

# SONGS OF LOVE ON A DECEMBER NIGHT

A NOVEL

DAVID ADAMS RICHARDS

DOUBLEDAY CANADA

PUBLISHED IN 2025 BY DOUBLEDAY CANADA



Doubleday Canada, an imprint of Penguin Random House Canada Limited
320 Front Street West, Suite 1400
Toronto, Ontario, M5V 3B6, Canada
penguinrandomhouse.ca



The authorized representative in the EU for product safety and compliance is
Penguin Random House Ireland, Morrison Chambers, 32 Nassau Street
Dublin, D02 YH68, Ireland, https://eu-contact.penguin.ie



Library and Archives Canada Cataloguing in Publication
Title: Songs of love on a December night / David Adams Richards.
Names: Richards, David Adams, author
Identifiers: Canadiana (print) 2025015384X | Canadiana (ebook) 20250153858 |
ISBN 9780385699211 (hardcover) | ISBN 9780385699228 (EPUB)
Subjects: LCGFT: Novels.
Classification: LCC PS8585.I17 S66 2025 | DDC C813/.54—dc23

Cover design by Andrew Roberts
Cover image: metelevan / Adobe Stock
Typeset by Terra Page

Printed in Canada

2 4 6 8 9 7 5 3

Penguin Random House
DOUBLEDAY CANADA

*For Lynn Henry, my friend*

"I can calculate the movement of the stars, but not the madness of men."

—SIR ISAAC NEWTON

"In all the world, people are only frightened of one thing, Weaver."

"And what is that, Pruty?" he had asked.

"Why, Weaver—don't you know? Of not loving enough."

THE SKY HAD DARKENED, AND THE HIGHWAY HAD intermittent sounds of traffic. The yard looked warm in the evening light. Against the sky, swallows flew. Gertie had noticed them when she came home. The traffic light flickered yellow against the evening. Then the rain pattered down against the veranda and the adolescent leaves of the elms.

Gertie was living in town but taking care of her father and sister, visiting the old house twenty-nine miles away four or five times a week. Her fiancé had been taken to jail, a few months before. She had been preparing for their wedding when he was arrested.

Two police officers had come to the door. Cappy Manse was one—a boy they knew who had gone to high school with them. She noticed a certain look of pleasure. It was as if he was saying: *Now I'm in charge.*

But the other officer spoke quite solemnly. "Mr. James Musselman—we are arresting you for the murder of your father."

His father had been killed six years before.

If he was not the son of a colonel, and the Colonel the son of a captain, and the captain the son of a First World War brigadier, would it have happened? His father had been not only a colonel but also a medical man—a doctor in Bosnia, and other horrendous places, where he had served not only servicemen and -women but civilians under fire.

Gertie believed Jamie did not do it. But she had no knowledge of how to prove it one way or the other.

HER FIANCÉ HAD A BRIGHT START IN LIFE. HIS FAMILY had money—and more than that, for she understood from what he had told her that many people had money. But his family were the Musselmans; his father was Colonel Musselman, and he was James Musselman. His father had been associated with many people. These associations allowed them a peculiar place here, one that overcame lack. That is, he might not have been among the richest, but he had the respect of many who were.

The family had travelled from one military base to another in both Canada and Europe. Conscientious, brave and resourceful, with at times little to show for years of service to their country. Jamie's father became a doctor, a medic in the field, volunteering once to take sick men across a contested ground between Serb and Croatian forces in a truck under fire. His father had treated many suffering from PTSD and perhaps, though he didn't say it, suffered from it himself. Colonel Musselman was not the same after Bosnia.

Jamie Musselman had never known a home for many years. And when he did know this home, a great house in the middle of town, there was a sharpness to the effect of it—its polish, its uniforms in the closet hanging under plastic on thick hangers, the white gloves in black dresser drawers, the sword lying in its sheath on velvet. It gave young Musselman the idea that he was a boy apart from others here. Or a part of those who came out of the woodwork at certain times.

He was the boy who knew his father kept a pistol in a locked drawer, and when young Musselman walked down spacious hallways, there were pictures of former family members in uniform as well, hung in out-of-the-way places. Going back to the Boer War, a Corporal Musselman, who may have been twenty years old at the time, sent off to an Africa he never came back from, and leaving a woman of nineteen with a child at home. A few pictures of horses, and a few of strange, uniformed men.

Then there was the other side of the family, notable as well for the blackened leather reins of shiny black Belgian horses, the huge iron mouth bits and the heavy shoes, the grand sleighs that carried the axe-blazoned tons of wood. There was that side, too—indomitable spirits of lumber and trade, who could put down their axes and pick up bayonets when needed.

Still, all of it had petered out with time, because time changes all. Canada became insipid, a country hollowed out by intellectual conceit and sanctimonious self-reflection. Canada wanted to be dissolved, it just didn't know how to do it without losing itself—a strange condition of trying to disappear without becoming invisible. But to the rest of the world, in many respects, it was.

The family changed with the times. The men grew old and died, their sons travelled, the women married, divorced, had troubles as well, and disappeared into the years, their dresses, hats and perfumes faded and retreating on forgotten trips in disappearing trains. One in Austria in the Second World War was said to have come out of a house with a small paring knife and attacked a soldier, was wounded and then hanged. Her picture was in his house too, a small picture in the corner of one of the upstairs rooms, a woman wearing a dark coat and small grey hat, standing on some forgotten street, looking with large eyes at the camera.

"Aunt Lydia," Jamie Musselman told her once.

The Maritimes too, that place where the family amassed their fortunes, became less and less significant to the wide world, and petered down to a small, forgotten part of our country.

They had been in the grand new house a year before Jamie's father's death. It all happened suddenly, spectacularly. His father died in his office from a bullet wound.

Jamie was a child who had already lost his mother some years ago. She was buried in Ontario—where they had lived before—in a cemetery in Hamilton. There was a bearing of duty about young Musselman; a responsibility or obligation to make up for something. Perhaps for this loss of his mother when he was nine years old.

He was seen with a wheelbarrow in his hand, doing his father's bidding, a few days after his father's death. It seemed he decided to simply carry on. That was so spectacularly sad to Mrs. Winnifred White, who lived across the road in the old Bunny house and said she had looked out the window and saw the boy wheeling a wheelbarrow with topsoil, which his father had been wheeling the week before, his thin legs in new khaki-coloured pants.

At first, he seemed to have no reaction to that death. Perhaps this went against him. One might know how the high school boys could pick up the scent of isolation and come after him, as a murderer of his father. There he is, they seemed to say without saying it, looking at him in a way to elicit fear from him—he being alone and slight, and they, of course, not being alone.

He was not like other army kids in that he had no illusions about his significance simply because he had travelled. He never mentioned his family much at all, this sandy-haired, thin child of a colonel.

There was the confrontation between him and a teacher, when he had first arrived.

"Oh, you've read Euripides, I suppose," the teacher had said, and other children laughed.

"Yes—I've read him," and he looked perplexed that he would have to defend himself in this way to a teacher.

The teacher did not like to be shown up by a mere boy, a newcomer to this place.

"You have? Well, where have you read him? Not in my school, you haven't."

"Yes, Euripides—I've read him in school."

"Where, pray tell?" the teacher asked.

"Greece," the boy said, not catching the significance of the geographical pinpointing of his own remark. The laughter was stifled, but then students looked toward the teacher.

"And what have you read by him?"

"*Iphigenia in Aulis*," he said.

The teacher who had mentioned Euripides by saying, "Oh that we might have the Helicon days of Euripides," had not in fact read Euripides and often mistook him for Socrates. He had not read *Iphigenia in Aulis*, would not know it was about the horror of human sacrifice and would not know that the story of Abraham and Isaac was one to counteract the blush of human sacrifice. But the boy, in some important ways, did. The teacher in his own life would go on, slowly, ponderously, and become saddened by the classroom and how it confined him, by his wife who left him, by his journey in the end, to his own end, in a small house at the edge of a one-way street. So he was very pleased when Cappy Manse laughed at this and said, "You didn't read no stupid book."

That day, Gertie had just come into the classroom, having missed the bus, and her hair was wet from the snow and the room was dark and chalk-scented, in the old Harkins school that is now gone. The teacher, seeing her, said, "Gertie, you're late *once more*, that's what you get for living in the boonies—take your seat!"

(The teacher had wanted the class to laugh at this as well.)

She noticed that boy then. There was a moment, in the half-dark corridor during a snow squall that very day, which had closed up the hallway in darkness with its leftover smell of stale noon hour, where she saw him standing alone and thought, *There's that boy again!*

He was clumsy at making friends. He stood near others so as not to intrude, and when someone looked at him, he would smile quickly, with a faint slice of hope. This came as a blight against him, as the days passed and the feeling of remoteness surrounded him—his dress, his manners, his thin body and hands.

Later came the constant rumours about him and his family. Where had those started? They hung in the air and flourished everywhere and anywhere at all. Among the high school boys, who decided they did not like him, and among the girls, always mimicking some idea or new prevalent philosophy, who decided to scapegoat him. There was a rumour that the wife, his mother, had committed suicide years ago over a captain. The captain tried to kill Colonel Musselman; Musselman escaped and ran as the captain fired a gun. This was not even close to being true, but the boy had heard the rumour about his mother. The source of this rumour was never revealed.

A colonel with his fiduciary complex, his orderly home brandishing its scents of polish and old-world honour. Its medical cabinets hidden, and his medical bag behind the seat in his car. Old-world honour—who would want that anymore? Military brass and a sword laid away on red velvet—who would ever need that? The flashes of memory of Kapyong—who would ever remember that? The other military had seemed to become more pronounced—the gloating, sexist, toxic kind had invaded the thoughts of countrymen. But Colonel Musselman was of a former breed. Or perhaps, if one thought of it, a breed set apart at the outset of military history.

And then, worse, the Colonel said things after his daily ten ounces of Scotch. After his wife died, he for the most part gave up his medical practice. He spoke in restrained measure but with curious force with his Scotch before him. He told the truth about the reserve near him, how money earmarked for education was taken by band members. Yet he did still go down there at night to deliver children.

Then, because of giving up his medical duties, and it seemed most other duties, he decided to resign over some policy that he felt was totally inadequate: the amount of, or lack of, preparedness in our north. Some said he was forced out, but the Colonel had been thinking of retiring for a long while. He was frustrated by the military, by so many brave men and women that he had treated over the years who had so little support.

Colonel Musselman kept a pistol he owned and some few hundred dollars that he was saving for his son in his desk. The idea between them was that for every twenty dollars his son saved toward a second-hand car, his father would put a hundred in the drawer. His father would of course make up the difference when his son graduated. (The father never really intended to obligate his son to honour this unwritten agreement, but his son did—taking jobs mowing lawns.) This was something the Colonel wanted to do for his son since the boy's mother had died, before they had moved here and the boy was left solitary.

The mother had had a friend, a captain, suffering from PTSD, who had been tortured in Bosnia, who came over to sit with her. Colonel Musselman was treating him and was his friend.

Who comforted whom, one may ask, on those long-ago days?

The captain would read to her while she lay out in the porch on late summer days, with the leaves rustling in the trees. He would read poems to her, and he read in his quiet voice stories of O. Henry and Guy de Maupassant. Then he turned to more religious leanings after a time, C.S. Lewis's work *On Joy*. That joy would be, and must be, everlasting—oh joy would be and must be everlasting. C.S. Lewis's book on the Psalms.

There in that house, she may have fallen a little in love with that voice of his without falling in love with him. That does so happen at times, in the light from a lamp and the sound of rain.

Mrs. Musselman died in the captain's arms, suddenly, unexpectedly, while he was reading to her from the book of Proverbs. The captain later committed suicide, another casualty of the hidden sickness that had infected our troops.

That was where the rumour started.

The Colonel moved with his son back to New Brunswick, and then, after a few years, retired. Except for emergency calls, he put his medical bag aside.

As for the son: "*The apple doesn't fall far from the tree—and anyway, he's not a real Miramichier.*"

The house was large and silent, and he, Jamie the boy, was seen alone on the veranda, and it seemed as if he was a castaway.

So, before she had ever known him, Gertie thought that a person like him was as out of the ordinary as his family was. He was friendless and perhaps already heartbroken. Of course, the

Maritimes, as Nowlan said, was a country of soldiers. And many of those were the children of the lost.

Then, suddenly, amid quasi-intellectual debates and Jamie working on an experiment about the polar ice cap, it came: His father died of a gunshot. At first the idea of suicide was all the talk. So this talk bled across the avenues and down the streets on the May afternoon. It dashed itself against the sunlit new paint of Mrs. Winnifred White's house, as if that too had something to do with it all. It caught one, in a momentary gesture of surprise: that large house at the bottom of a prosperous street.

And then the idea of a death in the *study*. It seemed a well-worn room, with a desk and important books. That is how many thought of it initially. That he died of self-inflicted wounds in his study, perhaps over the death of his wife.

The entire house seemed an object of death. And people empathized without knowing whom they were sorry for.

The police arrived and a yellow tape was placed round the extremities of the whole great house. People drove by that house late into the night, long after twilight ended and the stars were out in the sky. People stood on the sidewalk across the street, some taking pictures.

It was a warm night, and people were still across the street watching when the police took the boy first to the hospital and then, a day later, downtown for questioning at the small station.

So then, after a day or so, another rumour came.

The second rumour said the son had done it for money. The son had been shot in the left leg. He said it had happened when he had picked up the gun, and it went off. Money had been found under his pillow. So it all seemed to *fit*.

He had sandy blond hair. The sandy blond hair, looking so much like his dad, seemed to prove it. As if the same genetical makeup had caused the moment of hatred.

*What had gone on in that house?*

The sweet smell of the spring evening carried the saccharine smell of death, and filled one with a strange fullness, like flowers and the smell of paint; and then a dreadful edge to it—the slight frame of the son, with his khaki pants and brown belt, his eyes large and remote.

Mrs. White came over to the house with a small New Testament, and Jamie walked to school with it in his pocket. It was peculiar to see him eat his lone peanut butter sandwich, made by the maid, the first day he came back to school. He sat alone along the corridor wall, at the farther end of the hall, beyond the water fountain. The entire school was laden with a rather happy, exquisite possibility: Jamie had murdered his own father.

Some said he was of a cruel nature, disposed to killing robins for pleasure, that they had seen. At least, some boys had seen a dead robin at the bottom of a nest.

"Too bright by half," students said.

It was strange to see him, notice the small, transparent hairs on his small white arms, with the dark-coloured birthmark on his right forearm. And then, of course, the wounded leg—as he had struggled for the gun. "The sign," one girl, unwholesomely flaccid, who wore black eyeshadow and who suddenly admitted that she conducted many seances, said.

Most of the time Jamie was ignored. But then he was interrogated in the washroom by Cappy Manse and a few others.

"Why did you kill your father?" Cappy had asked him, out of the blue.

"Couldn't get nothin outta him!" Cappy Manse said, sniffing. "But did a good job twisting his finger back."

For the next month, Cappy made good and sure his victim knew he was there.

GERTIE'S OWN MOTHER, BEDRIDDEN FOR MONTHS IN that small house, died about the very time this was beginning. And Shamus took over the rearing of the young slip of a child and her twin sister. Gertie went to work as soon as she was old enough, on cold, dark nights in town, where Shamus followed her in his one pair of leather shoes, asking for money from his "best daughter."

"A real sweetheart—a noble little thing."

Her look when he first entered the door to ask for money was the look of someone who had naively mistaken her travel into town for an escape. But she could not, nor would she ever want to, escape her sister, Pruty. Besides, she was still in school and only a salesgirl at the store. Her hope of escaping her father, whom she always loved, was in fact delusional. She could never escape one and still be available to aid the other.

She was told just after she started working that Jamie Musselman wanted to jump off the Chatham Bridge. That he had yelled at his teacher.

"What had he yelled?"

"A very bad word. And he has only his old maid to care for him now."

The maid stayed in the house and took care of him. It was her obligation, suffering as she was from high blood pressure and insomnia and pains in her left foot. Yet she had cared for the boy before this, and she would care for him now.

"That is sad," Gertie said.

His face was so beautiful, but he did walk with a limp after the gunshot had permanently damaged muscles in his leg—and his swollen face came from one of the fist fights he, a Newcastle boy, had gotten into in Chatham.

Time took care of the travels to Chatham and the fights there, but time didn't heal the pain. The innuendos and suppositions had caused a crisis in the Musselman family in Nova Scotia, and the boy was taken away.

He was taken by his uncle to Halifax. Though people here had ideas about him, and spoke about him, nothing could really be proven. He was in the upstairs room, had heard a shot and gone into the room, picked the weapon up and was so distraught the gun had misfired into his leg. That was *his* explanation. But how flimsy a branch to hang on, people said. It was rumoured that police had found two hundred dollars under his pillow, in the room at the back of the large old home. The money, he said, he was saving for a second-hand car. The drawer of his father's desk was opened, and money was missing from there.

There was a certain agitation within the local police to charge him, and it hung in the air like a translucent spider's web. But they did not charge him yet.

Gertie was aware there were many things that precipitated the move to Halifax.

The girl Marsha, who did seances, said that he had confessed to her near the stone wall by the railway track, where there was an opening within a wall where students went to smoke. The police heard about her statement. So she was brought forward and questioned and said she knew many things that happened in the town.

She began to tell of things that happened; she said she knew more than the police. She said the boy had confided in her. She said she and the boy had a pact and this pact would last forever. That it was a pact between their very souls. She was a heavy-set young lady with dark eyeshadow and black lipstick. Her hair, black and straight, fell to below her shoulders.

This made it all seem plausible to some—that she knew something that she might someday reveal.

"Oh yes," she said, almost in a mystic state, "I know—so much more—I know." And her lips betrayed a certain smile of self-infatuation.

She told people that she and Jamie held seances and went for long walks in the woods and ate mushrooms and danced naked. She said that they spoke to long-dead First Nation men and women and had left each other special messages under rocks that only they knew about.

She looked serene as she spoke, and her voice drifted off as if she was in some sort of ecstasy or trance.

So started the terrible rumour at school of the pact between them. She said he told her he had stolen the money because he wanted to run away and have a coven, or some other such thing. That they always wore black and said a black mass on two occasions—and that priests were full of baloney.

So everyone listened to her, and when she was called to the principal's office, a whole group of young girls followed her down the corridor.

Two said: "We're her friends, we promised not to leave her."

They were young girls in distress—there were always young girls in distress, and it was usually those girls who were never in actual distress.

Marsha sat in the principal's office looking around with a peculiar smile that she was now the centre of attention. She would begin to chant and then stop abruptly, bring out lip chap from her pocket and soothe her lips. Then she looked through her purse and opened a stick of gum. The principal sat behind her desk. The drapes behind her were opened. It was May, but there was a cold rain falling.

"So, Marsha, you say you and Jamie Musselman are friends. Are you friends?"

"Oh yes—he confides in me—like he really and truly does, like not all the time—but like, hey man, you know, on occasion—and he was needing to tell me secrets."

She said the word "secrets" in a delightfully pejorative way.

She looked eagerly at the principal, as if she now had a new confidante and they were friends as well. Her face, in its urgency, seemed to push forward as she spoke.

"His father was even in Yugoslavia—so that's what he told me."

"Yes, his father was in the former Yugoslavia," the principal confirmed.

Marsha smiled as if this piece of information proved what she had been saying. She said the police would be talking to her, and she knew she must tell them all that she knew. It was like a television show about the FBI. This is what she said.

The idea was that they had shared secret messages, and he had written on a rock that he had killed his father, and they had both sworn that they would never tell, and they had a seance.

They then asked Jamie Musselman to come in.

She never retracted a thing when the boy told people it was a fabrication. He did not say lie—he said fabrication, because she was a girl and for some reason there was the semblance in his makeup of old-time chivalry that he had been brought up with—but a *fabrication* in the fact that he didn't even know her.

"So, you did not say that your souls were linked together forever?"

He looked at Marsha and then at the principal. "No—I did not say that."

"Or hide messages under rocks?"

"No, I don't think so?"

"Or have special meetings in the woods where you ate magic mushrooms?"

"No—not at all."

He said it so strangely—almost wondrously—as if he was hearing a strange kind of awful music and was wanting to decipher it.

"So, you didn't say you would meet again at the ends of the earth?"

"Oh no—I don't think I did so." He smiled at the absurdity.

The principal left the office. Marsha kept looking at him with a soft, acrimonious smile on her lips, an imperiousness that made her new-found celebrity shine forth in radiance. (And how many people in our lives do we know like this?)

"Hi Jamie," she said finally.

"Hello," he said.

The principal had phoned the police, and Constable Phyliss Matters arrived.

Phyliss Matters asked her under which rock they had hidden this message with the confession upon it, and if she could direct her to it.

"Oh yes," Marsha said.

And she stood, wearing a black dress and black nylon stockings with black ankle-high shoes, and into the corridor and down the stairs they went—quickly, very quickly, with Jamie being told to stay where he was in the principal's office, and a police constable left on guard in the hallway.

Once outside, Marsha became less certain and more reticent about the direction. But there were rocks at the edge of the football field.

And there Phyliss did ask which rock it might be. Marsha was suddenly uncertain which rock and was also uncertain if the confession was written on a rock or on a note buried beneath the rock.

Constable Phyliss Matters spoke to the young woman for ten minutes and had her retract at least part of the story, though Marsha did so grudgingly.

They walked back together across the grounds toward the brick school, students staring at them from upstairs windows and in the spaces between the two doors, and Constable Matters looked as one does who had caught on to a scam—a lie that seemed to infuse the air itself. In the drizzle of rain, Constable Matters's face looked wan and set, and small white hairs were visible on the underside of her chin.

In the next two days, Matters ordered all the rocks in that tumble of stones to be overturned.

Nothing was found.

So Gertie didn't know what was true, and for a long while she didn't see him after he had been taken away by his uncle to Halifax. Then one afternoon in early spring, almost a year later, with the snow melting and the streets filled with puddles of water clear enough to reflect the buildings that sat above them, she saw him standing outside Lounsbury's alone.

For some reason, though she never so much as spoke to him, she felt she would someday marry him.

In Nova Scotia Jamie stayed out of school and did not graduate. He wanted to graduate where his father and he had lived, he told people.

The maid still came to the house, to dust and make things right—an obligation for a family that had been blemished by scandal, but a family she was still loyal to.

He returned from Nova Scotia the next year and went back to school in order to graduate. He insisted that he do so.

He didn't speak to Gertie or anyone else. Rumblings that the father did not commit suicide but was murdered by the very son who sat two rows across from her in class were unnerving.

Then one day, as Gertie came out of the side door, the wind catching smoke from some chimney and the sky clouded, Jamie, standing near the side of the old elementary school building, said, "Will you come to my party?"

"Your party?"

"Yes, it's my birthday."

He told her it was his birthday but he had no one to invite, and if she might come, he would never forget it.

"I will return the favour," he said.

She did not even know that he knew who she was. A sudden sensation overcame her.

"But I will miss the bus downriver."

"Then I will take you home after. I have"—and here he did sound despairing—"my dad's car. It's a Mercedes, have you ever been in a Mercedes? I guess it's something." And he gave a quick smile once more.

Hesitantly, she walked with him, thinking every tenth step she was doing a very foolish thing. That he might do something horrid to her as well.

They entered the back door of his house. She sat in one of the rooms off the kitchen—she didn't quite remember—and he cut her a piece of chocolate cake, put it on what seemed to her a very expensive plate. And, worse, gave her orange juice to drink with it. (That was the horrid thing.)

"Do I sing 'Happy Birthday'?" she asked.

"No, you don't have to."

"Am I the only one invited to your party?"

"Yes—in the whole school, you are the only one I like," he said.

She was startled—and slightly frightened.

"You don't like anyone else?"

"No, I am not saying that. But what I mean to say is they do not like me, I imagine."

"Happy birthday to you," she whispered. She felt embarrassed. They sat in silence. She tried to fill the gap with conversation, but it did not go well.

And she couldn't help but notice two things about Jamie Musselman: his handsome face and his limp. She was surprised that he was turning seventeen, and she was eighteen.

But she had never in her life been in a house so large, with so many wise and expensive things in it.

After graduation, she took a permanent job at Lounsbury's, and Jamie Musselman was gone for almost a year.

So here it is:

He went away—people said to Europe—and when he returned, he asked her to marry him.

"I have no one," he said, "but if you were my wife, we could live in the house together—we might not even have to leave the house much if we didn't want to."

"What do you mean?"

"I mean I have enough money to stay in the house, and not go out—and you could stay with me—we could expand the pond to make a swimming pool, and there are lots of things I could do to make you happy. And there is one other thing I could do."

"And what is that?"

"I could tell you I didn't murder my father."

(As will be noted further along, Gertie was at this time engaged to an older man, a Mr. Bowels, who owned a store across the park. And that was another reason for hesitation.)

Still, after some time, she and Jamie were engaged, and then he was arrested.

Yet the circumstantial evidence was so great, proof of guilt did not seem to be the overriding factor. It was presided over by judge alone.

The judge took weeks and weeks to finally render his decision. It was written out in forty pages of deliberation and told in minute detail of the boy's actions that day—how he had gone out, had come home, had gone to the study, how money was discovered, how his leg had been wounded in a struggle.

There was no other conclusion the judge could come to.

"It may have been an accidental death—a death caused by misadventure—but I see no reason not to find Jamie Musselman guilty of the crime of manslaughter. Taking his age at the time of the crime, I assess it as a crime by a juvenile and sentence Mr. Musselman to not more than fifty-one months in prison."

No one—not even a judge—acts with impartiality in a case that has brought attention from the nation.

Many said he should have gotten life without parole. Few, a very few, said he might not have been guilty. One of the men who shed tears over it all was Shamus, Gertie's father.

During his trial, two factors persisted: He was angry at his father for the move from Ontario, where his mother was buried, and his father's insistence he go into the military as well. This, in fact, was what Marsha had said, and she attended the trial every day with three friends. People said she would be interviewed by the CBC and perhaps do a book about the whole thing, but that did not happen.

While he was incarcerated, Gertie would keep an eye on Pruty and her father. She would visit the house near Arron Brook. She would wait. She would visit him when she could. The village of Dorchester to her was as pitiable as the penitentiary on the hill; to her its road was bleak, and its houses bleak as well. And she was still barely an adult herself. In fact, she had been given as much a sentence as he.

Gertie's sister, Pruty, was confined to that house off Arron Brook Road, and there she wanted to be. The idea that her whole life had been spent there made her intent to remain. Besides, she knew her way around.

So Gertie visited her sister almost every day. Often bringing something to her—a chocolate bar, candy, often flowers. Orchids, and pink roses.

How she and Jamie met the second time, and came together before his arrest, is another story. A story that should be told in some detail.

—

Money, Gertie had discovered, was not an object for Jamie Musselman. When she mentioned it, Jamie simply shrugged and told her they had enough to do them.

He had known her through high school, but had not spoken to her except when he had invited her to his small, solitary birthday party. Well, once he had said *hello* in a quick, hushed way and disappeared around a corner when there was a grey afternoon and autumn smoke.

People said he had won all the awards in high school, but this in itself had a deleterious effect. At least, this is what Dannielle mentioned at the store.

"Why wouldn't he be winning all the awards—just to cover it all up, h'm?" She said this with a great deal of amusement at Gertie's naïveté. Dannielle, it was assumed, was having an affair with the boss, an overweight man with a moustache, and everyone knew it. But Dannielle did not know that everyone knew it.

Dannielle didn't like show-offs, or arrogant people, which she thought this Musselman was. But she was herself both vain and arrogant.

When Jamie came back after his year in Europe, Gertie was somewhat engaged to Mr. Mickey Bowels, who adored her and her sister, and whom she liked. But Mickey was quite a bit older. He was thirty-three, the local historian; he knew everything about the River—not a thing he didn't know.

Mickey doted on Gertie day and night, stood by the store where she worked after his own small store was closed, and tried to impress her without losing his dignity. He bought her a friendship ring. He had asked her to leave her job and come to work for him the day he had given her the ring—but she had hesitated. First of all, it was mainly a men's clothing store. Secondly, it might compromise what was to come.

She didn't say no, she simply had said, "Not now—perhaps next year," and reached up and kissed his cheek. She knew he couldn't afford to hire her; he already had old Mr. Williams working for him. Oh, it was love, ragged love, blessed love, but did she love him? Or was she waiting for the love that would come through the door and snatch her away?

One night, just two months after Mr. Bowels bought this friendship ring, Jamie Musselman appeared almost out of nowhere and asked her to go to a movie. It was strange, too, to see him *young like she was* (not old, or older like Mickey), his face youthful and his hair hanging slightly in front of his eyes. She looked down at his shoes and noticed he was wearing ludicrously bright red socks.

"I just got home from Europe, and you are the first one I came to see!"

She wanted to say no. She had to say no for *his* sake—for Mr. Mickey Bowels's sake.

But she didn't.

"Yes," she said, phoning him late that afternoon, her hand trembling, "let's you and I go to a movie."

"But I want to warn you—"

"About what?"

"You will be seen with me."

"I know," she said.

She did not say, "I know but that doesn't matter" or "That does not matter." She simply said, "I know," because this would cost her, in some way.

Then she had to tell Mr. Bowels she wouldn't be going home with him that night; she had to do something in town. It was the first time she had ever lied to him, or really to anyone. But all her joy at seeing Mr. Bowels—joy in a small measure—was gone now, replaced by anxiety and alarm that she might have to be loyal to him, when she didn't want to be.

She felt terribly guilty, because Mickey looked at her without the least feeling of being put out, or being a victim of guile.

"Oh, okay," he said.

Jamie took her after the bad movie, where they sat silently beside one another with a big bag of untouched popcorn between them, to his large house in town.

"Who owns this now?" she asked, not so much as a question but as a sudden strange acknowledgement that he had grown up in a world far different from her own. (Or at least so it appeared to her.)

"I do," he said. "I own many things now. I own a boat and a Ski-Doo and a jeep and a car. You see, after Dad died, I got many things—but I am just getting back here now, trying to get things organized."

He led her through the rooms, the polished corridors, past the ebony piano in the living room, the paintings on the walls, through the three floors and out to the upstairs balcony. Some of the back rooms were closed, with white sheets covering the furniture, and its darkness with the moon shining on the coverings of chairs and tables was somehow exceptional to her.

She noticed that for *all* the house, he lived entirely in three or four rooms upstairs. The kitchen, huge and open with pots and pans hanging on black hooks and a large stove with propane burners, was the only room in the downstairs he seemed to use. The living room was in darkness, and she caught it, as if through a shade, that paintings hung upon the walls there, their gilt frames seeming to catch her eyes as she passed by. It was as though she was floating on her legs and did not know why.

He told her his father had wanted him to be a lawyer. But after a year in Europe he decided he did not want to study law. Why was this? He didn't know. Perhaps he thought of law differently from others now that he had come into conflict with it.

"I don't know if I will ever practise law, though. It is always more subtle and uncertain than that, though, isn't it, less overt, more understated—maybe not explicit—that's a worry, do you think?"

It was the first time she had ever heard anyone speak like that.

"You could earn a bunch as a lawyer, I bet. Not like my dad, you wouldn't be gumboot'ener in the winter, you'd have a car," she said hesitantly, looking at him inquiringly. "Sides, you could make one of these here rooms into your office?"

"Money is not a problem," he said. "It will not be for me. Still," he added, "I have no illusions that I am liked here. But I was never liked anyway. It's impossible for me to be liked. I have the gilt of the outsider on me. It has always been so and will always be so. So, what do you think I should do?"

To her it was too fantastic to think about. He spoke a bit like Mickey Bowels when he was trying to inform her about the history of the Miramichi. Yet, as bright as Mickey was, this boy was far brighter.

Now she was suddenly being asked such a strange question about the *gilt of the outsider*.

Oh yes, she might say she was an outsider too, but not like him.

Then, to offset the enigmatic sensation of having him confess to not being liked and asking her what he might do, some *feeling* she did not think she deserved, especially with his handsome face looking as innocently upon her as Mickey Bowels's tired face had done just a short few hours before she grabbed Jamie's hand to comfort him.

But she saw the flash of Mickey Bowels's ring when she took his hand, and her reflection in the broad mirror above a small wooden counter that said, *You are being unfaithful.* Then she said, "Well, wouldn't that be up to you? I mean, how you live." She smiled and, taking a deep breath, added, "Anyway, I like you—if you think no one else do. I mean does. And I should be getting around home now. I mean, shouldn't I be getting around home now? I should be. I, well, I hardly know you as a fact."

Their faces were the same—his and Mickey's—in that they were trusting of her, of her beauty, and she recognized this. Until this moment she had felt something of a nobody—from upper Arron Brook, a place with little hope or destiny. Except in private moments, she felt fine to have come from there.

Now she felt sad for them both, and realized women had an immense power over men, that they must use wisely.

"Okay," he said, "I'll take you home soon."

Somehow, she was disappointed when he said this.

He took her downstairs and worked until he got the swollen door to the study opened.

"There," he said, as if this somehow solved something magnificent. "I'm not very good with boards and pliers, but I am very good at understanding."

"Understanding?"

"Oh yes, I am quite good at understanding."

He went and unhinged the French doors, that opened to the night air.

There was a smattering of dust when he opened the door. Still, the fresh night air, the fragrance of the lawn, drifted in. But he stared in a kind of penetrating anxiety into the darkness.

She curiously took the white sheet off the desk and opened the drawer—to see nothing but a small yellow pencil, and smell the enclosed scent of oak.

He responded to the sight of the pencil as if he now must say something about it.

"My dad's desk," he said, just as innocently as a boy of fourteen. "I was sure there was money in it—and the pencil was there to mark down what I had saved. We were saving for a car. I never thought of it until I was in Europe—that is, that the money was gone. The letter was also gone. The amount of money we had both saved was on the other side of the copy of his letter from the Department of Defence, about his resignation, but the pencil was here. When I told the police there had been money, they said they knew—that I had taken the money and hid it under my pillow. But I was saving my own money for a second-hand car—and my father was saving money toward it also. Do you understand?"

"No. I mean, when?"

"I remembered it when I was in southern France watching a bicycle race. That someone else had to have taken that money."

"Yes," she said, nodding her head.

"Well, it is one thing they didn't mention in the press—or this." And he took her to another door, opened it. "See?"

"See what?"

"The cabinet. They didn't mention that was broken into, either. I don't know where the letter where he had the amount of money written down went. The amount of money we had saved. Do you understand his letter of resignation might solve it? It would solve it for me. I know what was on it:

SAVINGS FOR JAMIE'S CAR

| Dad | Jamie |
|---|---|
| 1425 | 275 |

"Or something like that. You see, the 275 is the money they found under my pillow—well, except for a few dollars I spent that evening. Inside the envelope was his copy of the letter from the military accepting with regret his resignation.

"I've searched the house a dozen times. I asked the police if they had it. But they asked me if I had taken his money after I had fired the gun. Then they asked me if it was an accident. I said, 'I don't know,' because I wasn't in the room, but they perverted it to mean, *I didn't know if my shooting him was an accident*. That's what they perceived I meant. Then they said, 'We know you didn't mean to kill him.'

"'No, I didn't,' I said. Why did I say that? Because my implied inference was that not only did I not mean to kill him, I did *not* kill him. But it did not come out like that.

"So, everyone thought I was guilty because of that interview. Do you know Mr. Bowels? Mr. Bowels is a kind man—but even he has his doubts about me."

Her face turned away and, without being able not to, she lowered her eyes.

His face flushed, as if he knew she thought he was lying.

But she did not think he was lying. There was a moment when she thought, within a millisecond of looking at his face, that he was innocent. She squeezed his hand.

"That was before my uncle got involved, hired Anderson, and I was whisked away after Dad's funeral. My uncle walked in and said, 'Charge him or put him under my care.' He was a big, blustery man, my father's older brother, and never stood on ceremony. But now my uncle is dead, died of a stroke, Anderson is dead, died of cancer, and I may as well be dead. For my testimony is still there—still there. They will pervert it. That is, they still have me saying those things that they will now twist into a confession. That will certainly be the connotation, won't it?"

It was the first time she had heard the word "pervert" used in that way. The first time, or second or third, she had heard "connotation" in a sentence.

That made her feel as if she was in another realm, superior to, or at least different from, the ones she had been in before. Also, the thoughts expressed were somehow of a level higher than the ones she had been used to. No, that was not it at all. They were never higher, simply said differently. Yet she knew he thought about life on a different plane. A plane remarkably different from hers, where the why was always an inquiry.

His voice was in a way mesmerizing because she had never quite heard a voice like this before. His voice made her weak. It was almost as if he was taking her clothes off as he spoke. His voice could make her take her clothes off; she had never had that sensation before. But Jamie knew this about his voice—or at least it seemed he did.

And the more she fought it, the more she realized it. That she was seduced by his voice and wanted her clothes taken off.

She felt strange, too, to be in the room where the somewhat famous—yet mysterious—man had died of a gunshot. She looked up at the high ceiling, the crown moulding on its edges, the glass cabinet, and the picture of a man on horseback, covered in dust. A picture of an airplane high over the English Channel. It was a Spitfire, she was to learn, and it was high over the Channel in 1941, she was to learn, and it was Jamie's great-uncle, she was also to learn. A beautiful painting of a dory on the bay graced one wall.

He paused, picked up the pencil.

"Oh, never mind that," he said. "My family were lumbermen before they became officers. My grandfather made a lot of money in lumber and business, the sawmill at the Cove, you might remember it—near Russellville? And my father—the Colonel, as you know, was a medical doctor—their father invested with his brother in Halifax in tugboats and shipping. So, anyway, that's not important—we'll have money, you and I. I think I have somewhere around four million to be given to me sometime—maybe less—maybe three—but still, if I worked stocking shelves, that would be enough to get us by."

"What do you mean, *us*—you and I?" she thought she said. But in fact, she said nothing. She only looked at him, startled. The French doors were still opened, and people down on the street were passing by and some were looking into the house that no one except the maid had entered in almost a year. She wanted to leave the room but stood where she was.

And then he kissed her. And her mouth opened gently to his kiss, and she felt his tongue for a split second before he withdrew it. And she knew that she had hardly opened her mouth to Bowels when he kissed her good night. She felt weak and her legs began to buckle. She had heard of this—a girl's legs buckling—though it never occurred to her that her legs would. She felt she would be too strong.

"You are the first girl I ever really kissed," he said. "You don't get to kiss many girls when they think you murdered your father. They might want to—but they sort of shy away."

"Shhh," she said, "they'll hear," and she pointed to the people across King George Highway.

Both of them laughed. And he turned and closed the French doors. This was a very strange sight to people—after months of the house in darkness, or of the maid in the house with one small kitchen or hallway light, these many lights seemed brazen—even an attack of some kind, and young Jamie was back, and he had a girl—and that girl was Mickey Bowels's girl—at his house. In one swift moment, there she was, the interplay of which brought her to his house unknown, and one which could doom her forever.

Then he asked her to marry him.

"It's my first proposal," he said, "and perhaps my only one ever."

That is after the first poor movie of the first date, on the first night when he admitted half the town believed he was a murderer.

They walked out of the big office and along the hallway. She had thought he was taking her home. But he turned back upstairs. And she let him take her hand. She saw the cuffs of his white shirt, and his shirt collar, a bit twisted. But now he seemed to have an authority she had not realized. In fact, he could have made love to her in the dark at that moment on the stairs if he wanted. In fact, he was making love to her—in a strange, otherworldly way.

They were now on the third floor of the house, and she was looking far down at the street. She thought of Mr. Bowels and how much Pruty liked him, and his balding head, and his gentle, rustic smile, and the way he played the spoons and sang "Oh Danny Boy," tapping the spoons on the right knee of his best pants after Sunday communion on Saint Patrick's Day.

But Musselman, just as suddenly and unexpectedly, kissed her again. She felt strange, and her knees suddenly buckled again, so that he had to hold her up.

She thought of those obscured paintings downstairs in the living room and wondered what they said, and what life they spoke of. Paintings that to her were obscure—but for some showed a certain period of Americana in the late thirties. And then two nudes, painted twenty years apart by the same artist in Saint John, that emboldened in her a certain feeling of being cavalier, because of how flower petals covered them in certain places.

She also felt in some strange way she was in danger. So, she pulled back.

But then he pulled her toward him. She felt his hand over her naked breast. His left leg parted hers. She almost said, "Take my clothes off." Almost.

He kept his leg between her parted legs, and she suddenly was having an orgasm. He did not kiss her again, and he did not move, feeling her press herself against him, more and more urgently, and then she moved back, her face flushed.

"I got some dizzy," she said.

"Of course—yes, of course you did—so did I," he said. But he said so kindly.

She wanted to run away now—and wanted to stay forever. It was only the third orgasm in her life; the other two times, as a young girl, were by herself.

He removed his hand almost apologetically from her breast. She held on to his arms to keep herself upright.

"I'm ready to fall, I guess," she said.

There was a silence between them. Then he spoke. "Marry me tomorrow. You know you want to."

She laughed at his proposal and made a joke of it, but she backed away—not in panic, not in anything, but in alarm that he would joke with her as a child of poverty, which is exactly what her father had warned her about with certain boys from town. But he held tightly on to her hand, as if a plea of some kind.

"Oh yes, elope," she said, swinging her hand in his.

"Tonight, why not?" he said, his white lips pressed together.

"*Please*," she said, and she felt like a fraud the way it sounded.

"I promise I am not a murderer. I promise he did not commit suicide, either. I believe someone else was here and did the deed. It was in May—the French doors of his office could have opened and closed—the police trained their optics on me alone. They stepped over the crime scene as if it was a picnic—that is what Sergeant Delano was so concerned about before he died in Toronto—and then later Sergeant Becky Donaldson, she is not sure who did or did not do it—but she is certain the case was botched. Now the case is being handled by others. And she too is ready to retire."

He said nothing more about it and led her back down to the front hall.

When he drove her home, she asked to be let off at the Simon house as she had done the once before. She didn't want him to see where it was that she lived.

Of course, he knew where she lived, knew who her father was, and her family.

Those lights from his large ghost of a house, which cast brazenly down the steps and unto the soil, created a sensation, and caused the very case to be opened once more.

"Who took you to a movie—I have an obligation to know," her father asked the next morning, rubbing his nose and looking down suspiciously at the piece of black toast. The air was fresh except for the smell of black toast. "Movies now—staying out late and going to movies—that's the next thing now I'll have to put up with."

Her father pressed her until she told him. He looked alarmed. It took him a while to answer. Even his eyes watered a little.

"I want nothing to do with him in this family—we are not having nothing to do with murderers—are we, Pruty?"

"Pardon?"

"Murderers—we aren't having a whole lot to do with them. I mean as a rule—we don't invite them into our house, do we, Pruty?"

"Pardon?"

"Stop saying pardon, my little elf—but no, Gertie, he is not for you—and what will Mickey say? Mickey of all people—what will he say? Make me an egg, someone, will you? Mickey, what will he say? 'My betrothed loves a murderer, but she is still my betrothed'?"

At this she felt a sting; her heart deeply sank; she had almost completely forgotten about Mickey. And then a sudden shame overcame her as she remembered what had happened.

She began to prepare an egg. He wanted it sunny side up—unless you made it sunny side up, then he wanted the yoke broken—unless you broke the yoke, then he wanted it in butter—unless you made it in butter—

She made it sunny side up, and in butter.

"How can you just get over Mickey?" he said, looking skeptically at the egg. "Eh, Pruty? How could she? Did you ever hear him sing 'Oh Danny Boy'—tears to my little Irish eyes—well then—well then!"

"I pray for everyone," Pruty said.

"Of course you do, my little glow-worm, but that won't help until Gertie repents."

And he contrived to silently spoon the jam on his toast and not look her way, as if he was so surprised by this moral flaw that he no longer wished to speak. Then he crunched his toast and cut into his egg.

Her father actually was a well-known drunkard who would come into the store where she worked on weeknights and Saturday and not leave until she'd go to the coat room and get him money.

Then, after he'd taken the five dollars, she'd watch him go back out the door and cross the cold, blackened street to those characters he drank with who huddled against the side of Stothart's brick building. She had just started working permanently and did not wish to make a scene of any kind. And he knew this and traded upon it.

Their faces were in shadow too, against the buildings, squatting down against the cold wind, the smell of salt and snow and a bottle of wine, and watching them from the window from inside the store, she could smell the fabric of her best woollen skirt and crisp whitened blouse.

She would feel at a loss, and think her future was futile.

"I went to a movie with him," she said, "and I doubt very much if he is interested in me, or if I will ever see him again."

So, as we now know, five years after the robbery and death of Colonel Musselman, when she was certain she would marry Mickey, with his polka-dot tie and his soft voice, Gertie met Jamie for the second time. Now she began to ignore Mickey—became upset with how he spoke, told him at times she was busy and couldn't go to the Miramichi Historical Society meetings with him.

She did not want to act this way and yet found herself being unnecessarily cruel. In fact, in a strange way, this cruel streak came as a way to punish herself—to show that she was not entirely truthful to herself or to him.

But if she thought it through clearly, it had started with Jamie before the first date, as far back as high school.

He came to the store one afternoon looking for an electric heater for one of the upstairs rooms when he had first come back home from Halifax. To her, this very purchase made him seem too young to be on his own.

And as he lugged his heater away, she felt her heart go out to him.

That afternoon, Jamie had smiled at her blithely, quickly, and turned and left, carrying away his heater. The snow and rain came out of the sky. She watched him move by the window, as if he was covered in a dishonour of some kind because so many people spoke against him or his family.

One of the ghastly things he did, according to some of the gossips, like Dannielle, was kill his father and then *write* poems. This was revealed in the press at the time of his father's death, and one of Jamie's poems, "Death at an absurd moment," which had first been published in the school paper, was published there. But it was a poem in honour of his mother. Those who might have known him would have known this.

Shamus was all about how the murderer wrote poems and "*Poems, can't you imagine?*" But for her now, after the terrible way she had grown up, it was *love*. Yes, it was love.

One afternoon a few weeks after the movie, Mickey had been told by Dannielle to come to the store. In her urgent plea she had said: "Mickey, get over here now!"

Thinking something wrong with Gertie, he rushed out, leaving customers and the door open, ran across the park and saw something so unexpected that he was confused and speechless.

Jamie Musselman was kissing his girl, Gertie, and she had her arms around him, still wearing the friendship ring he had given her.

They were or thought they were hidden behind the store next to where she worked. Mickey looked into the store through the side window and saw Dannielle looking out at him, unmoved and indifferent as she first licked and then stuck price tags to small appliances.

Mickey moved into the corner between the two buildings and turned away.

He didn't see her for some time.

When Gertie came home from work two weeks later, daylight long and the robins chirping in the field they hopped upon, Mr. Mickey Bowels was sitting on the porch steps waiting with a little second-hand car that he had purchased for her.

Pruty had wheeled outside, and the sunlight glinted off her chair as Gertie came up the drive. But Mickey knew just by her walk up the drive that it was no use. Gertie walked toward them saying "Hello!" so loudly, and in a way in fear, it seemed to nullify any chance Mickey had, as she walked by them, her arms folded across her unbuttoned sweater, into the house.

Mickey waited on the steps until long after dark, and then he stood and walked away, leaving the car where it was.

Gertie didn't come to the upstairs bedroom window.

Pruty, getting up the haphazard ramp, wheeled her chair to the bottom of the stairs and said, "That was very and even terribly un-nice of you."

"I know," Gertie said, from behind her door. "No one knows more than me."

The next afternoon, Pruty saw the friendship ring lying on the side of the bathroom sink.

A week later, Jamie took her to his father's large house once more. Her bra was so white it seemed to shine in the sun, and her panties were light pink, and she suddenly lay back as he took them off.

"Don't come inside me," she whispered, "not yet."

Yes, it was love, ragged, lonely, forsaken and true.

His house was to be something special in our town, but was left unfinished. That is why some thought the idea of suicide improbable; there was still, on the back end, the unvarnished pinewood. And yet, in a way, suicide seemed the thing.

Now Jamie, the strange son, had returned and was alone in this house, and had stolen the first girlfriend Mickey Bowels had ever had.

Who would that sit well with?

Jamie said to her one night a few weeks later when they were sitting on chairs outside:

"I was in the room just after the shot. I ran to his room when I heard it. I yelled: 'Dad!'"

She could feel him shivering as he spoke of it. "You don't have to tell me," she said—half in hope that he wouldn't, half in dread that he would confess, even though she believed in his innocence.

"Someone had dropped the gun. And I grabbed the gun off the floor and I swear to God it went off into my leg, even before I got it level. The shot just went off. They said I would have to have pulled the trigger. Well, maybe I did, I don't remember. For a time I didn't even know that it had fired. Then I saw the blood on my leg as well. So I was gimping about holding my leg as the police came in, and still holding the gun. They put me on the floor with a gun to my head. They were so sure I had committed a crime. They will try to press charges."

"Press charges? They still want to press charges? No, I don't believe you."

But it was true. The new Crown prosecutor, with wavy blond hair and brave, enthusiastic strides, in new brown leather shoes, had reopened the case. Like many, he disliked Musselman; and like many, he had known Gertie and liked her quite a bit.

Gertie had fallen headlong into this, without knowing anything about him. And perhaps Jamie hadn't thought he would ever have to tell her.

GERTIE HAD BEEN BORN IN A HOUSE JUST OFF LOAD Road, a house freezing in the winter and filled with blinding heat, mugginess and flies in the summer. There was nothing she had ever seen of the great world. That is what many would say. But in fact her understanding of the world, her observations of the world, were as sophisticated as many who had travelled widely, and more sophisticated than some. She was at least as sophisticated as all those girls travelling to Europe with too many suitcases and rushing to catch trains on a Eurail Pass. She had not seen the leaning tower of Pisa, but she had read about it in those encyclopedias her mother had collected like treasure, a new one every third Saturday afternoon.

When she was younger, she would search all week to get fifty cents—which would at that time buy her and her sister each a bottle of pop. She went along the ditches searching for bottles, or she picked blueberries and, when older, babysat when she could.

Her father had a bulbous nose and darting, intelligent but shifting black eyes, and his feet were quite small. When his own wife was ill, he went to the priest every day, and begged God, and lit candles, but it didn't help.

"Her death is the worst that has happened to me since Pruty," he would tell people, blowing his nose, tears in his eyes. But then he spent four years in litigation insanely suing everyone for her death, even the bishop in Saint John, who he maintained didn't pray well enough for his constituents. Finally, no one wanted to speak to him about her, and when he mentioned her name—and how her doctor owed him money—*maybe even a million dollars*—people who were sitting at the tavern with him would get up and move their chairs. That doctor—the doctor who had visited her in the middle of the night, still wearing his pajama tops—was Colonel Musselman.

"Well, maybe not quite a million—half a million," he would say, trying to entice them back.

But the sad fact was that when his wife was dying, she lay in the back room on a cot, in a white, soiled nightgown, her thin legs with red kneecaps and blue varicose veins, and her feet narrow and long, with yellow toenails, and one night the children could hear her cursing him for hours:

"You miserable heap of misery," she called out over and over and over again. "You miserable heap of misery—blaming the doctor, who was the only kind man to me for years—yes, blame him—blame him—what life have you given any of us! What life—all your family were miserable—and I've spent my whole life here in this back end of nowhere taking care of the likes of you—YOU!"

His wife was English, and he told her when in England as a bosun in the navy that he owned Prince Edward Island. She came back to Canada and moved into this tiny yellow house with a small woodshed behind it. He then told her that he hadn't pointed at Prince Edward Island, but Sheldrake Island—and said he owned some land somewhere near it.

That particular night, Gertie heard her dad beg forgiveness.

She went to look in, and saw her father with his head down, sheepishly nodding, his nose running and his ears beet red, as her mother continued.

"You miserable heap of kleptomaniac misery, you did nothing but steal everything I had! My jewellery, my silverware, my cutlery, my bedspread. The gold bracelet my sister gave me when I left Liverpool—everything. I had honour and you squandered it—you squandered it! I kept you out of jail—and the only reason I did that was because of the girls!" She spoke raspingly and raised her head. "And all your life you did deals for a few dollars. You stole and cheated and lied and jacked horses up on gunpowder and tea—all for a few measly dollars at a horse haul, so our mare died of a heart attack—you will do it again—something will happen—something. You, you will do something! Because you are weak and need to be noticed. That's it—ha—you need to be noticed."

"Well, the mare won't die again—because well as you know, it is already dead. No, I promise I won't, my soul of honour—I won't do anything ever again. I will take care of the girls and you will be proud of me, and I won't be noticed by anyone."

She gasped and gasped and he tried to get in touch with the doctor again and he lifted her head and cried, and the girls sitting in the living room cried too.

The funeral was held on a cold November day, with black clouds, and Shamus's tie blew back, and his hair stood straight up, and his pants kept flapping at the grave.

When anyone came into the house, they would hear Pruty's wheelchair as she squeaked away from the TV. She would poke her head around the corner, looking intensely at who came in. Her lips pressed together, as if she was waiting for bad news. Her very poor eyes would narrow, and her lips would press until they were thin and white, and her body would hunch forward and shake. Then she would sit up and back away into the corner of the room, where it was dark and she was in shadow, like a turtle going back into its shell. With the chair out of sight, the sound of its squeaking wheels seemed to be a plea to whoever heard it.

At Christmas, Gertie put lights on the wheels so that they glittered and glowed and twinkled when Pruty wheeled to the darkened window to look out at the snowflakes or to see the windswept snow over their gravelled drive and the painted reindeer on the lawn. Gertie would dress both of them in pink party dresses and they would sit together, under the light of the tree, and wait all day for Christmas Eve. Or Gertie would wheel her down the church lane to church, and sometimes Shamus would come, stumbling behind them. The songs of celebration would elicit a grandeur in the cold. Shamus would stand at the back near the holy water font, near to the door, and the dark night would peer in when the door opened, and stragglers came in. Shamus was always one of the stragglers.

On July 1, a small Canadian flag would wave from its perch on the back handle of the wheelchair, and flutter in the wind if Pruty got outside. She kept writing letters to premiers and members of Parliament for better access to shopping malls, and petitioned for a bus for Arron Brook. She kept writing letters to staff members of various portfolios and waited for the mail. She kept little books on her shelf, too:

*How to Get a Man in Five Weeks.*

*The Man in My Life Could Be Yours.*

She would write to those in power, for she had so little; that is, like certain people, she was stung by the way some thought of her, and was determined to show her mettle.

"Why must we be without a bus to the greater Miramichi" was her plea, "and why must I have no access to a bus, even if it's the bus we don't have—so not only don't I have a bus, but I have no access to it even if I did have a bus."

Or, "I'm the only young woman bound to a wheelchair between here and Chatham Head—people should be more concerned about me than they are."

And she went on a march for more tolerance and compassion—where she shouted "Hurrah" and was pushed up a hill by a young boy, but forgotten there after everyone went home. She sat on the sidewalk in the drizzle coming down for three hours before Mickey Bowels came to fetch her home.

Once, she hiked to Chatham to see a rock band, all by herself, and spent the night searching for a place to sleep. It was the first time she got drunk, shouting with all the others and singing to the music.

Gertie told her once, when she was in junior high and Pruty had left school, that their situation could be reversed, but perhaps Pruty was given the disability for a strange and noble reason. Pruty from then on became more and more religious, which became more intense after Gertie started to date Jamie Musselman.

Still, unless her sister stayed near her, Pruty would be alone for days on end. Once, just a few months before Jamie Musselman was charged, when Gertie came to visit, Pruty, wheelchair tipped over, had been stranded on the floor for over two hours, trying to get her chair uprighted. She had pulled out the drawer, and all the pencils and elastics, and a few papers, fell upon her.

She had been trying to reach the counter to haul herself up. Her father couldn't be there *and* take care of his plans—his obligations were to the great outside world of our River, where everyone said he was a boaster, a snitch and a weasel but still a decent fellow all in all.

Pruty was Gertie's twin. She was born an hour later then Gertie. But she unfortunately was deformed. Her twisted legs did not fully grow, but she did look like Gertie. Many days they dressed the same. Gertie made sure of it—right until she was in high school. She tried to teach Pruty algebra and geography. She told her that her half-blind eyes weren't ugly, and her face was gentle and kind. She went to a school for the disabled, but she found herself quite a bit brighter than those there. She came back to Load Road, and stayed in the small room that was her existence. So, as often happens with intelligent shut-ins, she felt isolated and alone.

But she knew the very night Gertie lost her virginity. She said, "Ah, dammit, we are no longer the same," and smiled mischievously.

Pruty rarely got angry, but at times she would slam her fist, covered in a protective glove, on the wheel of her chair, and shout at Shamus, "Oh you—oh you—you took my money, you took it, you did, you did!"

"My, my, Pruty, you're just a little round ball of hate—worst I ever seen."

Sometimes her feet would be blistered because she had come to a skid when following him to the door and missed those small planks that allowed her access to the porch.

Gertie did not understand the world. She did not know how Jamie was bright enough that professors wrote him even at this young age pleading with him to take up law or medicine and calling his intelligence remarkable.

Sometimes she tried to join a conversation and became frightened and mute.

But she did know that, in the end, beyond all of it, he was *alone*.

Yes, he was alone and therefore he needed her.

She knew it when he wore his tan sports jacket with the grey tie and tan loafers and stood with other men in the rural settings on a brilliant October day, and they were in a group, and he was standing beside them, solitary. She did not know how her feelings matched at that moment the exacting universe, down to her heart beating, and seeing his bearing up, with his constrained face and his fitful, beautiful eyes.

That such a wound, done when he picked up the gun in terror, was somehow immutable proof that he was a sinner, and the prosecutor who had reopened the case believed it. So, one afternoon, they questioned him for an hour.

"Do you remember the Connell boy—he is the new prosecutor. He doesn't like me. However, I do know from how he spoke that he certainly likes you. He thinks I am leading you astray and he seems determined to prove it."

A morning later it was reported in the paper: JAMIE MUSSELMAN TO BE FORMALLY CHARGED.

The picture of a young man, no longer a boy, appeared alongside the picture of him as that boy, and a picture of the house as it was when it was roped off with yellow tape.

After reading about this (he was an inveterate reader of the newspaper), her father became worried and ashamed. Worried more and more as he thought of what all of this might come to.

He loved his daughters very much—as he had his wife—but he had been too weak and too influenced by bad manners to be able to show it like other fathers supposedly did. He was always in trouble. For years he came home at dinnertime and would lock all the doors and tell them to lie if anyone asked for him.

First it was hay—he stole a bunch of that. And then it was a few harnesses—a couple of those. And then, oh, a few hundred pounds of potatoes, and then four hamsters from a pet store, and then a horse—an actual horse—an old horse, however, and then meal for cattle. And then he netted twenty-nine salmon, and then—well, at every turn he said, "Pon my soul to God, this here is the very last time."

These were rural crimes, done along back roads, where fields and woods and streams separated barns and houses, and where miles of emptiness were punctuated by lonely wires running from pole to pole.

But now *this. This. This.*

He had been very careful around *her* before—with *him* in the picture; that is, Musselman. But after supper the day Musselman was found guilty, in the light that was diminishing and Pruty's small cactus plant leaning up against the blank kitchen window, he became sullen and arrogant.

He asked for a toothpick.

"Pruty, dear, wheel away there and get me my toothpick."

He decided, sucking on his toothpick, the lone little cactus plant suddenly looking ominous, that he must put a stop to this now!

"Well, he showed himself, didn't he," he said. "Yessirrie—he showed himself. Didn't he though! Did you see it, Pruty? Yes sirrrreee, I seen it coming. That prosecutor is a nice young lad, too—met him a dozen times, always smiles at me—likes you, Gertie, likes you. Asked after you, you know. Twice he asked after you—asked how you were doing. You could go out dancing with him, I betcha my bottom dollar."

This in fact was true. The prosecutor had asked after her, seeing her in town, and knowing who her father was.

Gertie didn't speak, she simply sat near Pruty with her head in her hands, her elbows on her knees, as the light continued to diminish, and the last robin tweeted and flew down along the creek.

But to Shamus, the diamond ring on her finger seemed to be the centrepiece of the entire room at that moment.

Suddenly, with the glare in his eyes like two shining viruses, and his face flushed, he said: "Let me see, sweetie pie—I bet it's not very much of a ring—not very important—them Musselmans was always cheap."

(He had never known any Musselman—not one. Only that Dr. Musselman himself had come to the house one night to see his wife when he, Shamus, was too drunk to get up from his bed.)

"No, it isn't cheap—well, here—" And she held it up, against the lights from the road, and it seemed to sparkle a second, and then she dropped it to her skirt.

Their house rattled with the passing transports in the night air.

Shamus, in a big red shirt, walked across the room and tried to take the diamond off her finger while lights from cars glittered along their window as they passed by on the road. He did not know why—he would never know why—but it plagued him, and if he removed it, if he could just forget everything, all might be well.

So, at first he told her to give him the ring. She said no. Then he asked if he could lick her finger. She said no.

Pruty tried to block his path with her wheelchair, but he went around it, first to the left, then to the right, and finally he stepped right over her head, knocking away her butterfly clip for her hair.

"Papa," Pruty said.

"She is not marrying a murderer!!"

"Papa," Pruty said. "Papa—stop it, Papa."

Until Orlif Speck came in with a new publication on the environmental strategy for migratory waterfowl. He always brought a copy of the small magazine for Pruty, Pruty being one of the people who attended environmental meetings at Orlif Speck's stone house.

He saw the man straddling Gertie as her small feet were kicking in their knitted slippers, with two small loose string laces flapping in the air.

He grabbed Shamus by the ears and dragged him off her.

"Please," he said. "Control thyself, sir." (He actually said "thyself.") And he continued, "Thou is a rascal."

He actually said "thou."

Orlif picked Gertie up. He looked at her strangely—as if for the first time he was seeing her. Oh, he knew she was the young girl that young boys like his son spoke about. But he was seeing her as a child. There were tears in her eyes, tears of embarrassment and shame.

Orlif went and sat on a small, rickety chair that, too small for him, seemed to heighten his sense of righteousness. But he had never done anything like this in his life. And sitting in his tweed jacket with the big patches, and his large, homely bow tie, he looked at their dreary little place with a renewed sense of purpose. He was an old man now, and except for teaching Plato, he had never done anything well.

"Maybe that boy didn't do it," he said.

And Shamus looked at them all, his face beet red and his hands shaking.

Then, turning swiftly as if stung by something, he rushed out the door and said something unintelligible when he slammed it.

"—Pruty," was the only word they heard.

ORLIF'S SON, WEAVER DE SPECK, WAS A REMARKABLE young man and always had other, more serious concerns. He was a social activist, with pale skin and long blond hair and white eyelashes. He had been to three universities. He was a philosopher and spoke in philosophical terms. He held his father in disdain, and his mother doted upon him.

His mother was a certain kind of woman, too, who had gotten a certain Mr. Beal released from jail, and who had gotten her own son out of trouble in Toronto. She had money that was independent of her husband Orlif's salary—but her features, the red lines on her face, showed her to be less well off than her son imagined. The money had been exhausted over many a whimsy and now her little family faced a kind of genteel poverty in a rural setting.

This is what had happened:

Six years before the opening of our story, Beal had stolen Ms. Speck's car. But in a moment of emotion, or perhaps because Beal had told her he was First Nation, she had asked for the charges to be dropped, and then gave sworn testimony that Beal had the loan of her car to do shopping.

You see, sometime earlier she had supported Beal's claim of being First Nation. She was the one who promoted it across our

River. It might not even have been spoken about if she had not promoted his claim, which in the end humiliated him.

She was with him for weeks, so that people said Beal was Vivian Speck's pet dog. If he ever heard that, God help the person. But he had not heard it. She had pressured Beal into radio and newspaper interviews—spoke for him, and told him what to do, and what he should say, and he became more and more confused and upset by her very support. Soon it was in the papers far more than he wanted.

Then it all went to ruin. His claim was discounted, and she hid from him. She did not answer his calls, and tried to disassociate herself from the bad publicity he was getting.

A week or so later, he stole her car, in fury that he had been used.

So, feeling responsible, she appeared at the police station, a woman no longer young, in a black sweater with frayed sleeves that she cupped in her hands, her face urgent and leaning into the officer as she spoke, her breath smelling of garlic. Garlic a new addition to her daily routine.

"Are you sure—quite sure, ma'am?" the officer asked her.

"Yes," she said. "Yes, I am sure. Of course I am sure—he had the loan of my car!"

So Beal was released.

Beal did not forgive what had happened to him, however. He had been laughed at. How Vivian was by his side day and night, whispering to him about what to do and say, and then left him alone when it was proved he was not First Nation.

Vivian had been Orlif's student. She had been bright and provocative and agitated by some terrible trials in her life. She had always stayed after class and spoke to him about philosophy and problems relating to equality. It was the age of a great struggle.

Her struggle, which intensified over the years—right up until the time she accused Orlif himself, and he lost a tenure-track job. He, Orlif, forgave her—as he had forgiven everything in his life. She had wanted to go to Europe, had wanted to leave, and if he had tenure, that would impede them from going. All of this had happened long ago.

They had lived together since then. And Orlif had acquiesced to his wife's commitment to change, because it all seemed to fit. One day she had taken his books in a wheelbarrow and wheeled them off somewhere. Because she told him they were "male inspired." He searched everywhere for his books, but could not find them, and ended up painting little jars and a statuette to put on his half-empty bookshelves. He discovered that he was good at doing so.

She so often had her way. And Beal, on her command, was released.

So it was said, and so it was done.

A month or so after this incident with the car, their son, Weaver de Speck, came home.

Beal and he met. They got together once or twice at the little tavern on the muddy road.

They just simply crossed paths one evening, and seemed first to notice each other and secondly to be attracted in some strange way.

After Weaver had been sanctioned and then expelled after an ethics board meeting at Ryerson, he had tried to stay in Toronto. He had told his mother he would have his book published, and some months after he had been expelled, he was both too ashamed to come home and too depressed to work.

They waited for this book. Weaver made up another story. And then another about this book.

"Yes, yes, it's all done—it's all ready."

But finally, he did come home. He did meet Beal. There was no book.

As far as the timeline goes, this was two weeks before the murder of Mr. Musselman.

Beal spoke to Weaver about his struggles—it's why he got the tattoo on his neck, because of his struggles—and Weaver felt he had a case, and a man, and a situation to write about. To give him the kind of notoriety he so wished to have. Of course, it was more subtle than that, and the emotions were not completely destructive. He did think of Beal's struggle against the social framework. He did think of Beal as someone society had abandoned.

Weaver had been expelled from Ryerson. So, in the last few months, all his plans had changed.

Vivian brought him home, paid for his ticket, paid again for his luggage to be shipped, helped him get his medicare transferred. His mother ran around for him—did everything she could to make up what she had not done in the past. Sometimes she tried to atone for her years of neglect, which, when it was happening, she didn't recognize as neglect at all.

Just as, when she had spoken against her husband, she had no idea it would impede his career, thinking that it would always be waiting for him, she neglected her son in a hundred ways, thinking it would all be made up to him.

Vivian had had buttons printed up:

*Vivian Speck, feminist, radical, friend.*

She still gave them out when people came to her house on Puddle Lane. Even elderly Winnifred White wore one. A law-abiding, elderly woman who Vivian Speck said was far too law-abiding.

"You might shake it up a bit," she would tell Winnifred. Sometimes at their meetings Winnifred would shake in her seat, as she listened to all the outrageous things people like Vivian Speck had managed to do and wished and wanted to do.

But long before Puddle Lane—no man's tenure was going to interfere with her.

She just needed to go to Europe to the great gathering of women in Rome. And he must come, and so too must Weaver. Orlif never got a chance at tenure again. He was here now at the little university working part-time. He had no tenure, just a yearly contract.

She often said she could have gone without him—and should have gone without him. For he did nothing but impede her plans.

But this was not true, for in her heart she could not exist without relying upon him. As he packed the bags, took care of the passports, arranged the travel, and very, very often slept by himself, this is what he knew.

That is why she betrayed him.

She had secretly lied to the administration to have his tenure refused. She lied about him and young students—it simply slipped off her tongue.

"Now you can come," she said, smiling delightfully.

So they went and then they came home.

The housework was never done, the child was left crying, and yes, there had been fights over who would take care of him. They hired nannies who didn't work out—and they went on with their great lives thinking their son would appreciate all they had achieved. But what they achieved was so minute, and all three of them seemed strangely separated from what they had intended to be.

After she discovered Beal was not First Nation and had done other criminal things, she had shied away from him. Although she put on a brave front, she needed to excuse herself from it all.

Once, a few days before the car was stolen, he came to her door, begging to see her, but she wouldn't answer it. She hid in the back room. Now and again the small curtain would move, and she would peek out.

Afterward she went to his aid when he stole the car, because she didn't want to be implicated as someone who had betrayed him.

Seeing her thin body as she tapped her fingers in apprehension, trying to put out fires she had started, one thought of Virginia Woolf envious, worried, brilliant, *circa* 1922. The Virginia Woolf who said, "As a woman I have no country."

"I didn't betray him—I didn't—never ever," she said as she left the police station that long-ago evening.

But our Mr. Beal, dangerous and wounded, felt betrayed.

After the murder of Colonel Musselman, both Beal and Weaver de Speck had left for some time. It wasn't looked at as peculiar; in fact it wasn't noticed at that time by anyone but Orlif himself.

Strangely, both were now back on the River.

They had come home after Jamie had been convicted and had been sent to prison.

In fact, both had gotten off the Scotia Limited within a day of one another after both being away. This was two or three weeks after Jamie Musselman had been found guilty. At first, they didn't seem to know one another—at first. And then one day they were seen on the sidewalk talking—briefly.

So then, on certain nights in the park, in the days that were starting to grow cold, near the fountain with its modest trickle of water, Weaver would sit on a board and stare across the street toward the river while he manoeuvred two small, smooth rocks in his hand, and Beal would show up. He would walk from the tavern and come over and stand by the fountain, and then he would walk to a bench near Weaver. Just near Weaver—not beside Weaver.

"We need to get that envelope with the letter back. Shamus doesn't have it—he doesn't know where it is. There is no way anyone can link us to anything—except that envelope with the letter and the money he wrote on the back that he was saving for his son. It was brought up in court—we must have taken it—so where is it?"

"I don't know. You told me to give Shamus the two hundred to keep his mouth shut. The letter must have been with the envelope."

"That's worse than anything!"

"Oh, even if it existed, it was probably burned years ago—"

"Or not!"

"Why did I go with you in the first place—why did I meet you? From what you told me, you were supposed to be in jail. You were going to sell that car, and Mom got you off. But the poor soul—well, once she brought a man into our house—to keep him from the cold—he ended up robbing us blind!"

Beal didn't like that comparison.

"Well, that was not me," he said, "so why in hell did you give him that letter?"

"I didn't. It must have been with the envelope that had the money. I just gave him the two hundred in the envelope like you said."

The night was cold, the sky was white. The little park was dreary where the wind scolded the small, dark branches. It was here Weaver had made fun of Pruty one day. And he remembered this as he sat juggling the stones. He shouldn't have done so—and perhaps that had caused everything else.

"I will look for it," Weaver said, "and get back to you."

"Little Nin is upset with me—with us. She is very upset—she does nothing but cry."

"Why—?"

"Why? Why do you think?"

So it was that night Weaver de Speck started his regular visits to Pruty. He would sit beside her and speak of the day he took her to the park and ask her if she still believed he was a terrible person.

"I never thought you were a terrible person, Weaver," she said. "I never thought so."

"I didn't mean the things I did that day, Pruty. I am more circumspect—I had two grams of hash that day—and then some beers. Well, you know yourself how that can hamper judgment? At any rate, I do say I am sorry! I shouldn't have asked you to get up and walk—did I say that—I don't quite remember?"

"I don't remember either, Weaver," she would lie, and then smile slightly. "You see, I don't even remember!"

He would visit when she was all alone—and once or twice she saw him looking through drawers and into cupboards and through the basket on top of the fridge.

"Whatever are you doing?"

"Oh, my dear, I am looking for a pen to write down my thoughts."

"Thoughts about what, Weaver? Thoughts about what?"

This went on for some weeks, and the young woman was beside herself—so much so she thought that maybe God would grant her a small miracle and she would walk down the aisle on her wedding day. She didn't know if it would be Weaver himself—but perhaps someone Weaver knew. Oh, of course—she was no fool—it was only a game she played with herself, that she would walk and someone would marry her.

"Did you ever see me at this house—a long time ago?" he asked her one night when they were alone and he had made her a marijuana cookie.

"No. If I did, I have forgotten. What night was it?" she asked, nibbling on her cookie so she felt numb throughout her body one moment and seemed to be floating about the room the next. One moment she could imagine her feet walking across the room by themselves, and she would watch them with great anticipation. Now and again she would giggle because Weaver looked like a clown. And at other times she would be subdued and very contemplative.

Her eyes in fact were quite beautiful—every bit as beautiful as Gertie's. And beyond the deep pain in them, there was an even deeper compassion. Pruty, too, did not wish to believe what she thought might have happened, all those days ago.

ONE NIGHT, SIX YEARS BEFORE, SOMEONE HAD COME TO Shamus's door. It was a May night, and at this place downriver it had rained, and the rain had made everything feel enclosed. Gertie and Pruty didn't see him—or them—it must have been two men at the door, one older and one younger—they only stayed a moment. It was a dark night, and the dark on upper Arron Road was exceedingly dark. Even from the bedroom window one could see only shadows. However, toward the river the sky was grey, and lighter grey farther over the water.

There was the sound of wind in the eave of the old house. Gertie was studying her history, about the Tudors and Sir Thomas More and his stand against the divorce of Catherine of Aragon, and could only hear them whispering.

Shamus had been on the fringes of this other world for years, not by design but by circumstance—that is, he was too weak not to be. It is what his poor wife knew and tried to cure him of, and he, Shamus, was sure he was cured of it all. "That nonsense," as he called it, "was just about over with." But then this had happened.

One of the men said, "Here it is. Take it—if you take it, you're as guilty as we are."

And he handed Shamus an old, worn envelope with some money.

So Shamus very quickly took this envelope with spots of blood upon it, and stuffed it into the drawer, and the men left. The envelope was addressed to Colonel Musselman.

As he left, one of the men said: "Nothing would have happened except for you. You are as much in this as we are."

Shamus followed them to the door, to ask them something, but they disappeared onto the pathway, still covered with spring mud, that led away from the high ground.

Later that same night, Gertie got a phone call from a high school friend who had heard of the suicide.

"That Jamie Musselman's father shot hisself with some kind of gun he had hid in his desk!" Then an hour and a half later, the friend telephoned once more. "They took that Jamie Musselman boy to the hospital and then they say they are going to take him on down to the police station."

The idea that it was murder came over the next few hours. People dropped in because they knew Gertie knew Jamie Musselman and wanted to talk to her about him. So, late at night, she came downstairs in her housecoat and pajamas and her old leather slippers and sat at the table.

She was an instant celebrity, more so if she could supply information. So then, what was he like, was he as strange as they said? She told them he was strange and unlike the other boys, and she was never sure about him.

"The whole house is surrounded by tape," people told her.

"That proves it's murder," someone said.

"Yes—well, they always do so."

"To ward off the curious—"

"Yes, too much curiosity."

Pruty wheeled out to the doorway between the living room and the kitchen and sat listening, her eyes wide and expressionless, unless one looked at them closely and one then saw them as eyes filled with wonder and fear, as if she was trying to understand the night in whole and not in part. But she didn't quite understand it.

"I hear the boy went bonkers and offed him with a pistol, then tried to kill himself by shooting himself in the leg!"

"That weren't it—weren't it, for God's sake. They had a bigger than average fight and the son wrestled the gun away after he were shot in the leg and then pointed it at his dad and said: 'This here is for Mom.'"

"Mom or Mommie? I heard he said, 'This here is for Mommie.'"

"I don't know—not so sure. Maybe he said 'This here is for Mommie—so long, pal.'"

"'So long, pal'—that's pretty cold."

"Yes sireee—yes sireee—this here is for Mommie—so long, pal. Them Musselmans were always crazy—the old lad there in Halifax threw someone off a tugboat."

"Well, there you go."

"The wife there—oh the wife, used to strip her panties off in front of the enlisted men and show her wire brush to them—on a daily basis, what I did hear."

Silence, and then the talk turned more and more disgusting, about the father and the boy, and the mother having an affair, and how she had walked about in bra and panties in front of enlisted men—and Shamus sat in his seat in the corner and was for the greater part silent. When he looked over at Pruty, she was staring at him, with her little mouth twisted in disappointment—and her eyes sparkled. But she didn't quite know what she knew.

This was the conversation around the table that appalling night, when Gertie had cream on her face, and Pruty peeked around the corner near the dark stairway, and there was night and the long-ago throated chirping of frogs. Then Pruty took her prayer beads that she had sent to the Vatican to get blessed by the Pope (so she believed that the Pope had personally blessed them) and prayed. She prayed fifteen Hail Marys and ten Our Fathers. People could see her in the light—at the back of the room, but only a little of her face, and her lips moving silently as the night passed. But how can one pray for something not to happen when it already has? That is the difficult position those petitioners are placed in. Worse for SHE whom they petitioned.

When people were quiet, they could hear the ticking of the clock and Pruty praying. But they didn't remain quiet. Everyone needed to know every detail.

They didn't mind saying disgusting things about a woman's bush in front of those two girls, and ended up using blasphemous words against God and man to prove they themselves were manly.

Shamus was quiet. When people looked at him, he smiled timidly. He even insisted he make the neighbours tea.

Later, when everyone had left, he took the envelope from the drawer and looked at the money—there were two one-hundred-dollar bills, crisp and shiny—and with this money an envelope listing the amount of money Jamie had saved—the name *Jamie* in pencil and the name *Dad*, side by side, separated by a pencil line. It was on the back of the envelope addressed to Colonel Musselman. It was a letter from the Department of Defence.

(The rest of the money had been taken by the accomplices. This was the envelope Beal remembered and asked Weaver about six years later.)

Shamus took the money and stuffed it into his pocket. He had no idea what to do with the envelope or the letter. The stove was lit, and he could throw it in. And he almost did. If he had, that might have changed the course of events for the entire family—and our entire River.

But thinking it was best to keep it, in case those two young rascals ever turned on him, he left it inside his drawer. It was a drawer no one looked in but him.

Then Shamus went outside and sat in the woodshed, shaking. All the clean cuts of wood he piled up seemed to curse him, because of their ordinary neatness.

The very gold slivers of birch seemed now to curse him. He tried to think of someone to blame this on. He had always been able to blame things on other people. Finally, when he couldn't think of anyone to blame it on, he blamed it on a bird.

It was a robin's fault.

He even said that, looking up at the sky through the window into the tattered clouds. "God, please, you know yourself and I don't lie—it were the robin's total fault!"

The little robin had fallen from a tree, out of its nest, and as usual Shamus was walking toward downtown at that time of the afternoon, which is where he often met Mickey Bowels to get a drive home.

He picked up the tiny half-feathered bird with its wing bones like little whitened sticks and reached up to put it into the nest. He believed God was watching him at this moment and would give him some kind of reward.

It wasn't easy or comfortable because the mother robin kept flying toward him and flying away, and he kept desperately trying to explain to the mother that he wanted only to put her chick back where it belonged.

As he was trying to explain this to the unfortunate mother, holding the half-naked, terrified baby, a tall, distinguished man standing behind him said, "You distract the mother, and I will put the youngster back."

And the distinguished man did just that. As Shamus waved the mother away, the fellow put the small chick back, with its three other siblings.

"There we go," the Colonel said. "Sometimes she will ignore the fallen bird if a human touches it—but I think she will realize it all ended well."

Shamus was busy trying to take spruce gum off his best pair of pants. Pants that Gertie and Pruty had chipped in to buy him for his birthday. He was born on April Fool's Day, but didn't like to mention this.

The Colonel stood there for a second and said: "You wouldn't help me move some flower boxes, would you? My son isn't home."

Shamus nodded. He recognized the doctor now, but didn't say so. He only thought of how the Colonel was at his house one night sometime before his wife died, and how he always felt unworthy.

There were twelve boxes to be placed along the back side of the house. The frames for these boxes had been repaired, but it did take time to get them inserted. The last few boxes were to be placed on either side of the French doors that opened in the front.

That is when he saw the money, because the Colonel took the key from under a mat and went into the room through those French doors to get Shamus twenty dollars. He should have refused the money. He shouldn't have mentioned he saw all this money in an envelope. But as fate would have it, he turned toward the town with the twenty in his hand.

The first person he met was Beal, who had walked up Jane Street after being across the river applying for a job. Beal was out of work and living in a small—tiny, really—apartment on Glow Street.

It was a desire to be liked by Beal, a hope of being considered worthy, that made him speak. Beal knew it. There were certain things he held against Shamus.

One evening when Shamus was bragging about everything he had done, all the fights he had been in, who he had told off, who cowered before him, Beal looked at Shamus across the tavern tables at the end of the night. The chairs were piled on top of the tables, and Shamus could only see Beal's dark black eyes staring at him. Shamus had sometimes laughed when others made fun of Beal when he was little—not a lot, but just the same he had. And now, well, now Beal was—Beal.

And Beal's dark, blistering eyes said he remembered this, said it across a row of tables and chairs.

Shamus was one of the people who said, "Thank God Beal is in jail—good place for him."

He would go about proclaiming that jail was the only place for Beal.

And then, when Vivian got Beal released, Shamus meeting him at the tavern said: "Oh, thank God you're out, Beal, good for you. Thank God—I told everyone—well almost everyone—pretty well everyone—that it was nothing but just one more injustice."

So, because of this, always wanting to make a good impression with those who were not good, the worst thing Shamus could have done, he did. He told Beal of the money in the Colonel's house.

"Do I have something for you," he said. He nodded and smiled as if Beal had been waiting for him to come through with some indication or proof of his ability. That both of them had been waiting for this meeting for years. In fact, perhaps this was true. But Beal simply stared at him.

So, Shamus said it again—and more urgently.

"I have something big for you if you wish," he said, and put a toothpick in his mouth and his hands in his pockets.

"What?" Beal said "what" as if he was angry with this intrusion.

So, almost out of breath, and without even thinking—he thought a lot in hindsight over this, looking at the hard brass rings on Beal's fingers—he explained that the Colonel had money stuffed away.

"It's easy pickins, Beal," he said, as if he was a character onstage, which is how he felt at that very moment.

Why was Beal out of jail? Shamus thought later. Why did Ms. Speck say it was a mistake and he didn't steal the car? Shamus thought later.

Perhaps it was because she had left her first husband years before, and had run away in the rain, and went to Orlif Speck. Then they married in a civil ceremony on the beach, with seagulls. Lots of seagulls and a sponge cake. That sponge cake was gone long ago, and those old seagulls were dead.

They had a son called Weaver de Speck—well, he put the *de* there himself. Their son had come back to them.

And the son Weaver had met Mr. Beal.

All of this played in old Shamus's mind later on that night. For he was not stupid, he was only weak.

His mother—that is, Weaver de Speck's mother, Vivian—was in the midst of a celebration. There was a German professor visiting. The problem was she had told everyone about Weaver's book.

Weaver had to pretend that it was on hold. The German professor, whom she had also told about his book, simply stared at Weaver, as if he was lying. So Weaver left the house most nights, did not go to the dinner in honour of this professor, or listen to his lecture.

And most nights when he went out, he ran into Mr. Beal. And they drank together.

And Shamus knew this too. Beal had been encouraged to tell his story, about his First Nation heritage, to the paper by Vivian herself.

"Tell it to the paper—I will help you," she had said with an urgency she often had when promoting her own participation. Her chest rattled when she breathed because for years she had smoked over two packs a day. And years of sadness.

But then something unforeseen happened.

Beal's story was discredited, and he felt humiliated by the very paper Vivian had insisted he go to.

The theft of the car came after this, and she had interceded.

Still, Shamus thought later when hindsight was always clear, if Beal had been in jail for the theft, he would not have met her son, and her son would not have been at Beal's later on that very strange and critical night.

At any rate, our Beal, standing on lower Jane Street, looked at Shamus cautiously a second, as if trying to determine why Shamus would give him this information. But Shamus was a child and he longed to impress a dangerous man.

And this childlikeness showed in the coat he wore, with the oblong wooden buttons, in the new white pants Gertie had bought him, and his new sneakers with big white bows.

Beal then went back to his apartment. His cousin, Little Nin, was there heating a can of soup. It was almost five thirty in the afternoon. The local news was on the radio.

Beal was thinking while looking out the window. He had to keep Little Nin with him, because he was the only family she had. She bothered him, she troubled him, and he had at times abused her; but in his own way, he was devoted to her. In his own way, and it was the way of a great many men, he wouldn't be able to exist without her—and loved her desperately. Though he did at times say he would throw her out or something else, he never did.

He was also about to be evicted from the small apartment in the old hotel. He owed some five hundred dollars in rent, and he had smashed both the front door and a window when he was angry over not being taken seriously about being First Nation. And, much worse, over being talked into giving an interview to the paper by Vivian Speck. The high point of his life had dissolved, and it had become a terrible humiliation.

Beal was not a young boy anymore; he was already in his late twenties. He had grade nine education.

Shamus said there "must be ten thousand there if there's a cent" and that no one would know. He also said (a part of gossip) that Musselman had a "strange piece" in Nelson and went over there most nights.

Beal thought about all of this as he sat on the old brown couch and said nothing to his little cousin, who had hoped he would get a job at the mill across the river.

Of course, there was only about fourteen hundred dollars in the drawer, but to Shamus it had seemed like a fortune.

At that very moment Shamus was home, sick that he had said anything, sick that he was such a mimic, and sicker that something might happen. He prayed to the God he did not believe in that nothing would happen. But he couldn't stand looking at his new pants that Gertie had bought him, and his new sneakers with the big bows. In fact, the sneaker box they had come in was now used for papers in the drawer.

"To Dad, love Gertie and Pruty" was on the box. In fact, it was while buying the sneakers that Gertie had first met Mickey Bowels.

*Nothing will happen*, he thought. *Nothing will happen.*

IT MIGHT NOT HAVE HAPPENED, EXCEPT FOR WEAVER de Speck. Beal had just about given up on it, was thinking that he was to take Little Nin to a movie and then report for the midnight shift, until he had a visit from that young man.

That distant night, the clock had ticked away. It was seven o'clock. At this time, young Jamie Musselman was at Zellers downtown buying glue for his model airplane. He was alone as usual, and he just made it into the store before it closed. He had bought a card for his dad's fifty-second birthday.

When he came out of Zellers, with the glue and the card in his hand, and started back toward Jane Street, he passed a man who had just driven to town, parked near the post office and was on his way to visit Beal, because he wanted to buy a little bit of hash oil, and maybe do some kind of story.

That is what he was thinking. Weaver de Speck's grand idea was to be a writer, who would shock people. His whole raison d'être was to shock, and shock well, and keep shocking. In order to "make them pay attention."

There was nothing sacred, and he was delighted there wasn't.

This particular night he was still smarting from what had happened at Ryerson. Or perhaps that he had told himself—and bragged to his mother—that by this time he would have a book published. He had told her that over a year ago, because over a year ago he thought by this time he would.

No one but his sad father seemed to try to prevent the kind of intellectual harm Weaver wanted to do, but Orlif seemed too beaten down by life's worries. Weaver wrote terrible things about premiers and police, about the army, and other writers—all people who he felt had injured his immense aptitude. And Orlif had found these articles in a drawer in his room. Weaver was deeply depressed about not being seen immediately as a great man—a replacement for Gandhi or Christ himself, poor Orlif told Vivian one night.

"I'm sure of it."

"What are you sure of?"

"He walks about as if he's Gandhi. If I say anything, he just smiles and shakes his head like Gandhi would. I think he thinks we should recognize him as Jesus. He preaches to us all the time about a new way of life, and goes about despising everyone."

"Nonsense—not Jesus," Vivian said. "Perhaps John the Baptist—I mean symbolically—"

But secretly Vivian was worried as well—worried about her child. In fact, she had started to smoke again, off and on. She had planned a great launch for his book at her house—had intended to call the local press—and all of a sudden he appeared with no book and no degree, and no attempt to tell her why. This made her, in her own erratic way, become enthralled by the German professor, who her husband had spent years trying to get for a visit. Weaver coming home from Ryerson coincided with this German visit, and caused a lot of anxiety. She had bragged to this German for days, and then had to admit Weaver's book was not forthcoming. Never had she been so humiliated. So, she determined to make it up to this German in some way.

Weaver was his mother's third pregnancy—she had aborted the other two. She didn't know if she would carry him to term but finally decided to do so. And she did so because her father said she wouldn't receive her inheritance if she did not.

"I'll keep the inheritance in my pocket until you pocket me a child."

And so she did. She hated and feared her father. She disliked her pregnancy. Her position as head of the pro-choice movement was compromised.

She had explained all of this one night to Weaver when he was still a child. It was during her time of commitment to truth—and honesty. This bogus feeling was a standard among many friends she was determined to impress.

She sat little Weaver down with a plate of cookies and took his hands in hers. A cigarette burned in the ashtray.

"Yes, dear—Mommie must tell you. The only reason I had you—and in fact I wouldn't have had you—but I did have you—was because your papa insisted I have some sort of child. Now, we thought of adopting—we did—seriously—but the children who one adopts are not at times of the best quality, and I wanted to have a child who came from where we knew—do you understand."

He simply stared at her. And she nervously picked up her cigarette.

Outside, it was a grey day and snow was falling. She put out her cigarette and nervously picked up and lit another one. Then she smoothed his hair, and said he was a pretty child.

Weaver did understand it. It took some time, but one day a year or so later it struck him as if he had been hit. She didn't want him, and she wanted nothing to interfere with her life. It came so suddenly he couldn't breathe.

And that's when this happened.

No one knew why he kicked walls. It usually happened when the monthly cheques were delivered. Twice he hid these cheques on his mother and father.

That's when he began to become unmanageable. She didn't know why.

So, one evening after he seemed upset and uncooperative, Vivian told some of her friends that she was exasperated, and had really wanted a girl.

"A girl would have completed my dream. A girl and only a girl."

"Girls are much better," Botsie, one of her outspoken friends, said with the frivolity most outspoken classless people have. "You might still have it come true."

A week later his mother took him aside.

She told him that now was the time to take certain hormone blockers and inhibitors, if he wished to express himself. Later it just might be too late. There was a way to do it, ending in orchiectomy, so she would leave him with this information.

Weaver de Speck was ten years old. He put his head down and wouldn't look at her. Twice she picked his head up, smiling and asking him what was wrong, and twice his head dropped and his eyes closed. She took his hand a moment. But he took his hand away.

Suddenly realizing her own desperate vanity, she stood and rushed from the room.

Two hours later she opened the door to that dark room, and he was still sitting where she had left him, with his head still lowered the way it had been. Never had so much shame engulfed him. He believed it was because he had kicked walls. At this moment in his life, nothing in the apartment in downtown Halifax seemed to have anything to do with love.

Within the next month he made sure he had three outfits, one red, one blue and one green. He wanted to surprise them, to show them both that he loved them, and wanted them to be proud of him.

Whether or not true—some said it was not true—his father seemed unable to influence much. He was almost ten years older than Vivian, and like many men who grew up under the influence of a mother, and of the university-sanctioned feminist movement, he was influenced terribly by his wife. Besides, she was younger, with a much more forceful personality.

Orlif was instrumental in his son's life because he was so often not there.

"Once I get tenure, Weaver, you will see—yes, my boy, you will definitely see a change in your dad—once I get tenure. Yes sir!"

As he grew, Weaver tried to be a boy on his own. He was more determined to be a boy than anyone Orlif knew, except Orlif did not know it then. He would bring home a hockey stick that he retrieved from a barrel or sometimes a puck that he found. But Orlif had little or no interest in sports, especially hockey. So Weaver was seen by himself most often, banging the puck against the garage door. He was alone most of the time.

He climbed trees, made a fort, and once he killed a weasel.

He was suspended in grade nine. The teacher was Ms. Lamond. All the boys loved her. She had wondrous breasts, which you could just make out when she bent over at a certain angle.

And he kept telling her he did. That is, that he loved her. That he wanted to run away with her. Once, he came up to her and showed her a hundred-dollar bill.

"I can get more where this came from," he said.

He kept following her home and waiting in her dooryard.

Then he realized he was not supposed to. And he was expelled.

He became interested in poetry and drama and played in summer stock for a few summers.

Years passed. Years went away.

He became a tall and rather strong young man—and was sent to psychiatrists until he stopped going at the age of seventeen.

Vivian, in order to be free, to show her mettle, had in some way destroyed them all.

Then he went to Ryerson, where he said he would be a writer. But he didn't stay there. It was all hushed up. Vivian might have known the full story, but she chose not to tell Orlif, and Orlif, so often in the dark, had to piece the story together bit by bit.

But that evening, before Weaver went to see Beal, he went across the park to the tavern and had a drink of beer with some money that his mother had given him. The cheques had stopped coming two years before, and he felt in agony for his parents, and the sadness he too had caused them. He promised his mother that he would pay the money back. That things were happening and he would be able to take care of himself. But Ryerson was his last stop, on many stops—York Drama School, a fine arts college in the States, Ryerson, and now back home again. And everywhere he went, he felt a certain dread that he had failed, and he needed to prove to himself that he would not fail again.

He had someone at Ryerson whom he liked—a young, dark-haired girl from Wisconsin, whom he had bought a ring for—and when he had taken it to her, she was sad, and said, "But Weaver, you know I go with Gavin Peters?"

"No you don't, not really. Why do you?"

"We are going to be married, Weaver—we are going to be married."

"*No*," he said.

So Gavin very much became an enemy—Gavin the new young writer who hardly knew him. He would follow Gavin around at a distance, and when Gavin looked behind him, Weaver would turn his head away, or stop and look in a window. He was like Orlif in this way. He found it most difficult to confront people.

Worse, Gavin's family had come from the Miramichi, and people had heard of him there.

Gavin himself had never considered Weaver de Speck a dreaded enemy. He simply did his work, day after day—had written some very promising things, and received an award. And was engaged to the girl Weaver was infatuated with, but neither Gavin nor the girl knew this. (Until he had tried to give her the ring.)

Tonight, at the Blackhorse Tavern, Weaver thought of his mother's own infatuation that had happened just a week or so before. "How could my father never say anything to that German! Tell him to go to hell."

But his mother had boasted so much about his book, and then, when it didn't happen, she was devastated in a way. And then, well, what could he say. At that same time, the German arrived, and she had to prove herself, and she was growing older. And it was all a disaster.

At any rate, when in Ryerson, he kept following the girl around, asked her out—until finally she had told him that she would tell Gavin.

"I don't want to be mean—but you wouldn't want to mess with Gavin." She had said, "He was a Golden Gloves boxer."

And he had turned and hurriedly walked away. In fact, he hid in his room, her words over and over again playing out amid the dark curtains and the desk lamp. He kept his head lowered just as he had that long-ago evening with his mother.

"If I do not do something soon—I will demand it of me. I will demand I do something."

So, back to Gavin. Both had found themselves by accident (if there are any) at Ryerson together. Weaver, to offset Gavin and his girl, had written a novel about Ryerson himself—and what a terrible fellow he was, all the way around. He just added things in as he went along. It all seemed very funny and tremendously good.

"I am sorry," the professor whom he gave the manuscript to wrote. "Because it is simply not true—he did not live like this. There is a great curse in the land and it has come upon us and it is in the form of accusation toward a past the accusers were not part of. But it gives notoriety to those who write it."

"Is that what you think I did?"

"I think writers from Newfoundland to Saskatoon do this—it's a kind of pandering."

He then handed the manuscript back, and in fact went and found a pristine manila envelope to do so—because he had accidentally torn the one the manuscript was previously in.

Weaver left the house and walked about in circles—in many circles—until he found a bar. He was devastated by this critique. He actually thought his professor would love the book. But he noticed that the professor had written and then had erased some lines. One was: "He channels Gavin Peters whenever he talks about the working class. He knows nothing about work or how men work at all. He knows little of how men work in cold or in ice, or on boxcars shovelling coal."

And another was: "All cruel people describe themselves as paragons of frankness—Tennessee Williams." That too was erased.

And also this line, erased furiously: "He writes about famous people so he can stand on the shoulders of those he maligns. Only the most self-serving of writers permit themselves this luxury." Weaver had to hold that up to the light to read it.

Stung deeply by his own imperfections, Weaver went to his room. But he was now deeply angered by the professor, and believed there was a case of bigotry here—the professor didn't understand his own sins in relation to our deplorable past. So he began to think of the professor's sins—yes, he defended too many of the culpable in his history course. The professor had defended that Anglican minister too! He had defended the Buckingham Palace guards wearing bear fur hats, defended hunting, defended soldiers—this, in fact, had caused a good amount of angst among certain of the most progressive students. And didn't he also say there were some kind teachers at residential schools?

It was this moment at Ryerson that would eventually lead Weaver home—to a place he didn't belong, to a place Gavin Peters's family was from, and he would become involved with people who at that moment he did not know.

He smoked one cigarette after the other and brooded. He had already told his mother he would have a book published by Coach House Press, that it was all in the works. That he had signed a contract. And she had told others and others had told others, who had wanted to meet him.

"We'll have a party for you when you come home for reading week—and you can meet some of my friends."

All his life this Professor Brown had lived by himself, entirely dependent on certain papers for his course on nineteenth- and twentieth-century European politics. For twenty-two years he had taught his course at Ryerson and was famous for teaching it. For twenty-two years he had added to his understanding of internecine European politics, and just recently had written fifteen or twenty more pages of meticulous research, especially on Germany's terrible position in 1914, and had corresponded with people there. They said he was an expert on the rise of the Bolsheviks in the Soviet Union as well. He was quiet and unassuming, and for the most part he didn't seek publicity. He had known Weaver's father. They had for a time shared a room at Dalhousie University. He knew Gavin's family as well.

So Professor Brown spoke about his own book the next time Weaver visited—not to brag about it, but to show that he showed deference to many of the people whose names he used, and did not try to exploit them. He was a friend with Margaret Thatcher and Angela Merkel.

"Perhaps some of the things you denounce were done for reasons you would at one time have applauded," he told Weaver de Speck.

He said this for Weaver's benefit because he liked him and thought highly of him.

One day, he told Weaver proudly that he would publish these years of notes in book form, and a very well-known historian in England thought he could find a publisher for him there. Perhaps within the year. And Gavin, who was fairly well-known now, would write an introduction for this.

"Wouldn't that be something if it really sold well?" the professor said, smiling naively amid a lifetime of books. That his book would in any way be published seemed to him the greatest of victories. "It's about the awful choice Kaiser Wilhelm was in a way forced to make—in 1914—and how all else in the twentieth century seemed to flow from this decision. Or was he forced to make it? That remains the question. What if he hadn't made it—would Stalin have risen to prominence—that is what this book wonders—and Hitler? You see, Weaver, sometimes decisions are also in the stars. But sometimes whatever we do affects the lives of many not yet born, or those born we do not yet know."

"Would you write an introduction for my book?" Weaver asked quickly. "I mean, if I revise it a bit—the book I just showed you." Weaver spoke hopefully, looking at the professor directly.

But the professor did not answer. He nodded, seemed to fumble about with his hands, looked at his old pocket watch, but he did not answer. Then he picked up his cane and inspected it (he used a cane at times because of gout).

Weaver was furious at the look the professor gave to that pocket watch, a watch given to him by a woman when he was twenty-one, and whom he never married, but lost to another.

*He is a bigot for sure—yes, it all shows*, he said to himself. He only said this because the age allowed it.

And he smiled bitterly at the man who asked him to stay and have a sherry. Then he said to himself: *Something has to be done. These people are out to ruin us, with their hypocrisies—I even saw him praying once—he didn't think I saw—but, ha, well, there you have it. There you have it—he prays.*

Then this happened, so unplanned that Weaver, even two years after, couldn't explain why he had done so. That next week, during the seminar, Weaver went into the study, took Professor Brown's papers—drafted on an old typewriter and annotated with thousands of pen marks—and read them over. He read on one page the suicide of Stalin's wife and, flipping back forty-five pages, the rise of an obscure party headed by Adolf Hitler.

Yes, it was all there—the Kaiser's decision to enter Belgium, and the untold grief in the years to follow; the horrid fight for Verdun and the Battle of the Somme.

To him, though he realized the professor's hundreds of hours of work, the relentless toil of this professor who had done nothing to him, except loan him money and help him find a room when he first came—and wore this professor the same awful tweed jacket he had worn for twenty years—Weaver realized he was holding something foreign and very remote to himself in his hands. But what if he himself could use it in some way?

What if this could become his book? That is, make it more relative to today, less staid and blinkered. Improve it! Besides, it was only a draft, and he whimsically thought he could finish it himself.

Impulsively, he took the papers, put them under his coat, left the apartment and brought them home. He was worried, even panicked that he had done so. Why had he done so? He wanted to read them over. He wanted to see if he could do something with them himself. But he wouldn't use all of it—only the best parts. He telephoned his mother and said, "My book will be published soon. Are you proud of that? Everyone thinks I am a failure. Well, wait and see!"

There was such emptiness inside him when he hung up the phone, he wished to die.

The next time he went to Brown's house, the place was torn apart. Two young first-year students, a boy and a girl, were going through papers in the study, the cabinets in the library were opened, and all the desk drawers had been turned upside down.

So Weaver joined in, and helped the professor look for these papers for days, always willing to give his opinion on where the papers might be. The professor was beside himself with worry, and twice he got drunk, stumbling about his apartment in a fog. It took him nothing to get drunk; a few drinks of sherry and he stumbled about. On happier occasions this was a joke among his students.

"I made no copy," was all he could say.

"I made no copy."

Then he would pause and say with tears in his eyes, "Did I mention—I made no copy. What an idiot I am to still use a typewriter and make no copy—what does it show? I will tell you, Weaver, it shows arrogance. It is my fault—because it shows arrogance. That's why I lost Shelly"—this was the love he had lost—"this is why, yes, too proud to ask her out—too—too—too proud. And you know—well—you know I opened a car door, thinking what was I thinking, and there she was with my friend—her breasts naked—a day in the sun swimming—and I was late working on my master's about the Industrial Revolution. I am so, so sorry."

He stumbled away.

People asked Weaver to stay with this Professor Brown, who might do himself injury. "You are someone he greatly admires," people told him.

Weaver slept on the black leather couch in the very room he had stolen the papers from.

He decided he would spend a while looking, and then find the papers himself and bring them back. He would tell people he was in contact with certain people, and did a deal with them, on promise of anonymity, and would not reveal his sources.

So this is what he did. He told the professor he might be able to help. He then asked Professor Brown for a thousand dollars that he said was what his contact wanted.

"I will get them for you," he said. He waited for the thousand dollars, took it and left. At the door, Professor Brown, tears streaming down his wrinkled face, gave him a hug.

Two days later, he went to the professor's house, filled with new information. "I'll have those papers tomorrow," he said, "or the next day for sure!"

However, security from the university was there, and so were the police.

All those papers had been found hidden in his room. The room Professor Brown had helped him acquire.

Gavin had also been asked to search for them. (It took him four hours to decide only someone at that seminar could have taken them. After Weaver had asked for the thousand dollars, Gavin asked campus security and the police to search Weaver's room. They had both a warrant and a key.) And Gavin had brought them back to the professor that day.

When Weaver came into the house holding two coffees in his hands, the papers were sitting on the table in the hallway, copious and riddled with pen marks, and oddly, even more yellowed by time. At first Weaver didn't understand what he was looking at: three men, and a batch of old papers.

The professor did not press charges, and when Weaver finally apologized, saying he did it as an experiment for future writing, the professor only said:

"Yes well yes, an experiment—okay, yes—you were my favourite student—yes—bright—very—yes, okay, thank you—a mistake—we all make mistakes—yes—thank you—yes, you see, I had no copy—that was the only thing—other than that—but I had no copy—anyways, and you mentioned my girl to your friends, about the girl I lost—I should have known then—you told secrets about me, and I told no secrets about you—honour—it was honour—and yes, as you said, she was bereft of clothes, her young breasts—yes—and I had no copy—you see. You said a man like me should not have children—yes—you said that as well—everything gets back to one, you see—and other things, unpleasant things—you said you saw me praying, with a rosary—well yes—I do, do so, forgive me. I prayed that these papers would come back to me. They did do so. They came back. I said the rosary—foolish—you are so wise to call me a fool. No, please keep the thousand dollars—I insist—for your help in this—yes—okay, it's yours."

And he closed his eyes as Weaver shook his hand. So Weaver added, "Yes, it's not you, professor, but you must admit your fondness for Ryerson himself. You see—his name—you see, I was simply protesting, in a way, to further our journey toward reconciliation," and he looked at everyone and nodded.

Weaver stayed in the house an uncomfortable length of time, saying he would help straighten everything out. But no one spoke to or addressed him, and finally he left, never sure of what he wanted to prove.

*I will kill myself*, Weaver thought.

Gavin came to visit him (Professor Brown insisted he do so) and asked him if he could help in any way, gave him the name of an editor at Coach House he knew, and offered to speak to people at Ryerson if he could.

"I'll read the novel for you if you like?" he said.

Weaver kept his head down, tears in his eyes, and waved the offer away.

But that made it worse. He couldn't look at Gavin. He discovered he couldn't speak. What he had done now manifested itself in how Gavin stood to leave, holding out his hand.

"It's all been rectified," Gavin said. "We all make mistakes, we can all be forgiven!"

Weaver wore his T-shirt that stated STOP OIL NOW. But in Toronto, on those cold, endless streets, he always tried to find a place where it was warm. And who in the world would blame him, when the temperature dropped, and the wind blew against the lost grey buildings.

Then the letter arrived, telling him he was no longer welcome in his room.

Now Weaver thought of all of this at the tavern. He thought of everything. He thought of the French teacher he had followed home. He remembered the German professor a few weeks ago, saying, "Oh, once you are older, my young man, you will understand," and pinching his cheek, and then winking at his mother.

It was that wink and his mother's seductive smile—that's what troubled him. And the way she had said: "Yes, professor—I know."

The way she said, "I know."

He had looked from one to the other, glanced at poor Orlif and felt desperate. Horrid.

His mother and father were now living modestly—and he the benefactor of their inheritance. Did he even remember his grandfather? Only once or twice. A strange remembrance of a man in an office, of his mother Vivian trying to please him, sitting on a chair and Weaver playing with a toy in the corner. Poor Vivian trying to please a man she could not please—had a son in order to please him. The office smelled of cigars, and a kind of staleness, with papers and leather chairs, and calendar pictures of ladies. And Orlif standing there, looking out of place amid it all—with a young, hypersensitive wife who had expected so much more from him.

So, Weaver met Mr. Beal because his mother had said to the German professor, "What a rogue Beal is. He's like you, professor—a real individual."

Vivian wanted to parade her knowledge of men like Beal, yet if he ever showed his dangerous side, she would flee. In fact, so would the German professor.

Orlif simply fussed with his pipe in the corner, nodded and said: "Professor, when can we have a talk—I have an essay I'd like to show you."

But Vivian wanted to show the professor her paintings, and they went upstairs.

They went upstairs and ten minutes passed, and then twenty. Now and then Orlif would glance up those stairs, and then over at his son.

Weaver at that moment was in misery. Still, they came back down, and nothing was said.

Her son, the product of her revolutionary fantasies; her husband, their victim.

But Orlif did say this the next morning to his son: "I want you to promise me one thing, son—and only one: that you will not become too chummy with our Mr. Beal."

"Why?"

"I'm not sure why. I thought of something last night—I'm not sure what—but I beg you not to."

After two beer, Weaver finally went off to meet a dangerous man. He wasn't even thinking of going there—that is, he was headed for the old Ritchie Wharf where there was a plaque to local writers.

How had it all come about? He was desperately hoping when they were installing those plaques that they would have one of him. But that had not happened. Gavin, who had relatives downriver, was on one of the plaques. The award he had received for his book, *Wayward Sons*, about the Miramichiers in the Crimea War, was mentioned in quotes. And a citation: "A level of true bravery persists in his written word."

Tonight, Vivian said she knew Gavin's people—but had not cared for them. He had blurted, "Oh, I know him—I've never been impressed." Then he had asked for money to go to town.

Orlif said, "Are you going to town? I thought we might play a game of chess."

But Weaver just shook his head and left.

He stood in the evening air for a moment looking at the plaque where Gavin's name was.

Gavin never said a man should not have a child in order to hurt and harm him. He never spoke down to anyone who said the rosary. Gavin once said: "If Johnny Tapia and Roberto Durán can say the rosary, I think Professor Brown should be able to as well." All of this flitted in poor Weaver's mind. The idea that the plaque noted Gavin's bravery disturbed him.

Across the street, he saw Beal's light go on.

He turned in that direction.

That day, after his talk with Shamus, Beal went home.

Beal had been the talk of many people in our town over the last year or so.

He had boxes of papers on First Nation claims. He had tried many times to get in to see the Minister of Indigenous Affairs and was once handcuffed and led away. He had made a name for himself—and was by now known to have been involved in many and various crimes. Earlier in the year he had petitioned the courts for his birth record. That's when Weaver's mother came in, taking over and helping him prove he was First Nation. She rallied for him, had a group formed on his behalf, petitioned the local Catholic church for his documents. She had no knowledge of what she was doing, but smoking again almost two packs a day—and demanding she be listened to by the premier himself—it all seemed more possible to Beal than before.

"Oh yes, you will be definitely thrust in the public eye. I will thrust you in the public eye—I have connections everywhere. I will be your thruster."

At first this pleased Beal very much. Like some powerful men, he was naive, even at times childlike.

This was when the doctor, Colonel Musselman, came in.

Colonel Musselman had delivered him. Beal had not been born where he had claimed, the reserve. (And this is what the reserve was in fact trying to tell him.)

Now, after his name was in the paper, his claim discounted, the premier ignoring Vivian's petitions, Beal felt humiliated by everyone. The worst thing happened that could have happened: He had been laughed at. And Vivian, sensing she had helped cause it, tried to distance herself from all that went on. She did not answer her phone when he called. When he took her car, she once again realized she had to rally for him or be a laughingstock herself.

Weaver de Speck knocked on the old, blackened door of Beal's little apartment, looking for the hash oil that would calm his nerves.

If it hadn't been for Weaver's knock, Beal would have gone out to a movie Little Nin wanted to see. A Disney movie with little hobbits in it. She had wanted to see it for a long time, and Beal had promised her! Then he was going to start a midnight shift. Little Nin, all excited, had gotten him the job.

But Weaver came in.

"Don't open the door," Little Nin said.

But Beal told her to go answer it.

The opening of that door changed all their lives.

BEAL COULD HAVE HAD A JOB IN CONSTRUCTION ACROSS the river that very day. Little Nin had pleaded with a foreman who told her, yes, if he came to see him, Beal would be hired. He could start the midnight shift. Beal had gone there too, the day before. But it was Nin who had gotten him the job.

It was better than working the boats, better than cutting pulp.

She had run all the way back across the bridge, her small hands clenched in joy. But he had hesitated. Shamus had said ten thousand dollars. That would last him some months. If all went well, he could still make the midnight shift.

"No one will be home—they are never home in the evening. The boy goes to the library, and the Colonel goes out. Play your cards right," Shamus had said.

There was something else as well. Beal was still humiliated by his own name in the paper. Everything had been a mistake. He shouldn't have listened to Vivian Speck, but she told him of her broad provincial influence in all these matters.

A reporter had revealed this when he began to validate his claim. They had contacted Colonel Musselman, who had been the doctor the night Beal was born, to a young white woman from Arron Brook. She had been made pregnant by a young white man who came in on a ship, the *Lambeth-Othello* out of Liverpool,

England. The woman, along with other ladies, would meet the boats that came in from England, Spain and Germany.

It had happened—his birth, that is—on the Renous highway, when she had been kicked out of home, and Colonel Musselman—who wasn't a colonel then—had happened to drive into the small restaurant where Beal's mother was in labour. It was a winter night; a storm had come and everyone was stuck there, and her water broke when she was in the bathroom.

Musselman, having just become a doctor, was the physician. The woman told him the boy's father had gone back to Liverpool months before, and perhaps did not know what condition he had left her in. She, Beal's mother, was a young woman who met the foreign sailors for money.

"What fool I," his mother said. She was a scared little waif of a thing, that is how she was described. A poor soul of seventeen who died in childbirth.

So, people knew how his mother became pregnant. And now the whole River did.

His picture was on the front page of the local paper. In big letters, it said the reporter had the EXCLUSIVE.

Beal asked to have another interview—he kept phoning the reporter. He followed her until she told him she would phone Detective Matters.

Perhaps that was why he stole the car, but he didn't even know. He only knew that Vivian left him, that she didn't support him when he most needed her support.

Now those boxes of papers showed he was not educated enough to handle what he had tried to. He believed he was First Nation and wanted status and money—but he would not get either. They no longer allowed him on the reserve, even to pick up some clothes he had left there.

He was furious that he had been exposed and exploited by things he himself had never known or understood.

Little Nin followed him about like a lost soul, telling him not to mind the stares of people. That they stared at her too.

He had met Little Nin in the park, the week after Vivian came to his aid, and they now lived together. In many ways Vivian tried to illuminate a strange kind of independence from her domineering father by doing these mighty things. She had left his den and his office and his large suburban home to prove it. She had a son to collect her inheritance, but her main interest in all the years Weaver was growing was a kind of conventional activism that put her on occasion in the papers, as an achiever. She had in fact received an honorary doctorate some years past. And was most proud of it.

"A woman who is the conscience of so many of us today," the citation said, in part.

But all of this was flagging now. And when she phoned a woman whom she had once been close to in those grave and socialist days in university, the woman no longer seemed to remember her.

Beal got out of jail and met Little Nin. They had an on-again, off-again relationship. Sometimes Beal had no place to stay. But there was no doubt—in spite of everything—that he loved her.

The very day Beal and she had met in the park, Little Nin had been supposed to meet that youngster Jamie Musselman, who had told her he would read a poem by Dylan Thomas to her. She did not know who Dylan Thomas was, but was waiting for Musselman when Beal came along. This was her famous cousin, and for a while she forgot about the young boy who had helped her so much with lessons and other things.

Why hadn't Beal taken that job across the river? When Shamus said Colonel Musselman's name, it stung deep in his heart. He had been laughed at by everyone. So had his mother. He knew it wasn't Musselman's fault, but he couldn't stand being laughed at.

"No, no, no—the boy is mistaken—he is not First Nation."

He had been laughed at as a boy by everyone, and he had tried to make those who had laughed at him as a lonely child feel frightened of who he was as a man. And he had almost succeeded—almost.

But worse was the interviewer. When he asked how this journalist came in possession of certain knowledge, the reporter simply said—as if she had rehearsed it with her boss—"Oh, that's private information."

The way she said it was so glibly dismissive of him that if he wasn't on the phone but in her presence, he would have struck her.

And the boxes of papers that sat all about him—all those legal documents collected over the years to prove who he might be—now seemed to insult him. Worse, he never knew who he was. Because of the fact a First Nations woman, Mrs. Samuel, had helped raise him, he had, in his own mind, lived a lie.

Weaver told him about his own plight, which was lack of money. He would like to get some money and go to Europe—but things weren't going well. Weaver tried to sound very cavalier and offhand as he spoke of his trouble, as if one should know of his trouble, a man as cultured as he having to be here in this little town.

"I can't stay here—there's nothing for me here—except my parents—but I'd be far better on my own. I have to get some money—so maybe I could sell some hash—if you have some I could sell—you know, for you—on a percentage?"

Beal looked at him a long moment, then looked at Little Nin, who was looking at both of them from under her eyebrows.

"Or maybe something else?" Weaver asked.

So, after a moment, though he hesitated, Beal told Weaver what Shamus had said, about a lot of money in Musselman's house.

"There is a place with a lot of money—I am thinking I might just take it—to even up a score."

There was a slight pause. Weaver thought it over a second. The very first thing he thought was to say no. No. But he didn't say that.

"I'll go," he said. "I'll go with you."

He was thinking that this might be the very book he could write, one about the inside cubicles of a thief's mind. He thought he would simply observe—and then write about it, without implicating himself. The book had already formed in his mind.

"I'll go."

For the rest of his life, he would wonder what jaded idea of shocking people made him say such a venal thing. In fact, as strange as it was, this was the beginning of his journey toward redemption. The journey to forgo this world for one better. It would not be noticed by him for a long while. But perhaps, toward the end, it would be realized by him that, like so many of us, the road to redemption begins with terror.

There was a line in Professor Brown's manuscript that Weaver suddenly remembered: *The terror we have heard of has entered our town.* It was a reference to the Nazis of 1933, but Professor Brown had taken the line from the movie *M*.

At this moment he wanted to back out, to say he had thought better of it. But he did not. And he suddenly looked frightened.

Beal, who was no one's fool, and blamed Vivian for his being laughed at—for encouraging him to go to the paper, and now having her son with him—put on his jacket and his boots. He looked at Weaver seriously and lit a cigarette with the flip of his lighter.

"Are you sure?" he said. "It mightn't be easy."

At this moment Little Nin looked at him, Weaver, with imploring eyes, without speaking. She had two little studs over her eyebrows and her eyes looked brave and sad.

Darkness had by now entered through the walls, and they left.

"It won't take long?" Weaver asked, as if to mitigate his unease.

Little Nin following behind them like a sad little ghost with big sneakers. (Her sneakers were much bigger than her actual feet.) All the way there she was trying to talk them out of it. Of going to see hobbits.

Weaver was, he believed, only doing this for a story—but if a crime happened, what a story he could write! He got caught up with something at Ryerson, but this would prove it!

He followed along thinking of his course in journalism, his novel, Professor Brown, Gavin's success, his mother's disappointment in him, his father's lack of spine, and all other things.

They headed away one behind the other, Little Nin saying, "Let's go to the movie instead, guys—okay?"

Weaver only remembered the terror of the Colonel coming into the room. They had been told he was out seeking a certain woman's favour from across the river.

Beal had taken the gun from the drawer, along with the envelope, thinking there was ten thousand dollars in it. He had little use for the gun, but he knew where he could sell it—and then he looked up and saw the Colonel. The gun immediately went off, and the bullet pierced the man's forehead. The Colonel simply started to fall backwards, and then crumbled unto the floor against the back wall. All of this happened in ten seconds.

Beal could say he didn't mean for it to happen, because he didn't; the gun had a hair trigger and he had put almost no pressure on it. And Weaver could say he didn't really intend to be there, but he was. Both of them, a few hours before, had no knowledge they would ever be together and ever be here.

Beal tossed the gun away just as the boy, Jamie Musselman, was rushing down the stairs.

"Dad, what's wrong?" they heard.

For some reason, when they got to the bushes that led to a path that led down toward old Strawberry Marsh, Nin fell, and Weaver de Speck tumbled over her, covering his pants with mud. Later, they heard a police siren and saw an ambulance rush by. There was blood spatter on the bills—and for some reason on Weaver de Speck's shirt.

Little Nin begged them to go to the police. In fact, she thought that was where they were heading when they got to the town square. They sat by the fountain as they watched the ambulance, and then Beal said, "Let's go."

They all jumped into Vivian's car, parked as it was near the post office, and, with Beal driving, drove along the river toward Load Road.

"What a mess," Beal kept saying, and he asked Little Nin, who was bawling, to not think of it anymore.

"Don't think of it no more—it's over."

Perhaps Vivian did not know what in the world she had done when she had petitioned successfully for Beal's freedom. As she declared to the stunned police, "My destiny is to help all the downtrodden in this regard. I have been a warrior for justice."

Orlif had a premonition Beal would someday come back to haunt them both. But he had existed all his life in a state of incomprehensible innocence brought on by years of aloof study, and he never knew how to disagree. In fact, he knew how to disagree. At times he said: "Oh ho—wait until tomorrow, then I'll tell her."

Especially when she went away a whole day and night—with the professor from Germany.

SOME YEARS PASSED, AND IT SEEMED FORGOTTEN. WEAVER de Speck left town, and travelled here and there, to India, and ending in Europe, and Beal and Little Nin went out west, where he worked in the oil patch for a while and she worked as a maid at a motel.

Until Jamie Musselman was found guilty.

After that happened, they both came back—a day behind one another. Weaver had been in France—and Beal, north of Edmonton. Weaver had written home for money on occasion.

He came back—as all do to the Miramichi. He came home.

Beal followed Little Nin a day later. That is, Little Nin was compelled to come back, after Jamie was convicted, and Beal was compelled to follow.

People still remembered Little Nin with studs in her eyebrows and a ring in her lip. And of course they remembered Mr. Beal.

One night a few months after Jamie Musselman was convicted, Vivian and Weaver were at home. Orlif had made popcorn and was sitting in the corner—not in his usual chair, either, but in a smaller, out-of-the-way chair near the small stove, nibbling on popcorn he had cupped in his right hand. The stove was on, and it was cozy. Orlif and his wife were living in some moderation now—both had never handled money well—and they had indulged Weaver for many years. Especially sending him money in Europe.

Orlif was puzzled first because he liked the little priest Father Benjamin, and he was not supposed to. That is, Vivian often told him how he should feel. Like some intellectual men who married their students, he was sometimes at a loss because at one point she seemed so much more attuned to the modern world. But Orlif was always at a loss, and Vivian, though often at a loss herself, kept up a brave front of never being so. Now she had formed a committee—and as such, this committee had a certain activist bent, and as such, she had already spoken about the little priest and how he should be viewed. She did this only because of spite. The Church hadn't helped with Beal and hadn't listened to her list of demands six years before. Still, the Catholic Church was horrid and all decent people, especially the more educated, knew it.

Orlif, unfortunately, had met Father Benjamin and liked him. "I do like him—I do—I mean, I like him a little. What I mean to say is, I like him as much as I am allowed to like him—and will like him no more than that."

Weaver told them he was writing something quite spectacular. He stated that he didn't think the investigation into the death of Colonel Musselman was being handled well. He said this because he had learned Gavin had taken an interest in the case and had visited both the River, where he had stayed with relatives, and the house. But in truth, Weaver felt very guilty that Jamie had been sent to prison. He was also worried that the very reason he had gone to that house was now being investigated by Gavin himself.

He was angry about what might come of it all.

Angry that Gavin's connections to this River were through people Weaver did not know—but perhaps should have known.

Certain aspects of Weaver's interest in the case also bothered Orlif very much. A deep worry had entered him over the last fortnight. All of this had made him wish to talk to the priest—or talk to someone about his fear, his waking up two nights in a row in a cold sweat.

As for the priest, Father Benjamin, there was a lot of skepticism about him as far as Vivian was concerned. A man who had lived in the orphanage run by the sisters who knew Mother Teresa?

But Orlif found the little Indian man's journey quite fascinating—even inspiring. Not too many people he knew were left on the side of the road in a cardboard box, while tigers roamed nearby.

"Yes," he would sometimes say to Vivian, "in a cardboard box—that was all he had—and let me tell you—at three years old, to go seeking your fortune in a cardboard box, that's not a lot."

Orlif had been trying to come to grips with the case that had been the talk of the River for months. The case of young Musselman. He truly wondered about it. Sometimes Orlif would stop pruning his garden and think out loud and say, "I am not certain he is guilty."

Sometimes he would get up in the middle of the night, and have a pee, and light his pipe, and sit outside and say, "No, I don't think he is guilty."

There were certain things that had plagued him about it. And Orlif Speck had written them down on a sheet of white paper. Unlike certain professors, he did not belong to any set or group for safety, partly because he too had been laughed at in the philosophy department a good deal and ate his lunch, out of a paper bag, in his office by himself.

It had all started with a certain event.

A few weeks before the murder of Colonel Musselman, Orlif had invited a poet activist from Germany, an Hegelian of some note, and the poet activist was very displeased with him—told him he wasn't a true Hegelian. Poor Orlif had always thought he was a true Hegelian. On another topic, two of the professors bullied him and he never knew how to react. He would sit in the office and be perplexed. And he could hear them as they giggled.

Orlif was always perplexed. He sent his son letters which were never answered. He sent him an essay or two he found informative. Weaver de Speck would rarely comment.

One night a week or two after the Hegelian was there, Orlif woke, sat on the edge of his bed and thought. The moon shone down over the scrub trees in their back lot, and he could see the lone fence post far off. Beyond the moon there were two or three stars. And he awoke to a certain dread. He remembered that whole night his wife was not with him; she had driven the German to the airport and had not returned. A whole day and night.

He had phoned the airport to see if the plane had left.

"Oh, I'm sorry, sir, the plane is grounded until tomorrow evening—passengers have been given vouchers to a hotel."

And yet Orlif didn't want to think of what he might think of.

But he could not stop thinking as he sat at the edge of his bed.

*Yes,* he thought, *and then some nights later there was the murder.*

He remembered Weaver the night the Colonel was killed—coming home very late.

That day, the day after they heard Colonel Musselman had been killed, Weaver had stayed in his room. Why? He usually went out. Nor did he eat—he only played with his food, his favourite Moroccan chicken that his mother specially made for his homecoming from Ryerson.

He thought something was wrong with Weaver and did not know exactly what, so he said, as they had sat at the table, "Did you hear of the kerfuffle, Weaver? Were you up in town?"

"No, I was not," Weaver said. "What happened up there?"

So, though he was no expert—as the poor man always said about everything, "Of course, I am no expert"—he kept coming back to that—why would a sixteen-year-old boy assembling an airplane model of a 1941 Spitfire casually walk downstairs and murder his dad, who had taught him all he could about Spitfires?

Now that Weaver was back this second time, he thought of all these events again.

Then he thought of something peculiar that was mentioned at trial. The French doors were opened. So why would that be? The police first said they were closed, and then at the trial said they were opened a little.

They said it was because the son was thinking of fleeing—but was that the case? For he did not flee at all, and he was nowhere near the French doors.

Orlif knew his son was in town because of the slip from Nick's Convenience, where he had bought a pack of cigarettes.

Still, he wouldn't allow himself to believe anything more.

The murder happened some days after his wife had driven the Hegelian to the airport and had not come home—just about the same week.

Orlif tried to put all of that out of his mind too. In fact, he could be mistaken. He was still trying to navigate a car when he drove. He hardly drove. Often Vivian drove him if he needed to go somewhere. But he was attempting to drive now. "Still trying to get the hang of it," he would say when the cops pulled him over.

"Yes, well, turn your blinker off. It's been on for the last three miles."

"Oh, I see. Well, as I say, I'm still trying to get the hang of it."

But he had to get the hang of it.

For day after day he drove past the Musselman house. Sometimes he would park near the house and walk down the street. Sometimes he would carry a sketch pad and draw the house with his pen.

People wanted the boy guilty—but that did not mean the boy was. The prosecutor had a thing for Gertie—Orlif could tell—yes, Orlif wasn't a fool—and the prosecutor was doing this, as he said, "to protect those who innocently believed in this fellow."

The prosecutor would make sure he left the courtroom by the door that would take him into the hall, so he would meet Gertie on the way out—and he would make sure he met her on the way in. He would stop her and say something, trying to hold her attention, and pass by quickly enough so as not to compromise his office.

Orlif knew he too had been betrayed on that night long ago—for that's what the Hegelian did with Vivian and Vivian had done with the Hegelian.

"Yes, I know," he would say to himself, cleaning his pipe, "I certainly know—what do I know?" He would look into the pipe bowl and frown. "Well, I know something."

Orlif's confusion always showed—showed in his little twisted bow tie and his sad face, his greying long hair and his gentle hands. It showed in his wife's disappointment in him, and his solitude, and the horrid memory of her driving away with the Hegelian—and then coming back the next afternoon.

It showed also in his walking with a cane at night and sometimes coming back late and going to bed in the spare room. It showed in his not being allowed to smoke his pipe in the house and having to sit by the stream to do so.

It showed in Weaver saying, "Why didn't you protect me that time, Dad? That is when I needed you to—when they were laughing at me at school because I loved my French teacher."

And one night, thinking of this, his mind plagued by many things—how his students talked among themselves as he was trying to teach Euripides, and how they shrugged when he asked them to be attentive; how, when he went into the common room, he knew by the way the conversation shifted that they had been talking about him—he began to piece together Weaver's travels during the time he was in town that night: the tavern, the park—the sudden, sudden money he had for a while after that night. It was all elliptical and then it began to hammer into him, blow by blow by blow.

He might not have thought anything, but that summer—the summer after the murder—their septic tank had backed up, and Orlif had to go and find the buried septic tank using a metal rod, dig it up and check the line back to the house. And what did he find in that line—that summer after the murder—but bills covered in filth that must have been flushed down the toilet. They had been torn so they would fit. But the old septic system was too weak, and it backed up.

The perplexity on his face showed as he walked in his garden looking at his cucumbers, checking the radishes and hoping for the tomatoes.

"No, it cannot be," he said, and then, angry at himself for his suspicion of both Weaver and his wife, he said, "Oh dear me, it cannot be!"

Their house was a memorial to past battles. Woodstock posters. A picture in the far corner of Tommy Douglas, and a speech written by Vivian Speck against nuclear weapons that Vivian had framed and put on the wall. It was her big moment as a fourth-year student. Then there was her honorary doctorate from Acadia.

Three cobs of Indian corn sat on the bookshelf. After she went away with the Hegelian for a night, Orlif said, "It is not nuclear weapons that ever caused a war. It never was the spear or the arrow either. It wasn't a blunderbuss or a cannon. It was not Oppenheimer who caused disaster over the skies of Hiroshima. It was both of us leaving Weaver locked behind a door when you went to exalt at a meeting of your peers—and me too, when I had a bloody class. And though we did it by accident, we did it more than once—until—until we don't know him anymore. It was me wearing a suit and tie over my flesh and bones and making jokes about religion so those I wished to impress would be impressed—and it was me not realizing that my destiny lay outside all of that—my destiny lay somewhere in the future—in connection with some terrible event I would have no control over." Then he added, "So there."

But he said nothing about the Hegelian.

Those things they had on their walls seemed to elicit the feeling they both tried to have, a feeling of right-minded thinking.

That is, when you entered their place—and little Pruty noticed this—it was a place where you thought first that these people elicited the right kind of opinions. But sooner or later one found, or at least Pruty did, a certain doubt in the air. Somewhere, hidden among the cobs of Indian corn, Mrs. Winnifred White felt that way too. Whenever she came to a meeting, she would start to shake, and tremble, and end up trembling and shaking.

THIS HAD HAPPENED DURING WEAVER DE SPECK'S FIRST time home, just before the murder of Musselman.

It seemed so innocuous, his coming back home where he said he had plans to do better and be better, and act better. And they both believed him.

Still, on a cool early May day, young Speck—well, they said that he burned a Canadian flag in the park, and had lit part of a bible on fire. It was a stupid prank by a youngster trying to show off.

"What kind of bible?" some asked.

"The good kind," others answered.

Orlif heard Pruty was with him and had become very upset. The Canadian flag was on the back of her wheelchair. And she had been proud of it.

Why she was even with him was a mystery to herself.

He had taken the car after it was brought back to the yard, and he had picked her up, saying he would take her for a drive. Secretly, he had wanted to take Gertie for a drive. But Gertie was not home.

So Pruty took her purse and a few dollars she had and put on a new hat.

He drove her to town. But soon she became worried. He drove too fast, and spoke about things she didn't understand, even though she tried to smile.

"How much Nietzsche have you read lately?" he inquired.

"I'm not so sure, Weaver sir," she said.

"Well—certainly Aristotle—"

"No—but your dad mentioned—and I even think at one time he mentioned—yes, he did—he mentioned Aristotle—yes—so, yes, I did hear of a Mr. Aristotle. Where does he live?"

And Weaver laughed at this. "Let's get some beer," he said.

"No, thank you, Weaver—please to take me home now."

"Oh, not yet," Weaver said. And he went and got some beer and drank a few pints. Then he wheeled her to the park.

"Would you like some hash? I have some good stuff here."

"No, thank you. Please to take me home, Sir Weaver. I pray you will take me home, please."

"Pray—you know God is dead, of course," Weaver said.

"Please to take me home—or to Lounsbury's store—my sister is working there, Weaver, and I can go home with her."

"I said not yet—not yet—wait—my little crippled cupcake."

"Pardon?"

"I said wait—not yet, my little crippled cupcake."

"What are we waiting for, Weaver?"

"Time to run out, Pruty," he said. He looked very distraught and said he did not know why he had been ousted from Ryerson—that it wasn't his fault things happened. He said he didn't know why he was back here—for what reason did he end up here!

He told her she lived in a dumb town with some very dumb people.

"You are dumb, the town is dumb, the people are dumb."

So, without knowing why, he had caused her to panic and cry.

Orlif had thought that Weaver coming back home that first time was an accident waiting to happen. Anger filled the house when he spoke—and his eyes wouldn't look at you directly, especially at his mother. He always lowered them when he spoke, and turned away as he did.

"Weaver is an accident waiting to happen," Orlif would say at the oddest times. In mid-afternoon, as he brushed Vivian's shoulder, "Excuse me—shhh—Weaver is an accident waiting to happen." Then he would jump back, hoping she wouldn't slap him.

At night, as Professor Speck put on his nightshirt (he had always worn a nightshirt), he would lament, "Shhhh—between you and me and the bedpost—Weaver is an accident waiting to happen."

"Why?"

He paused a moment, looked at her and spoke as if he was relaying urgent information that would make him more important to her—his voice had that kind of tone—especially once he said, "But it came to my attention."

"I do love him, I love him forever, and I will love him forever, but it came to my attention he was on drugs or something in the park yesterday and burned a few pages of a bible, and a flag or something—and that girl in the wheelchair, Pruty, was wheeling about trying to get him to stop, and crying. It was her flag, and he took it and burned it. He was angry about being back here. And so others came over to stop him. But one of the young men there—who worked the boats—did not at all take kindly to it, picked Weaver up and shook him, saying, 'Mind your manners.'

"They said Weaver was very drunk—and it's not the first time, either, since he's been home. In fact, he's been drunk often since he got home."

"I'm sure he was only trying to say something—well, important. Symbolically—of importance—do you think?" Vivian said.

"Well, I think I might say a prayer for him—"

She paused, putting cream on her hands, and looked at him. "But for God's sake, you don't believe in Catholicism?" Vivian asked.

This caught him up. "No—of course not." He sat on the edge of the bed and stared at the corner of the wall in thought. Then he looked at her without his glasses, which made his eyes squint. "Still, sometimes I wonder if Weaver isn't similar to a lot of mimics. Mimics only do one thing—it's the only thing Catholicism may have taught me—"

"What do mimics do?"

"Oh—they destroy—they dig our graves."

"Nonsense. It was a lark—with that girl—just a joke. Weaver is very gifted—that's the problem. He was far, far too gifted for Ryerson. That's why he's home now."

He looked at his socks in a stupor. But then he added, "I haven't done my best for Weaver—that's the shame of it."

"What do you mean?"

"I only wish him to be fine and noble. I failed."

"Why? In my mind he is too noble—that's the problem—he's too noble."

He stared at her, paused and then continued. "Still, I know how you feel, Vivian, I do—and I respect how you feel. I do. But I do say there were some good priests—that's all I am saying. One helped me when I was a boy, after my father died. In fact, he saved my life. I was going to jump off a cliff, at Boy Scouts—into the ocean—about a hundred-foot drop."

"Yes, you told me before," Vivian said. "I am not saying they are all crooked—but the Vatican has more money than tea in China. They are a horrid people, Catholics."

"Well, what if a good priest is accused—like that Anglican minister Weaver wrote about? Well, he wasn't the only one who wrote about it. Remember, it was the thing going on up there? That Anglican bishop or something?

"But they found out he didn't molest a girl, he only made her a cucumber sandwich and she was an Inuit girl and allergic to cucumbers and broke out in welts and sneezes—that's all it was. I made a girl a cucumber sandwich—I mean, I must have at one time. I know there is lots of abuse done to Inuit girls, lots of abuse, I know—but in this case he was innocent—and, well—he was innocent."

"But—who really knows," Vivian said. And she got into bed and rubbed her feet, and lay with her back to him. "He might be innocent today and charged tomorrow. Besides, I'm for charging them anyway, just as Weaver is, a young man far ahead of his time."

Orlif thought more about what he had heard that morning. That Weaver had taken that little girl to the park—that little Pruty—and burned the flag on the back of her wheelchair. That he then saw the bible that the Salvation Army chaplain had accidentally left on a bench and picked it up. By this time, he was drunk.

"Stand up and walk, if you believe in Jesus. Yes, stand up and walk—and then I will believe that God is not dead as a nit. If you can do so, I will believe. Well—come on, my little blighted flower, my little twinkletoes, stand up."

Poor Pruty was crying and shaking and said she had thought he was nice and had promised her a milkshake.

Then a young man who worked the boats went over to Pruty and lifted her up and, putting her feet on his, walked her across to the fountain, and put water on her forehead to revive her, for she was in terrible pain and distress, and said: "You see, she is walking now. So why don't you believe, loudmouth."

Until that moment, Orlif and Vivian had not known their son ever got "lit up like a lantern," or ever "had a skinful," or was ever "drunk to the gills," or took some "sophisticated pills."

That was the rumour about it all—a week or two before the murder. It was the one rumour all over town about Mr. Weaver de Speck.

This is what Orlif mentioned to Vivian just before the German professor came.

Everything at that moment was still relatively good.

After the murder happened, Weaver went away, and now, after Jamie Musselman was convicted, he and Beal had returned.

Little Nin came home from her job as a cleaning maid in a motel out west. She was the same Little Nin with her kind eyes, small feet with big sneakers, and pins in her face.

And Beal had followed. Because he had to follow. The more he said, "I'll show her," or, "She better smarten up," or, "I'll kick her up the arsehole," the more Beal realized he was lost without her. Like many tough men (or so-called tough men) it was a woman—not much more than a girl—that tore his heart in two.

Orlif, who spoke almost to no one now and lived a solitary life, saw his son again back home, in his early thirties, with nothing to show for all his travels, or all his studies, or all their hopes in him. Orlif did not know what the answer was. In fact, he smoked his pipe alone and at times there were tears in his eyes.

Vivian admitted to Orlif a few years back that she had told Weaver that she had hoped for a girl—that her father demanded she have a child in order to get her inheritance of 2.7 million dollars. And so, after two abortions, she decided to have Weaver. But after hoping for a girl—she had him.

She would never mention it again—but she admitted that she had mentioned it to him.

"I never saw Weaver look so sad," she said. But she couldn't bring herself to blame herself over it all.

"But you see," she explained, lighting a menthol cigarette, "he was kicking walls—do you remember?—so I felt compelled—you see—oh, Orlif, don't look at me like that—like a complete pedestrian—times have changed."

And she left the room.

Orlif was quite upset when he heard this. Orlif tried to forgive her because he realized it was the price for living with her—and he did love her.

Vivian told Orlif not to go out that night. She saw him putting on his coat. She told him he would catch his death and she wasn't going to take care of him. Rain lashed the window of their little stone house, and the wind blew down against the bay water, and the old buoy blinked out in desolate moments.

So Orlif waited until she went into the bedroom and took his pipe and left.

It was a terrible night, and yet it fired him with a kind of melancholy hope that all would be well—that he would face the coming storm, whatever it might be.

There was a story Orlif heard on that dark and stormy night (yes, it was a dark and stormy night). He had gone out for a walk—and he said to himself, *I will go to the tavern and she won't stop me.*

So, timidly, he walked in. He was hoping that Weaver would be there—but Weaver had gone to the tavern in town. Timidly, Orlif sat down at a table, unbuttoned his soaking windbreaker, and this is the conversation he overheard.

He pretended he didn't want to overhear it, but he did. There was hardly a soul in at this time of night. Some of the chairs were piled on the tables, and now and again the lights of a car passing by near the windows. He could hear the rain against the tin porch roof, and wind rattled the double-paned glass.

There was someone besides himself having a beer, and Orlif sat at the table nearest his and ordered one as well.

It was the man Mickey Bowels, and he was speaking to the waiter. There was no one else in the tavern at this time. The lights were dim, the pool table was covered, and many of the chairs were upturned on the tables. And this is what Mickey Bowels said:

"When I was younger, my mother died. I was in my teens at the time. She went over the bridge in a car. Orville McDurmot tried to save her. The ice was weak, and he couldn't get out far enough—and his uncle Lorne tried to get a dory up at one of the cottages—it was heroic of them—and I wrote them both to thank them, a long time ago.

"Anyway, I started to go to church, asking for Mom to speak to me—even if one sentence—or two—just say something, *hello*, or say that she was *all right*. I asked her to please tell me—but no words came. I didn't do this for me but for Dad. Dad had gone into a terrible depression.

"The priest came to our house—and the worst of it was, the priest had no answer. He was a placid-faced little man who had drifted away from his own hopes and dreams. My father finally swore at him, told him not to come back and stopped going to church. I didn't question this. It was no matter to me. And still isn't. There are saints who never go to church, and sometimes they are the better for it.

"Church was the loser as far as my father was concerned, with a twenty-dollar-a-week offering for over thirty years.

"I never cared for church, and at times I still don't. I think it has infected itself with matters that are beneath the world it pretends to elicit. My father never swore or said anything indecent in his life before that as far as I can remember. But he began to. He began to swear day and night. He swore at other drivers. He swore in the grocery store over the price of bologna. He became a drinker. He hung about with some women, and they got him drunk at Beal's and took his money, and once he woke up in an alley robbed. I know Rueben Sores did it—Beal's friend Rueben Sores—but I can't be sure. He lost the money he had and looked like a derelict. He slept on store steps downtown.

"He began to be thrown in jail. What is worse, I think, was the hurt look on the police officers' faces when they had to arrest him. They certainly didn't wish to do so."

The waiter picked up Mickey's two empty draft glasses and went to the tap and poured him two more. And this is when Orlif took a little sip of beer and moved his chair closer.

The man Mickey Bowels—a country bumpkin with his broad face, a laceration from an errant shovel on his cheek—was telling them something very private. But it was night and dark and Mickey had been drinking because of Gertie and the boy Jamie Musselman who was now in jail.

So he continued when the waiter came back.

"The ground was cold where she was buried. The ground was cold." He seemed to trail off here. "I walked in the snow and the wind to the graveyard. My mom did not like the dark, so I put up little lights by her grave, so she wouldn't be scared. I never wanted my mom to be scared, I tell you that! I was not myself either. At times I would set out at night trying to find my father—trying to rally his spirits and bring him home.

"I planned to do something very great for her. That is, become important.

"But I didn't get much done. The year passed, and then another. I went to university for two years just to get out of town, and while there I realized that all the bright people were like me—*atheists*." Here he glanced suddenly and apologetically at Orlif, and Orlif nodded.

"I was wondering—" Orlif began, but the waiter cleared his throat, and so Orlif stopped speaking.

"There was a whole bucketful of atheists at university. They were caught up in the insulated inexperience of the time. You may ask was it insulated naïveté, and I will say yes—it was mimicry too. There was just too many people doing and saying the same things. The trick was to say them more cleverly than others.

"Many of the girls laughed loudly at anything they said had diminished them in the previous world—housework, vacuum cleaners, being a housewife. That is, as far as they were concerned, they were very much independent and very brave. So, often they retaliated against the world by mocking those who brought them into it.

"Then I realized as I walked up the courtyard and into morning class that the university had taken religion out of me. Instead of finding truth in the host at church, I found it in self-reverential Professor Ferrari and others who thought the church was fantasy made for simpletons like my mother. So I began to think of my mother and what she believed, and how tender she was, and kind. And I wondered then, what I had done to become important, and would she want that?"

Orlif was quiet. He opened up a book he had brought with him and pretended to read. For this is what he often did at the tavern, for he had no one to speak to. And Mickey continued his tale.

"So I tried to act like the youngsters who were there. They too knew more than Saint Paul, for sure—the laughter about what priests said was infectious. Why was I ashamed at all this? I do not know. Oh, I did know, of course—the worst kind of insult on the human soul is that of mockery. Blake knew it, so did Yeats. That if you look closely, irreverence is part of the student's universe—whether they admit it or not."

Here he stopped speaking and looked at them, and they glanced at each other.

"But," Mickey said, "as I studied more and went to study hall or the library, I realized that some of the really bright people—that mattered to me, in what they wrote—believed somewhat in God, at least in the possibility of God.

"So, over the year, I began to read C.S. Lewis and others. I began to say to myself, after I read *Screwtape Proposes a Toast*, that if C.S. Lewis is telling the truth, then what he believes must also be true. What I discovered," he said politely, "was that the Church does not need me—but I just might need it. And why might I need it?"

"I don't know—why might you need it?" Professor Speck asked.

"Pruty is why I might need it, and my strength from it to help Pruty, who has few things in her life—and less love than most. Oh, people do love her, but people are tied up in their own concerns as well. You see, that day when she was in the park—and I am not picking on him—but your son said, 'If you believe in Jesus, stand up and walk.' He was teasing her and he was drunk—he burned her little flag. And all she had wanted was to go with a nice boy and have a milkshake.

"Later—you see, the bible that was sitting on a bench was left there by the Salvation Army guy, Mr. Harrison, who went into the tavern to collect donations. He did this once a week and had simply left his bible on the bench. Your son saw it and said he would burn the bible. He didn't burn the whole bible—just some pages. Pruty, to prove he was wrong, tried to lift herself out of the chair—and she couldn't do it."

"And could you help her?" Professor Speck asked.

"I could help her—with love, but only if I believe."

"Why is that, for heaven's sake?"

"No one can have love who does not believe!"

"I love—" Speck said.

"Therefore, you believe," Mickey said.

"Well, Mickey, I hope you find peace," the old waiter said. He was baffled by the story. But he knew Mickey had quit university all those years ago, to come home and take care of his father.

"I did find some peace, but that is not the story," he suddenly said, blushing. "The story I want to tell is about my father. After I came home to take care of him—and managed to open my store—"

"Your father?"

"You see, my father didn't get around to fixing the loose steering on her car—he had promised to do so, but he never did. That is what was told to me. And he couldn't admit it. It would have taken him an hour, and he simply forgot.

"He didn't think of her old Pontiac, took everything in stride until it was too late. That's why he drank and was thrown in jail, because of guilt.

"In a rash moment, I told Dad what the investigation found: that she wasn't able to correct the steering as she went around the turn toward the bridge.

"He just stared at me, and tears came down his face. He was no longer himself. He had wanted to sue the government, you see—sue them for how terrible that turn was going onto the bridge. He wanted to do that because of human guilt.

"But after I had explained what I had discovered, he just sat silently staring at me. He was as thin as a rail, and he had lost his teeth—he looked just a little like an elf."

"He did? An elf, you say?" Professor Speck said, and he had a strange grin on his face at that moment, and so did the waiter. A grin that often comes to people at the most awful moments.

"Yes," Mickey said innocently, "so I knew he would die soon. He was seventy-two years old. Perhaps I knew it before he did. That he would drop off at any moment.

"'How could she ever forgive me,' he whispered, and tears flooded his eyes.

"Then, about a week after that—I had my own apartment on Water Street, living away from Pa—"

"You were at that time living away from Pa?" Professor Speck said.

"Yes," Mickey continued. "So I went to see him again. He was in the little den, sitting alone, in the huge chair, by the window, with his huge black ashtray sitting beside him filled with a multiple array of cigarette butts.

"I realized he was a frail old man who had hated the last eight years, blamed himself, blamed God, blamed the bridge, blamed the province, the government, blamed hockey coaches, blamed everyone.

"But that day there was a change."

Bowels paused a second, tried to control his voice, then continued. "Yes. He looked up and said to me, 'Look at this.' So I looked at it. It was a picture of Mom. She was in a field downriver, filled with flowers, and the sun was shining on her hair—she was a girl of about nineteen—the year he met her. At the bottom of the picture, written in my mom's handwriting: *I'm here waiting for you!*

"He told me he hadn't seen that picture in fifty years. She had given it to him when he was in the Merchant Marines. He had forgotten all about it. He couldn't even tell me if he remembered seeing it in all that time.

"It was strange how he found it. He had come into the den, started to feel faint and fell against the wall beside the old bookshelf. One of the old books on popular mechanics fell, and out of it the very tip of the picture appeared. He wasn't sure what it was. He was on his knees beside the book, and he hauled on the tip of the picture.

"He took the picture from the book and saw her the way she once was long ago, sitting in a field of flowers, in a summer dress, and read: *I'm here waiting for you!*

"What I will never forget is the pure radiance, the love that filled the picture. I guess I will never forget that—because it looked as if the picture was brushed up by her death."

"Brushed up?"

"You know—enhanced. There was a strange enhancement in it—a feeling of joy. After all our human suffering, there is joy."

He paused and looked at them awkwardly. Then he said, very quietly: "Oh, I know I said way too much. I spoke too sillily. My father died a few days later. Still, I never doubted again."

"You never doubted what?" Professor Speck asked, confused and troubled by the story.

Mickey didn't answer. He looked like a huge country boy. And from his look you could tell that all of his hopes, or most of his hopes, had been dashed in life, like the loss of Gertie. He was a solitary man, the world passing him by.

"The suffering, you see, is with Pruty—but someday Pruty will have joy—joy forever and ever. And I believe she will—"

"Will what?"

"Oh—she will save the world—in some fashion—even if it's just a small one."

The next night, Orlif, though he hadn't planned to, told Vivian that story as best as he could remember.

"You were at the tavern? And that is where you heard this story?!"

He nodded.

She went back to needlepoint and said there was entirely too much suffering in the story. It wasn't bad, but it did have too much suffering. She felt Weaver would be able to tell him a much better story.

"Weaver did have a story—that book—I am not sure what happened to it. He was so certain of it. But perhaps he felt it wasn't ready and wanted a finer story to introduce himself," Vivian said.

"Perhaps."

Orlif knew it wasn't the whole bible, it was a few pages from Revelation that Weaver had torn out. Some people were upset about the flag, and replaced it. And Mickey, Orlif told his wife later that day, after all the kids had gone, had helped Mr. Harrison retrieve the pages. A few could not be saved, the page about the Four Horsemen of the Apocalypse.

"I am very surprised Weaver would do that," Orlif said. "I mean, just as a matter of literature—the bible is written quite well." Then he said, "I hate to bring this up—but I think Weaver is not so angry at me, but at you." Then he reflected, "Or at both of us—or at himself."

The wind blew hard against the little house as Orlif spoke, and the stars were far away and almost like blisters, and then the clouds covered them after Orlif spoke. That is, as Orlif spoke, the stars were there, and once Vivian began to speak, they were covered, and the wind blew harshly.

Inspired to counter all this depression, Vivian mentioned a great man, some years ago, who reached One with the One, and Wholeness with the Whole. And that man, the German had told her, was Hegel.

That put an end to the conversation. And Vivian went back to being silent.

She poured water into her small multicoloured teapot she had specially ordered from Pakistan and put her nose down to smell the brittle tea leaves. Her last determination to be relevant in the world had happened with Beal, as it had happened beforehand with many others. And Orlif usually watched in silence. He wanted to mention something—he wanted to say: "Well then—where did you go with that German Hegelian, if you don't mind my asking?"

But he felt he wasn't up to it. He was never up to it. He wished he was. That is, to tell her he no longer believed in her revolution. Whatever revolution it was.

First it was women, then gays, then combatting AIDS, lately it was Indigenous. But that, as Speck found out, hadn't gone well. So now she shifted—against the Catholics and all their sins. But he had been brought up a Catholic, though he hardly mentioned it—and when there were jokes about them, he would always laugh the loudest—especially amongst other professors, just to show his mettle.

Speck still retained much of his Australian accent, and it was always noticeable when he became impassioned about things. In fact, all along Arron Road, they called him "Kangaroo Man." And they had called Weaver "Joey"—when he came back after university. And they called the Chinese couple who had moved here some time before "Meandering Madeirans."

They called Pruty "Wagon Wheels" and Gertie "Gold Rush

Gertie" after an obscure 1934 movie, because she had become engaged to a wealthy man and left Mickey Bowels. So the whole place had nicknames that floated above the heads of those who wore them without them at times knowing that these names floated in the air.

Orlif had left Australia as a young man and settled first in England, then in Wales, then in the US, and finally in Canada. And this was part of his diaspora, and the reason for his feelings of alienation. And in so doing, he picked up enough of the mantra of the left in order to reorder his world.

"I love Trotsky," he once confessed. Then he said, "I like Trotsky." Then, after a few years, he said, "I still think our Mr. Trotsky was on the right track—yes—on the right track."

Finally, he said, "Trotsky was, I believe, a mass murderer."

He wore a T-shirt with a picture of Che Guevara. Then, one day, he took it off and tucked it away. There was a picture of Ho Chi Minh on his dresser. He one day put it in the closet. But he still thought everything through as much as he could.

"The West is no better," he would say, and look proudly about when he said it. "The West is no better—ho ho—well, let me tell you—the West is no better."

But no one spoke to him anymore, so usually he would speak to himself. Sometimes when he was smoking his pipe, he would say, "Ho ho, the West is no better, I will tell you that."

Therefore, he still believed in some way that the whole landscape would and must change. And he had instructed his son in all of this—and so had his wife.

But now—now, what had happened? He was just another lost soul—always worried, like he was with the Hegelian, that he didn't quite measure up.

"No—I don't quite measure up—wish I did," he had said to the German Hegelian in an off-the-cuff moment, and the German had smiled and looked over at Vivian.

"I bet *you* measure up," Vivian had said.

And it was all horrible.

Orlif had never been able to find a home, it seemed, anywhere. So he became interested not in physical landscapes but political ones.

And he, with his wife's help, had written their book, and they were quite sure it was a needed and highly effective guide to change.

The book was called *A Highly Effective Guide to Change*.

When his son came back for the second and, as it was to be, last time, Orlif had given it to him in the hope that he would make the distant past up in some way. That he would become closer to him.

That was the hope—that was the one real hope that poor Orlif had.

"I wrote a book as well—well, I am not sure of it—just a draft. I am thinking you might take a look at it. The university press said they might publish it—but so far I haven't heard back from them. I go rather hard on our reliance on plastics—and on the combustible engine, I'm afraid—rather hard on the combustible engine—and I go rather hard on pesticides—yes, there is a chapter on pesticides. Vivian, of course, helped on many things, and you'll be very interested in what I say about equal pay for equal work."

So he waited in the henhouse—yes, they had a small henhouse—and he sat in his tweed jacket and his casual suit pants and puffed on his pipe and waited for some glorious exultation to come from Weaver de Speck.

But his son said nothing about it. In fact, he never mentioned it. And when Orlif mentioned it at supper two weeks later, Weaver paused for a second, picked up the ketchup and, as he was shaking it, said, "I couldn't finish it—"

"Couldn't finish it?"

"Sorry, couldn't finish—pass the pickles—it."

"Well, where is it?"

"Where is what?"

"The book, Weaver—the book—my manuscript. Where is it?"

"I don't know. I might have tossed it."

"Tossed it—"

"Yes, I might have tossed it out."

Orlif would go about the house muttering, "Couldn't finish it—pass the pickle—tossed it—tossed it—couldn't—pass the pickles."

The book was about establishing a universal guaranteed minimum wage for every man, woman and child—even toddlers. "Yes, even toddlers," Orlif said, to show his radical side. "Yes, even toddlers would get $24,000 a year if they couldn't get a job."

He did have another copy, however—but when he went back to the book and looked at it, it was only a sheepish collection of what others had said before, and in a rash moment he threw it into the fire. The embers lasted a long time—and Vivian watched them burn, sitting in a chair, her knuckles up against her chin, her legs half-opened, so that a rush of tormented desire filled him. But then she said, "Well, just another pipe dream of yours." And then she added, "So, give up the pipe."

He said that he was afraid his son disliked him.

"Well, if he does, it's your fault!" Vivian said. "Men are disappointing—"

"I am—*not*—disappointing—I am not. Am I disappointing?"

"Afraid so," Vivian said. "Look what happened to your book. What will you ever do now to prove yourself in any way?"

He said nothing for almost an hour. He went away and worked on his carving, which he did every evening.

Then he entered the room again and, startling her, continued, "Yes, you are, Vivian, completely earnest—like a little earnest mole—we couldn't get a person more so. Yes, what you are is a carbon copy feminist—you've zippered up the hide of liberation and are dishonest. But you envy as many women as you do men. That's why we had to go to Europe when I was ready for tenure—to see Botsie and Sue. We caught every train in France trying to find Botsie and Sue—for they just might have been doing something that might have left you out."

He looked absolutely stunned that he had said this. Then he went and stood behind a chair and pretended to read an article.

For a long time, she didn't answer. He had hurt her. He didn't mean to. But he had. Botsie and Sue had never paid attention to her—both had been published in peer-reviewed journals. They were the two she had so wanted to befriend in those small little cocoons at university, so long ago. He had never before brought them up.

Then, sniffing her tea and turning and walking away, she said, as if she had been saving it up: "No, it was men—like you, Orlif. I simply told him that if he was as upset with you as I was, that if he wanted, he could have a sex change. Besides, I thought it would be quite revolutionary."

"Revolutionary—"

"Yes—but he didn't want it."

For minutes, the clock ticked, and nothing was said. What she had said drew the air from him.

"That is quite odious," he said, and then, amending it, he added, "At any rate, it might be considered odious by some." Then he said, "But of course not for Botsie and Sue."

Then he continued perusing the article on bats. Now Vivian spoke, angry that she had related this incident and wanting to mitigate its impact. "No—you have always been a coward—why don't you just admit it." She said this victoriously, as if everything else she had mentioned was beside the point.

"Oh—you expressed all of that before—and then you helped me lose a tenured position just at that time—when you were angry—and I simply said nothing. Yes, I remember Botsie and Sue and Europe. Then we had to pack our bags—remember, Weaver had a little backpack—and away we went. And the position I wanted did not materialize. At first you wanted to leave me behind, but then you demanded we both go. You had your father insist that I go with you, because—"

"Because why?" Vivian said.

"Because you are afraid," he said. "You are afraid of the world. And your father knew it."

"You weren't right for that position anyway—that's what we decided—you weren't right. You were the one who said, 'Vivian, I don't think I am right for the part—I don't think I will take this job.'"

"I gave up everything so we could go to some godforsaken place like Paris. Then I never got a decent offer again. And the only reason is because some friends of yours were travelling—hopscotching about Europe with suitcases and maps—and you didn't want to be the one left out. And you kept writing them, and going to post offices, and waiting in cities for them to answer. And poor little Weaver tagging along and me growing a moustache, and you penny-pinching and saying I couldn't buy tobacco for my pipe. Finally, you realized you didn't want me with you—after I had given up everything because you had demanded I go. Then your father wrote you and we scurried back."

"I never scurried over anything in my life."

"Oh, you scurried. You scurried. You were and are a scurrier. You couldn't even take time out to pee—hurrying and rushing about to get trains, and then to Heathrow, where you got into an argument with an Air Canada representative and tried to get a refund—I remember."

"Oh, you would remember all the dross, and not the pure treasure I was after."

"Well, it was never the same afterwards—no matter what," he said. "Not between us. It could never be the same after. I shouldn't have gone—I should have really put my foot down."

She looked at him, turned to stare, her eyes like pencil points. "As your students all know, Orlif—nothing you say matters. Did you ever notice how little your life really matters—how everyone laughs at you? Remember how you planned for months to have Professor Stengel? I don't think he noticed you." She said this in her sweetest and deadliest voice, and then turned and pretended to be trimming a houseplant.

All of this after thirty-five years of marriage.

There was a long and horrible silence between them. His eyes blurred as he perused his article on bats.

Then Orlif commented, "No wonder—no wonder—it has happened."

"No wonder what has happened?"

"It has happened."

"What is it? What is it that has happened?"

But he didn't say. Then he added, "I've never seen anyone quite as sad as our son, our once-beautiful son—and our bickering is probably why. I think he wants us to feel terror—he wants to frighten you—and me if he can. So what do you think? Those meetings you took him to—so often speaking vile things about men—and he a little boy—I am unsure if that was helpful."

But she had gone into the far room and would not listen to him again today. And he went back to his carving.

He sat on the very trunk that he had carried at one time in Europe, pushing it and hauling it toward a train, while Weaver sat upon it, wearing a small cap, and she, Vivian, walked on ahead, hoping to catch Botsie and Sue amidst the clatter of Europe's myriad of trainyards and streets.

There was only one person in the whole region who was kind to Orlif, and that's who he thought of now. Pruty.

She was the one who listened to him, who spoke to him, who was kind to him, who told him jokes. Who said, "Now, professor, tell me about that guy who you was talking about—you got impassioned about."

"Oh—well, he was Cicero—and he wrote some very famous things—and so did Seneca—Nero killed him. Did you hear of Nero?"

"Oh yes, I have—he killed Saint Paul." And she took his hand and held it and smiled at his old eyes and said, "You know more than a hundred others!"

And he was pleased that at least one person thought so.

Orlif had gotten Pruty Dr. Heatherington—a doctor who was in a good deal of demand on the River (very much in demand because of his belief in opioids and antidepressants, in nortriptyline, gabapentin and all sorts of anti-anxiety medication). And though he said he was skeptical, he did finally say he would take her case.

Heatherington had looked over her file from the other doctors and realized no one was helping this woman the way he might be able to. As he closed the second file and placed it before him on his desk, he muttered about certain failures of direction. And this spurred him on to take her case and find a contemporary civilized resolution. He had decided on a solution before he had ever met her. The history of her family, an added and incisive segment of her file, pointed in only one direction.

"Medically assisted suicide."

He hadn't divulged this yet, but he would.

Hers was a case study within a voluminous theory, that certain people—many people that he had seen since he had moved here from London, Ontario—these people who sat in hospital waiting rooms and crowded them day and night, could be sooner or later subject to this emboldened relief.

Pruty waited on this service, not yet aware of what this service was.

Orlif smiled open-heartedly and tried to touch his son's arm. His face was filled with good intentions and his hand trembled just a bit. His whole life, spent in the classroom with uninterested students, codified in that caring look. A look of good intentions that never seemed to matter anymore. He was this night trying to have his son stay in and speak to him. But Weaver wanted to go.

What Orlif did have—hidden from everyone, even Vivian—was the filthy bills that had been flushed down the toilet two or three days after the murder. Earlier in the year, he knew Weaver had remembered that money too—and had tried to follow the line to see if he might find it. He watched Weaver for an hour one day, as he tried to spirit that line above the ground, and then became frustrated and kicked at the soil.

And when Orlif looked at Weaver now, his eyes seemed to say, *I have that ball of money hidden.*

That is, Orlif had been put in a kind of prison as well, deviating from logic in order to find an answer that would mitigate.

It was growing cold. The day was flat and grey, and the water in Little Hackett Brook had slowed its meandering.

"I love you," Orlif called after him. "Take your jacket, it's getting cold—and there is frost in the garden. And never mind an old man like me." Then he added, "No one else does."

He went back inside. He had vacuumed the floor earlier and now he smoothed the tablecloth and set the table, rubbing the spoons and forks and knives with a cloth, one at a time, as he did every evening. He set them down, and took the plates, rubbed them too, set them at a particularly correct distance from one another, and lit the candle. But this evening he didn't whistle his usual tune.

*WHY WAS I NOT BAPTIZED?* WEAVER THOUGHT. *DOES SHE care that little? What if it's true?* He was frightened now, as if his soul was moving through darkness. He was also disturbed when the thought of Mr. Musselman's body decomposing overcame him. He tried never to think of it.

*What falls off first? The nose—yes, probably the nose—the toes too—fingers as well—eyes, yes—eyes.*

He remembered Sophie, this girl who had wanted to paint him. They were in her room—this was in Halifax—and she simply took off her calico dress. It was in the summer too, and hot too. He had just turned eighteen.

"I don't want to get paint on it," she said. "Get on the bed and I will paint you—take off your shirt—okay?"

She moved toward him. Her panties were almost see-through.

"Here we go," she said.

Why hadn't he realized this was an offering? Her offering. He put his arms behind his head like she asked, and when he did, his hand went under the pillow, and he felt—what—a rosary.

He couldn't believe she, Sophie, would have a rosary, and he jumped up, stood confused, picked up his shirt.

"I say it at night when I'm alone," she told him. As he turned, he could see her breasts, see the mysterious beauty of the hair between her legs.

But he simply nodded quickly and left.

She ran to the door and said, "Wait—"

But he didn't. He felt very self-righteous.

No, he had certainly been confused about so much in his life. And now this Sophie, who had offered herself to him, was a well-known artist in the region, and he had gone to one of her exhibitions. He wanted to kiss her, he wanted to start over, but she was living with someone else, and simply shook his hand. In her shaking his hand, he remembered his self-righteousness and her tolerance.

So tonight he moved out into the dark. He tried to light a cigarette, and in anger threw it down in the dirt. He thought of that woman Janie McLeary and how she had had to baptize her child—and the woman from the gum road who did the same, before she was murdered in 1934.

Yes—why was all that important?

"Is there, then, anything true about Catholicism?" he asked. Probably not, but what if there was?

That night could never change—and no dismissal of the faith could change it.

De Speck met Beal in the tavern just off the Load Road, that tavern that smelled of hash and smoke and mud. They didn't sit at the same table, but at tables kitty-corner to one another. And they spoke quite softly.

Beal told him he had followed Nin home, back to the Miramichi, because she was so upset with young Musselman being convicted. She was coming home to help him, knowing he wasn't guilty, but not knowing what to do.

"I couldn't get her to let it go—couldn't convince her," Beal said. "I told her it was an accident—and that, anyways, the Colonel killed my mother—when I was born—so it was even-steven. My mother was just a girl—I go put flowers on her grave—they said in jail that I was a kind of psychopath, but no—I am not. They have said everything they could about me. I didn't mean to harm anyone—it just happened."

"Where is she now? I'll convince her—she'll listen to me," Weaver said.

"She has gone," Beal said. "That little idiot who I gave my life for—almost my life—not quite my life, but close to it. You don't know, but from the time she was a child I took care of her—no one else cared—no one."

"Nin is gone?"

"Yes, Nin—I can't find her—pins in her face and all. Wherever she is, I need to find her. She has gone loopy—she is talking about confession. She knew him, you know—he was nice to her, so she says, so she is all discombobulated about it."

"Who did she know?"

"That Jamie Musselman." Then Beal said, "That envelope—that letter at Shamus's—will make us both culpable. We are in the clear if we find it—it can't be that hard to find."

Weaver said, "It's all turning bad—Pruty knows something too—"

He told Beal she was in the other room when they entered the kitchen of Shamus's house that long-ago night. He could see her feet, with a Mickey Mouse blanket over her legs—the steel footrest gleaming just beyond the light. He told Beal he had been going to see Pruty two or three times a week, and rifling through the place as much as he could, looking for that envelope with the list of monies.

"She is in pain all the time—she tries not to show it."

Beal thought for a moment, and asked, "Pruty, the little crippled one?"

"Yes."

"She is in pain?"

"Oh, I think so, yes."

"That's too bad. What does she know?"

"She knows about that envelope—I am sure. Well, I am more than sure."

"How?"

"She spoke to my father about it—or at least, I think she might have—who's to know—she doesn't know all that it signifies, but she knows more than she should."

Beal said nothing, so Weaver continued whispering into the low tavern lights.

"Dr. Heatherington is her doctor. My dad managed to get him for her. I went to see him on a few occasions—he is a fine man. A progressive. You know what I mean—progressive? I believe he is hoping Pruty will take medical assisted suicide as an option. I mean, it is an option. He is going to try and convince her that it's for the best. He would be doing her a favour—or at least I hope he would.

"She can't live like she is. Heatherington and I have both decided her life must be a drudgery. You see, I spoke to him—long ago—the day after I was in the park with her, you know—and he said that this would be the best thing for her. At least, I think this is what Heatherington is thinking."

Beal looked at him in some astonishment. Weaver was sitting sideways to him, and pretending to be looking toward the poker machine with all the lights.

"You can just decide that?"

"Yes, if we have to," Weaver said.

"So that will solve it? I mean, she will kill herself? Then no one will know of that letter?"

"Don't think I want that—it's nothing like that—we are just thinking of her. He has performed this before. He's progressive, as I just said. He did it to an older woman in Ferry Road. He just said she relaxed and went to sleep—her leg kicked once—or twice—two little kicks. And then she said her last words."

"And what were her last words?"

"'God forgive me.'"

Beal thought this over. "But how can you decide for someone else—?"

"It depends on who that someone is. Pruty is locked in that house. You know that. Heatherington knows how to navigate this for her. He will convince her—it will take a month or so—but by Christmas she might be gone."

Beal said, "I know a man who rescued a young girl from jumping off a bridge. Should he have let her do it?"

"I don't know what you mean."

"Well, he risked his life climbing the girder to save her. Risked his life in kindness and love."

"That is different."

"No, I don't think it was—for maybe if they can do it to Pruty, they can do it to all of us. And who gets to decide—that is the same as killing—" Beal said, whispering, "Dr. Musselman."

"It's not nearly the same," Weaver said. "It's far more sophisticated."

Beal was quiet.

What was said was that Heatherington had lost his son in a snowmobiling accident, and had turned against everyone, and everything, in his new quest for the absolute truth.

"Is Vivian for suicide?" Beal asked.

"Well—yes—in cases like this."

"And is she for abortion?"

"Why?" Weaver asked.

"I don't know—maybe I don't understand things the way you do."

"How is that?"

But he said nothing more about it. He seemed genuinely disturbed by this new world—this world where he had collected boxes of information hoping to be accepted.

Yet he was the murderer—no one else—and it was what Little Nin told him—he could not wish it away.

"Let us both go to confession," Little Nin had pleaded one night. That was back at Easter, Palm Sunday, and she had found a palm lying in the street under a light as the day was waning, and brought it home, and placed it on the small window ledge.

Years ago, he remembered hearing people saying that people like Little Nin shouldn't have been born, because they had no societal skills. His longing for Little Nin now came over him. If she should not have been born, then the world itself should not have.

So, Beal told Weaver this: Jamie Musselman had been Little Nin's friend when she was in school. Though she had already missed two grades and was only in grade nine.

She had been alone and thrown out of her house. She lived down beyond the rocks and had no family to speak of. Little Nin, during all of this time, when her cousin was in and out of court and jail, was left alone.

So, before he knew Gertie, Jamie Musselman knew her. He was her friend, snuck food out of his fridge for her. He let her stay in the dollhouse that was in their backyard. That is, the dollhouse, once a plaything of a young girl whose father was a judge, was almost as big as any house Nin had lived in.

He brought her blankets, and a bowl of Rice Krispies in the morning, carrying the bowl in his right hand, with a towel and a washbasin in his left.

"I need to pee," she said one morning. "Where can I pee? And I need a change of underwear."

Jamie Musselman went downtown and, out of his savings, bought her three pairs of pink underwear and a pair of jeans. He brought them back to the dollhouse for her.

Then he took her into the little guest bathroom in the back room of the main house. The one with the black-and-white tiled floor. It smelled of stale Lysol and old soap. No one used it, and he told her she could have a bath there.

But Beal got out of jail, "sprung free" by Vivian.

And everything from that moment on changed dramatically in everyone's life. Though none of them knew it then. All of this happened as if there would be no consequence, and the world would still spin around the sun, while these few small people would cling to their dreams.

So then Little Nin no longer spoke to Jamie Musselman, and he no longer knew where she was.

He went back to school and to his studies and she was forgotten.

He saw her now and again, but only at a distance. Once in a while he would wave to her, but she didn't seem to notice him. This was another consequence of Beal having been reprieved, that Vivian did not seem to know.

Afterward, Little Nin had been instrumental in the terrible robbery. She helped show Beal where the French doors were—where a key to them was hidden under the mat. For the next number of months, she did not even remember it. Then she woke with a start one night and said, "Oh, my good God."

And she lived for months in a daze and never forgave herself.

They went away and she worked as a maid in the Sleepy Nook, a small motel north of Edmonton. One day she read a leftover *Globe and Mail* and there, on page five, was the story of her friend being convicted. And she read the report by Gavin Peters published the next day as well.

"Has there been a miscarriage of justice?"

Gavin had deep associations with the Miramichi and New Brunswick, which Weaver did not know, until he saw the plaque to him at Ritchie Wharf.

When Musselman was convicted, Nin was determined to come back home. Jamie had been her friend, one of the few people to be kind to her, and she could not just forget him.

So she left Beal and he followed her. He told her one night that they could go away and start a better life—and he would never bother anyone again. It seemed if she just forgot about what had happened, he would.

"I can change for you," he said he had told her. "I will. I can change for you, please."

But there could be no change without acknowledging what had come before.

She had not been to church since her confirmation. At that time—the time of her confirmation—her grammy had dressed her in a white dress, and she listened to the story of Joan of Arc. A man told this story, that Joan of Arc was betrayed by the very king Charles VII she had helped put back on the throne. That she was captured outside the gates of Paris when she fell from her horse.

"I believe this day we have burned a saint," is what stuck in her mind. And the little girl—that is, Little Nin, who was about five feet tall and wore big, big sneakers—was awestruck by this. She received her confirmation and decided she would go to church every day. However, she did not make it back for nine years. That was when she decided she had to confess to this terrible sin. And it was the memory of the story of Joan of Arc that allowed it.

The priest, a man almost as tiny as she was, a man who had come from Bulga, India, said, "You confessed to me. Now you should confess to the police so that young man will be free. As you said, he helped you long ago. He was so very kind to you. It is a terrible thing to have him in prison."

"I know," Nin said, "I know—so give me some Hail Marys—I will say some Hail Marys and be free—maybe I will say as many as twenty-four or twenty-five Hail Marys."

"I will give you Hail Marys—but I do not think it will free you. You should tell the truth to the police. I think Mary might wish you to do so. And do you know there are many, many, many people who do not believe in the Virgin Mary—they hoot and laugh and bellow at her. I have heard them many times—they in fact try to shame her, to prove the devil right—but I believe that you do believe."

"Yes, I do—but I want to go away. I will escape and go away, and I will never sin again. I will become as pure as I can manage under the circumstances."

"The burden will not be alleviated by going away," the priest kindly said, in his quiet singsong voice. "You went away after the crime—you told me so—so, how did that alleviate one thing? You had to come back. You were compelled to come back."

Jamie was supposed to meet her the night Beal met her in the park.

He was going to read to her from a book called *The Collected Poems of Dylan Thomas.*

He was her friend and helped her. But he had been kept in after school by the English teacher, who disliked him. That was how everything else came to be.

And thinking of this, she said: "I will go to the police—I will—I will pray some more and then I will go."

Beal was a lost human, betrayed by the world—remembering things no one should have to remember. And so, secretly, Little Nin did love him. In fact, as harsh as her life had been, she loved no one else.

One night when he was very drunk, Beal had told Nin to take off her clothes, and she hesitated, but after some coaxing, she did do so.

"Take them off—and stand up and let me see you," he said. "Remember, you and I are alone in this world."

And that was true enough. They were alone in the world, and they needed each other.

She stripped for him, and his comment was, "Your hair—is reddish there—but it is lovely. Turn around—ah—your behind is so—so lovely too—now turn back. Ah—your breasts, my dear—are large for your size, so—so wondrous. Now go to the bed and lie down."

And she did so. She lay on the bed. And, finally, Beal went into the room and lay beside her. It was snowing, and a gale wind washed against the window—and one could hear the trees grate as she lost her virginity. She told him that she was a virgin—but she didn't tell him about the jail cell those nights when he was not there to protect her. And what had happened to her.

She wrote in her little scrapbook that this was the first time. And it was sacred—so those terrible things that happened in jail didn't matter anymore.

She would never tell him the difference, the secret, and she prayed that he would never find out.

Beal bought clothes for her—jackets and pants and blouses. This was a month or so before she ran across the bridge, happy she had gotten him a job.

Then came the robbery—the travelling away and coming back after the boy was found guilty. Like Weaver de Speck, whom Beal thought he would never see again, they arrived back to this place within two days of one another.

Beal told Weaver that it was a warm September night, and he and Little Nin were close to the bridge overlooking the river near Arron Brook. The bells were ringing for seven o'clock mass, and their old car had broken down.

The next day, she left. He awoke with no one beside him. Her small white socks had fallen under the dresser, and the dresser drawer was bare. A certain terror entered him, and he sat immobile.

"Nin," he whispered. "Please, Nin—please—answer me."

He phoned her cell. There was nothing, simply a beep.

But he was heartsick, not because of her leaving, but because of the reason for it—the terrible thing—and Musselman in jail.

If Nin was with him, then he would be okay—he would be able to handle the world—because as strange as it all may seem to others, he deeply loved her.

Everything was allowed in today's world except goodness, kindness and simplicity. That is, all the things both Little Nin and Pruty seemed to stand for and tried in their own way to celebrate. To hold and catch, as elusive as they may be.

"I don't know why she don't trust me no more—all the good things I did for her—I mean, off and on—not all at once—but there you have it—off and on," Beal said.

He told Weaver he took off her clothes in the apartment and made her sit in the chair naked all day. Even if she peed. That was to keep her in line—because she was worried about the robbery and what had happened.

She told him she had heard a shot.

"Ha—admit you didn't hear a shot."

"No."

"Admit there was no shot."

"Can I get up now?"

"No, not until you admit you didn't hear no shot."

But Beal always gave her clothes back later. And later he would beg forgiveness, say she was driving him crazy and that she didn't hear a shot.

"Yes, if you ever saw Little Nin naked," he told Weaver, "but let me tell you—it is sacred—I felt it was sacred—don't laugh at me for saying this—and don't tell anyone else or I will get mad—but that first night she took off her clothes and stood before me, with the gale force wind, it was—sacred. I should have treated her better—do you understand me? I shouldn't have gotten her mixed up in this."

This meeting came about because they had learned someone had stabbed Musselman in the library of the prison—a hoodlum with a teardrop tattoo. This is what bothered Beal.

"I know that guy—out west—he came here because they wanted to kill him out there. Beating a boy like that—who makes model airplanes and reads poems—I can imagine if that guy came at me," Beal said. "Come at me—I tell you that."

"What would you have done?" Weaver asked.

Beal shrugged. "He never would have," Beal answered.

This bothered him very much—that Musselman had been stabbed.

But there was something else that he had just discovered.

A few nights ago, he went into Bowels's store to ask him if he had seen Nin Burns. Bowels told him not in a long time and he was worried about her too.

Then Bowels told him he knew something else.

"If you know something about me, say so," Beal said.

Bowels told him when he was a boy of seven, his father and he got stuck in the halfway house on the Renous highway in a great storm that had swept in from Quebec.

"You were born that night," Bowels said, as he was going over his accounts, now and again looking up at Beal and then back at the page.

"I was?" Beal asked.

"Musselman was there and did everything—everything he could—and managed to save you."

"To save me?"

"Yes, to save you—you. Your mother had died—he worked desperately to save her too—he kept saying over and over her blood pressure had dropped, and he couldn't do anything. I simply remember this young girl on the floor with blood on her legs, and her eyes staring—and then the fact that you weren't breathing either—and Dr. Musselman giving you mouth-to-mouth, while your body looked grey—and finally your little chest started to breathe—little by little—and Musselman yelling instructions at my mom, who was helping him keep you alive. He kept you alive for a day and a night in that storm before the paramedics got to you. Musselman stayed awake to keep you alive."

"You were there."

"Yes," Bowels said quietly, "I was there. Years later, you broke into my store—and you beat my father."

"I didn't," Beal said.

But Bowels didn't answer.

"No, it wasn't me," Beal said. But he too was now heartsick.

It was true, as well, when Weaver had told Little Nin some weeks before that he himself had nothing whatsoever to do with it, that the crime committed was not his doing (this was when they met for the first time after finding themselves back on the

River), she had simply sighed, and looked at him with dark, understanding eyes, and said:

"No—you too—Weaver—you too. You were there too. We are all culpable. And now Jamie Musselman, who only wanted to read me a poem, is in jail."

And for all his grand learning over her, his three universities, and his petitioning to get Ryerson's name removed from Ryerson, and his writing about the rights of others in order to have his name known, those simple words rang true.

"You know, Nin, I am a revolutionary," he told her.

"Ahh, Weaver," she had said. "Whatever does that matter now?"

And she said nothing more.

After he had left Bowels's store that night, Beal secretly wanted to hear, perhaps for the very first time: *You are forgiven.*

He didn't know that Bowels in his own way had already done so.

"Can't something else be done?" he asked himself, in the dark, on the corner of a windy street, thinking of Pruty.

Then he said, "Please, God. You are supposed to take care of us. What did you do?"

WEAVER TOOK A WALK DOWN THE CHURCH LANE. DAY WAS breaking and seagulls roamed over the graveyard and cried out toward the island. He walked along the beach eating a peach, and if anyone saw him, as he walked near Sheldrake Island, they would see, as the sun came out, a man alone—but, in the innocent way he carefully ate his peach and looked at the seabirds in the sky, a man the great world still loved and had compassion for.

Little Nin, through the small window in the basement of the church, in a room with old candles, and a sawhorse, and a small toilet, and a cot, and an old picture of Father Morrissey, and an old picture of Father Conners, and a small icon of the Madonna over her cot, could see him—could see he ate the peach. She wanted, Little Nin did, to run to him, to cry out to him, to ask him to take her to the police.

But she was frightened. So, she silently watched Weaver de Speck skip stones against the waves coming in to wrestle with the shore. The day was cloudy.

When did it all begin? he asked himself, between the stones he was skipping.

It was your betrayal of Professor Brown—your leaving Ryerson, your coming home by train. Or was it long before that? Was it not then, when he believed it was his right to bring down the powerful—those he considered obnoxious—like that hypocritical bishop that he did rail against? That he believed he had no reason to be kind or caring? And hadn't he believed it would make him so well-known, his mother and father would be ashamed they had ever doubted him. Didn't he feel betrayed?

But why was he taking the walk?

Because of Gavin's recent exposé in the *Globe*, about this case. It was published three days ago, after the boy had been stabbed.

"This is utterly shameful. I believe," Gavin wrote, "this case should be reopened. There are simply too many inconsistencies. I believe the boy is innocent—and two, perhaps three other people were involved. That it was an intrusion into the house looking for money. The mat was overturned, the key was missing. The door was ajar, the desk was ransacked. The criminals were young—that is why I believe there was more than one—they came from outside."

Professor Brown's book had just been published as well, and had a good review in *The Times Literary Supplement*, and a friend of his mother who was at the house just two days before said:

"Oh, wasn't he a professor of yours, Weaver? You must be terribly proud. What a professor to have!"

Weaver desperately tried to release himself of any guilt, or of being a party to the crime he wrote about. It was not, nor could he ever say it was, his fault. But suddenly this happened—he thought of the first-year course on theology he had taken years ago.

Lucifer became Satan—and what did the word "*Satan*" mean? The accuser. And who ever accused more than those who murdered or tried to shame others?

This is what he had learned from Father Kingston. The only thing he had learned from that awful course.

Still, he kept saying he was not party to the crime.

He had written *Never admit you were there*, and then had torn the note up in twenty pieces and thrown it into his garbage can.

No, he didn't want, nor was he inclined sexually, to become a woman. But at times he just didn't seem to know how to be a man.

He turned back toward his house, and Little Nin watched him go.

That afternoon, after reading Gavin's article, Professor Orlif Speck came and sat beside him. He looked out the window, at the trees blowing in the great wind, and finally he said, "Son—I would like to call you son—do you mind?"

Weaver shrugged. "Yes—I am your son—you can call me that!"

"Son, my father had a little budgie bird. I had forgotten this—until Mickey Bowels spoke about his own father, and then I remembered my father. I had forgotten my father—but a similar thing happened to me—not the same as Bowels, but similar. It was a terrible—well, I won't get into it now."

"Good, don't go into it," Weaver de Speck said, and then, to offset Bowels's story, which he had heard from his mother, he said, "Hocus de pocus."

"What is—hocus de pocus?"

"Bowels's 'story'—I mean—as you said yourself, I wasn't baptized—you said yourself it didn't matter."

"I am thinking it does matter—it could matter—perhaps it might matter." Orlif said, "Still, if it matters or not, it is strange, isn't it? That is, it made me think of my father."

"Why?"

"He lost his job, my father—and he had worked all his life for me and Mom—and he was cast out as if he was nothing. And soon—well, it's different with me than Bowels. You see, my mom took me away from Dad. I am not blaming her particularly. But she was scared of having nothing—and she was a good-looking woman—and the man who fired Dad took an interest in her, you know, a sexual interest—and he bought her clothes and took her to dinner, and laughed loud and wore a pinky ring, and had a gold watch, and drove a sports car. We lived in a small town outside of Sydney, Australia, and I was young—very young. And my dad was alone—very much alone—very, very much alone. He wore one of those bush hats, and khaki shorts, and walked with a cane. I remember Mom going out that first night with Dad's former boss—and how she ran about the house, looking for a brooch, and how she borrowed a mink stole though it was thirty degrees—and how she rushed to the door—and rushed down the steps to the car, with him honking the horn—I remember it so much. And then coming home—and he on the couch with her, when I came out to see if she was home—he on the couch—"

"So—listen," Weaver said. "Perhaps she couldn't live with your dad anymore. Perhaps things were bad between them. So you can't blame her."

"No no no no no, son—I would never do so—but please listen, Weaver. No—you see, you are named after him—Weaver McNair."

"Not Speck?"

"No—that was the other man's name—the man my mother took up with—he was a Speck—but I never forgot my father. My mother wanted me to forget him—I will tell you that—she wanted me to. I remember when I saw him walking along a street—we were riding in her car—and I said, 'There's Dad,' and she slapped my hands and said, 'He is not your dad—Fulsome Speck is.' So I became a Speck—in fact, nothing but a Speck—but you see, the interests I have in philosophy—came in fact from my father—so much came from my father—and I was hoping that you would have some interest in my life. I waited vainly for that. I know you wish to be famous—in some way—but you have to have compassion while you do. You and Dr. Heatherington were overheard speaking about the euthanasia of little Pruty—as if it was the best way to end her life. Is that an ideal of yours?"

Weaver didn't answer for a moment, then looked over his father's head and said, "I don't know—I don't know. I thought I knew—even a few weeks ago—but I no longer know—so what is this about?"

"It's about my father," Orlif answered with a sudden startling command. "I remember him, diligently taking a course in economics. He lost our house and lived in a small room, with a budgie bird, and was taking a course in economics. He believed he would get Mom back. He washed his socks in a little communal sink, and brushed his suit jacket and ironed his shirt, and went diligently to the community college, a man with big red hands and strong arms from working in the fields, and shearing sheep on a farm south of Brisbane, now determined to better himself to get Mommie back. You see, that's the problem."

"What is—?"

"I can never not love my father."

"Well, no one told you not to."

"My mother did," Professor Speck whispered, and his lips trembled. "My mother did. But the courts allowed me to visit him. There was a huge fight over that—and an insinuation—I will not mention the insinuation, it is too horrible. But I got to visit him in the little room, and he sat in a chair and spoke to me, as if he was nervous, and the little budgie bird sat on his shoulder. He would tell me about the economics course he was taking, saying, 'You see, son—economics is life—that is what they say. Why, without our economy, things in Australia would be quite different—yes, quite different all the way around.' And he would always have a treat for me waiting on the small table. Sometimes it was the same treat for months on end, but it showed that he always thought of me. And I felt so sorry for him."

"Why—he made his own bed, let him lie in it," Weaver said. He said this to show he was more mentally developed, far less sentimental, and had bigger fish to fry. But in many ways, he no longer believed what he said, and he was angry with himself for saying it.

"Oh—yes—well, you are right—of course that's the way it must be. I know that—why, your mother is a first- or second-generation feminist—so how could I not—make their own bed—yes—that's what it is—second-generation feminists are all for making up your own bed—but I still feel a little sad for him."

"I see," Weaver said. He went to say something more but felt he couldn't. He remembered Pruty telling him two days ago that she would be there if he wanted to talk about anything.

"About what, Pruty?" he had asked.

"About your unhappiness," Pruty had said. "We must continue to work on your unhappiness."

"He flunked his economics course at the community college, he didn't know much about it. One day, when I went to visit, the little paper that said he had failed was sitting on the table, next to the present he bought me. I saw his white shirt and his suit pants hanging in the closet. And his shoes in the corner. Outside, it was terribly hot, far hotter than it gets here—and no air conditioning. But I was used to it then.

"He didn't speak much that day. He took me out to buy a soda pop—that's what he called it. 'Come, son, I will buy you a soda pop.' I remember his face, red and kind and sweating, and a fly landing on his wrist, and the candy cane–coloured straws the waitress put in our Coke as we sat in the booth. And he played a song—I don't remember what song. I think it was from the big band era—of course, it had to be. He took me back to the room and showed me all the tricks he had taught that little bird, how it could drink out of a cup, and how it would sit on his shoulder, and when he said, 'Up,' it would fly up to his head. 'You see,' he said, 'you see?' And I was so proud of him when I was eight years old. He looked at me as if he was amazed himself, he had taught it all these things.

"At any rate, a week later he was killed—however it was, I don't know. I mean, I don't know because no one told me. I still remember a fly on his wrist, and his kind face. And his economics course, where he would become a whiz and get Mommie to love him again.

"'Oh, we will all live together again,' he would say. I never saw the budgie bird again."

There was a pause, and there were tears in Professor Speck's eyes. They rolled down his cheeks. And suddenly Weaver felt strange, and he reached out and took his father's arm.

"I see," he said. Then he let go of the arm quickly.

Orlif blew his nose, and then looked down at his shoes. "Mom, you see, had a bad time as well. Our protector and provider—the man named Speck—soon took up with a secretary at the office—his office—a few years later. A little blonde who wore a white blouse with three buttons undone. I remember. Yes—at twelve years of age, one begins to see such. Mom now found herself trying to do everything she could to please him, but to no avail.

"And one day we followed them into Sydney and saw them together at Bondi Beach—and Mom standing there on the sand in her high heels with her nylons having that black strip up the back, and the wind blowing sand, and me there with my fries and vinegar in a little cardboard tray listening to the hullabaloo, and my mother, her face blotched and red—and it was—well, it wasn't pleasant. And I thought—where do lies begin, and when do they end, and if they do not end, how in the world can we exist as men and women? The worst is the lie we tell ourselves."

Weaver was embarrassed, and he said, "Well, what in the world does that have to do with me?"

And Professor Speck smiled guiltily and said, "Why—everything, son. Everything in the world. That what you partook in for the sake of your career—is—is—shameful?"

"What did I do?"

Orlif fumbled about in his pants pocket—his pants always seemed a size too big—and hauled out a piece of paper, and handed it to his son.

It was the drawing he had done of the Musselman house, some months before. His lips pressed together, and his eyes blinked rapidly.

His son took the drawing, folded it and placed it upon the table near Vivian's ashtray.

Orlif tried to pat Weaver's hand, but his son, showing deep embarrassment, shied away, stood and left the room.

Three days later, when Weaver was out, Orlif saw that torn note of his son's in his wastepaper basket. He took it out, and painfully put it back together. It took him almost three hours.

*Never admit you were there.*

He taped it together and put it with the money that he had gotten from the sewer line.

Later, he sat at his little desk carving a duck. He liked to carve rabbits and ducks. He had given a carved rabbit to Pruty and he had given some to the church to be given away to children. He put his initials on the bottom of them, *OS*—and even doing this made him feel like he was bragging too much. He didn't want to be immodest. Once, Vivian took all his carvings and hid them when she knew he was giving them away to raffles at the church.

She was angry at him because they had become outcasts among the people she most wanted to impress. She had wanted him to be a great generational professor and she a grand generational activist. Now, almost no one knew her anymore.

Secretly, she kept waiting for an invitation to Professor Smythe's house for his Christmas soirée—that was the professor who seemed so intrepidly aware. And she had hoped to align herself with his views.

Orlif knew why she became so interested in the German environmentalist when he visited. Because poor Orlif had failed her in all the grand things she imagined for them. Every time she berated him, he knew that he had failed her. Her determination to sit beside the German at dinner proved it. Her rushing about to help Mr. Beal proved it. And in every way she acted there was a betrayal of him as a man, and a promise of more failure for herself, and he was silent.

So he kept carving away a woman in repose—a woman of substance and strength, a woman who would love and care, perhaps, for him in the end, hoping that this time he would make the one perfect gift to give to someone who cared for who he was.

Weaver left the stone house and walked up the heavy black road. It was a terrible feeling to feel free one moment and to be burdened by this boy's incarceration the next. He was pulled away from Europe by it; it was as if a magnet had hauled him back home, across those deep trenches of black ocean, the moment Jamie had been found guilty.

The last thing he was prepared for was to have Gavin interested in this case! Gavin himself. And saying what Weaver was going to say but having none of the responsibility.

He walked to the path, which was about three hundred yards from Load Road, and turned up through dark spruce and poplar trees cracking at their tops in the autumn wind. He walked Load Road for about a hundred yards. Just before he came to the back of the old house, he stopped and moved through an ancient footpath to the left.

Here Weaver stood in silence, waiting for a light to go on. That is Gertie's bedroom light. He had been lucky enough to have walked by one night on his way to the tavern and just by happenstance had seen her in her underwear. Her body, which seemed so slight in its clothes, was magnificent in her white bikini panties.

He realized she spent two or three nights a week with her sister and her father. Her father, Shamus, often slept in his big leather comfort chair in front of the television. The chair had a tear in the back and stuffing protruded. His bedroom was up the stairs at the top of the house, and often he didn't want to climb them. The kitchen was to the right of the living room. There was a small makeshift bedroom off the kitchen and Pruty slept in that small room. But just up three stairs off the first landing to the left was Gertie's bedroom, and where Weaver stood was in direct eyeline to the parting in the drapes which allowed him to see her. Yes, he had seen her in her snug white bikini underwear and one night he had seen her put lotion on her sunburned shoulders and naked breasts. It was very nice. But he hadn't seen her since. It was odd how she enticed him. He had first seen her sister, Pruty, at one of the meetings and then bathing at Savage's shore one morning. Mickey Bowels had taken her from her wheelchair and was holding her up in the water. Then he watched Mickey put her into her wheelchair, cover her with a beach towel and push her back toward the road. And Speck said:

"Ah, what a magnificent face that girl has—too bad about her legs."

Later that day, through the swath of August heat, he saw the same girl walk toward him, as if a miracle had just happened. How could that be? The same brilliant dark eyes, the same white, unblemished beauty in the face. He stared at her almost open-mouthed as she passed by. It was over a month later before he realized what the discrepancy was.

Tonight, like other nights, he waited for this beauty to come into her bedroom and strip herself naked. But she did not. All he could see through the lower window was Pruty with her head nodding and her hands folded around some superstitious Catholic rosary. Dr. Heatherington had been hoping to speak to her about end of life to relieve her suffering. And suddenly seeing her through the window, Weaver despised himself, and maybe Heatherington more. But to understand why, perhaps we must visit the day before.

THE DAY BEFORE, WEAVER HAD TAKEN PRUTY FOR A WALK.

"I can take you—Where would you like to go?"

"Do you mind taking me to the bathroom so I can have a pee?"

And he did so.

He found her hat and her mittens and began pushing the wheelchair up along Load Road and then cutting through an out-of-the-way back path, while Pruty, her little pink hat pulled down over her eyes and her small pink gloves tapping in time to some imaginary song, was telling him how much she appreciated this—and how kind he was. Telling him Shamus was forgetful and should have been home.

Weaver kept giving her puffs of hash, too, because she took it for the pain, and she was singing.

Finally, they came close to Pattern Cliff with its drop down to where Little Hackett ran into Arron Brook, and he stopped the wheelchair so that her feet dangled over. He hadn't meant to be so careless—he just hadn't known the path ran out.

He stopped it so abruptly she almost lurched forward, and he held her back with his arm. She took his hand as he held her back. She looked at him, and as he looked down at her, she smiled a sweet, crinkly smile. Her smile was always so noble, because of all the pain she had suffered in her life, that he smiled back.

"Thank you for smiling at me, Pruty—so few girls do."

"I will smile at you always, Weaver, you don't have to worry. Did you know this is the suicide place—where people suicide themselves?"

"No."

"That's what they say."

"Well, I am sorry I was careless."

"No, please don't worry anymore—you worry in your very soul. I can tell."

"Oh, I have my whole life in front of me, Pruty—many, many grand things I intend to do."

"Weaver, none of us know tomorrow what it is we will ever do."

He turned the chair around and the cold wind came over them.

On the way back to her home, he suddenly stopped and said, "It is awful for you to be left alone, Pruty—but you know"—and here he began to push the chair again—"I was left alone when I was a child—and you know—I started kicking walls—and I am beginning to remember it all—for the first time. Since I came home, it is all coming back. And it is coming back to me in terrible rushes. For instance, my mother was obligated in her work—and so was Dad—and I was left to my own devices. Do you think it is strange that I forgot that for many years and now it is flooding back? How I was dragged to certain meetings—how my mother told me that she was embarrassed by my father—"

"Ahh," she said.

"What do you mean, Pruty?"

"I am so sorry—for then, who are you allowed to love, your mother or father, and which one will you be loyal to? For you see, that is what is being asked," she said, and she reached back with her hand to take his hand, but he didn't take it. So she continued:

"I ended up being loyal to my father—not because he was good, or because my mother didn't suffer by his hand, but because he was and is alone, and forgotten and growing old. And my mother, who I loved, is gone."

"If I tell you something, will you laugh?" he asked.

"Of course not—unless it is funny—"

"I have not been baptized, as I told you. I wonder if it would change things if I was? You see, my mother only had me in order to receive her inheritance—my grandfather wanted her to have a child. He was a terrible man to her—or so she said. But she acquiesced to his demands. We were once quite rich, so then I was the price she had to pay, and so she paid it. She was somewhat embarrassed when she was herself pregnant, because she had fought so hard against that kind of—that kind of—tradition."

"Tradition?"

"Yes, tradition. So, when I was young, I was left alone. I started to act out. Sometimes I would change clothes two or three times a day just so my mom and dad would notice me. Sometimes I dressed all in green and then an hour later I'd come into the room and be dressed all in orange. At supper I would appear all in red—right down to my shoes. You see, I stole some money from them—and bought these outfits. I also tried to run away. I jumped a freight train. But I came home again.

"She was at that time Vivian Speck—she had no time to spare—no time at all. For me. And my father—was trying so hard for tenure."

"Ahh," Pruty said.

He pushed on down the path. He tried to sound as if this was all a kind of joke easily gotten over. That he decried the idea of self-pity. And yet he said this: "I have no one to talk to about this.

I remember I was scared and alone—a man used to take me upstairs—I never told my parents. So when my parents came home, I would rush into my room and come out, and dress all in red—so they would notice me. I was seven or eight and started kicking people. Then bigger boys used to get me at school and force me to eat pickles. And I broke out in a rash. One day I ate about a dozen pickles. I am just starting to remember it all. It took you to make me remember it—and realize I too am a human being."

Then he said, "Yes, we had the inheritance because of me—and no one knows. I was the object that got them the money. You see, I didn't know I was a human being. I did not know until I started to talk to you. And so—I am sorry—about the park—I am. I am sorry."

"I know that, Weaver—I know that," Pruty said, looking down at the path and the alders and the puddles as they passed by.

"I am sorry about many other things too—but you see—I am hoping things will change—I am hoping—but perhaps it is too late."

"Did you ever think of getting baptized?" Pruty asked.

"No. Well, why? It's useless now anyway—and what would it ever matter? A bit of silly water on the forehead."

"You told me last week and again today you weren't baptized, so you must have thought about it. You said you were the object of their inheritance. Become baptized and you will be the object of a greater inheritance."

He tried to dismiss it. But Pruty wouldn't.

"I have made some boughs for Christmas. You might get baptized. You could come to midnight mass—when it comes—that would be good. We always have warm cider at the community centre after—that's real good." She said it as if she was hoping to find something kind to say and was somewhat at a loss.

And the wheelchair squeaked along, and the pathway was frozen, and she reached behind and took his hand.

"Hold my hand, Pruty. No woman in years has held my hand."

There were tears in his eyes, and he said it was from the cold.

There were tears in her eyes, and it was from joy.

THE TROUBLE WITH GAVIN'S REPORT IN THE *GLOBE* WAS that it was all true—and, worse, was now being taken seriously by the RCMP and the major crimes division. And so Weaver's plan to come forward with a giant revelation—like a book of revelations—was now compromised. It was best to be silent, for if he spoke—or until he confessed—they would simply say he was following Gavin's report.

"This was never a good or honourable arrest. It was done with much overlooked and much decided by notion rather than fact."

That was Gavin's opening line.

It was quite a bit like Weaver's opening: "Many facts were missed, much was assumed, and the actual events overlooked."

The road was silent, the dark night enclosed him in its mute oblivion to his wishes. He went to find Mr. Beal, because he had to. He had no one else. He showed him the article Gavin had written.

Beal had bought himself a new jacket and cap and had a new pair of jeans. The new jeans showed in some way his naïveté, with the cuffs turned up precisely. He said he wanted to look good when Nin came home.

Then he added, "What will she do when she can't handle anything and gets all mixed up with numbers—and goes to try and get her welfare?"

Beal looked at Weaver as if Weaver would understand and nodded quite contemplatively as he looked at the article.

"Nin was right. She told me we had to come back. She was right." Then Beal said, "God bless her—"

He looked startled. He didn't know why he had said that, he just did.

Nin was a little ragamuffin, a girl on the street, wandering from one place in town to the other, looking forever for a chance to be loved. When she was quite young, she had neither tampons nor Kotex and she would hide in the bushes. That is when she befriended young Musselman, who supplied her when she needed to be.

She spent time in the old Wandlyn, spent time in a room at the tavern, before she had met Beal. She used to go to Mickey's store in winter and stand near the hot air register. Mickey remembered her white face would change to pink, and she would go back outside into the January afternoon then come back in later, shivering again. He would tell her to help him put jeans and socks on the shelves and give her a pair of socks and a woollen shirt and a ten-dollar bill. He also let her stay in a room for a while—and, as always, people began to talk.

Beal and she were cousins, perhaps first cousins (and, though ludicrous, some maintained half-brother and -sister—and also, it was said, lovers, and she was indebted to him).

Weaver left, throwing Gavin's article into the garbage. They had all heard Jamie Musselman had stepped in between two prisoners in the library to protect one from being stabbed. Weaver was now infuriated with himself—with everyone. Where in the world might he go? Is this what he imagined when he saw that stupid plaque in honour of his rival, who never thought of him as one?

On the way back from the tavern, he dropped into the house to see Pruty.

She told him that she believed Dr. Heatherington was going to ask her something special when he came to see her.

"Do you know my doctor?"

"Oh yes."

"Well, he told me he was going to ask me something special. Do you think he likes me?"

"Of course he likes you."

She paused, thought a moment, looking up at him somewhat mischievously.

"I think so too," Pruty said, placing her hands on her lap and sighing. "What do you think he will ask me? Maybe even on a date, or something like that there. He even bought me a milk-shake and everything. Oh, I know I'm being silly—but I like making things up. I sit here most of the time by myself, so I like to make things up—so I wonder at times what he will ask."

"I am not sure," Weaver said, "what he will ask."

Pruty paused a moment, and whispered: "But I wouldn't go—on a date with him—if you—if you were mad at me, if I went on a date with him. Do you know what I mean, Weaver? If you were to get mad cause I was out on a date with him—do you know what I mean? I mean, if you like me so you would be mad if I went on a date with someone else and everything like that there? I mean, I know I make things up in my head, so don't mind me."

Weaver looked at her and touched her face with his hand.

"No, dear, I wouldn't be angry—you do what you wish—but, no matter what he asks, only what you want. Only what you want! Do you understand? And say a prayer always before you do. I mean, I see you saying prayers, so it might be good, if you believe in that, to say a prayer before you do."

His lips trembled. He looked down at her legs in their white leotards and tattered dress with the pin in the middle. He was once again trying not to cry.

And she said, "Because—I wouldn't ever want you to get upset—for what I think is—well, forgive me for saying it, for I'm a big dreamer at times—that you like me a little bit too."

That same night, Father Benjamin brought Little Nin her supper of beans and wieners and tea and sat with her for many moments. He talked about being bitten by a snake when he was young, and how an old man at the orphanage sucked out the wound, and they hauled him in a cart for a day and a half when he was delirious, and in his delirium he was sure the Virgin came to him and put her hand over the snakebite and that is why he lived. And perhaps Nin didn't believe him—but that is what he thought, at any rate. And he told her he was so afraid of freezing to death when he got here that he hid in a closet with a blanket over him. He said in Mumbai there were 14 million people and 300 million rats. She listened to him, nodding, and eating beans and wieners and saying,

"Oh, my good God,"

and

"What kind of snake was it?"

and

"How many tigers did you see?"

and

"Why do bishops wear such funny hats?"

and

"You would be a good man whether you was a priest or not,"

and

"I love Beal."

And he told her he knew she loved Beal, but that the boy—the young boy she knew, who had helped her long ago—had been stabbed, in the prison library, whose window overlooked a desolate land—and if she did love, then she must try to have courage. And then he gave her a book.

He made sure he got it for her because she had spoken of it often: Dylan Thomas. *Collected Poems.*

As Mickey Bowels had tried to tell Mr. Speck that little rustic story, he was really saying neither they nor he could really change the eternal mystery and the longing of the human heart. He was trying to say nothing but simplicity and kindness mattered.

And each day Vivian Speck and Orlif woke to this sad and inevitable truth, with their son whom they deeply loved, who was now somehow inflamed with a journey into a darkness they did not understand. They tried desperately to understand and had various opinions, and even phoned a psychologist, who spoke to them of grave times, about the youth of the world seeing the fallacy of the moment.

"Yes, they are seeing the fallacy of the moment."

"They are—the fallacy of the moment—how are they seeing the fallacy of the moment—what moment?"

"There are in this day to day—all kinds of moments—and they are seeing the fallacy of the individual moments."

"The individual moments—I see."

Vivian said she understood the psychologist far better than Orlif ever would. In fact, as time passed, she berated him for everything that he said or did. The problem with Weaver was, she insisted, Orlif himself.

"I remember what you said about that!"

"When?"

"March of '83, I wanted to leave you at that moment—start my life anew—be anew—be fresh and new—saddled as I was with an old man—like you. It wasn't fair, was it?"

"No, it wasn't fair."

"So, you do admit it wasn't fair."

"No—you are right, nothing seemed to be—fair."

"You've failed in everything—admit it."

"Yes—I have pretty much failed in everything."

Vivian was now and then coughing up blood and woke at night with a rasp in her throat, and he ran downstairs to make her lemon tea, and tried to hide her cigarettes, and told her that if she lied about how much she smoked, her nose would grow. But Vivian was her own person and would do what she must. So, Weaver and she, whom he both loved, were in trouble and he was at a loss at how to heal them.

It was perhaps why Orlif Speck started to go back to church, just now and again—on the sly, so no one but the congregation of small village working men and women knew. It started when they had asked him to carve some sheep and cows for the manger. And after he carved four sheep and three cows, he put them into a shopping bag and took them down to the church. Then, because he was so welcomed and people didn't think he was such a complete failure, he stayed for mass.

There in the church, the statue of the Virgin quite plain, and the old wooden pews where a thousand people had prayed, it all seemed hopelessly rural, poor and, worse, too suspiciously Catholic. And the last thing he ever wanted to be was a hypocrite. Worse, though he believed everyone in the world was a hypocrite in some way, he didn't wish to be called one.

He had tried to get away from that—yes, he had! The bishops

had bothered not only Little Nin but bothered him as well. He looked upon them as the masters of non-disclosure, simpering pieties and convention. But they were not the Church. They, as much as they met with each other in the Council of Bishops, were not the faith. The faith was much grander, ethereal, and captured the entire universe for whoever wanted it.

Did he find the peace he was so looking for at the age of sixty-seven?

Not as long as he had the ball of money. Not as long as Gavin had written in the *Globe* that he believed there were three people involved, perhaps two men and a woman. Of course, for the moment, this made those who had convicted Jamie Musselman more unwavering and narrow, more hard-hearted; and all of them claimed the right person was convicted and the case was closed.

The night Weaver came back from seeing Beal at the tavern, Orlif was about to ask him about the strange way he and Beal had returned home just after Musselman was found guilty, but Weaver spoke first.

He said, "Dad, I want you to know—you never protected me—never. One day I was alone—about eight—and two boys were hitting me—bigger boys—and you weren't there—you were at class." But this was a lie. It wasn't two boys, it was that man upstairs—and poor Weaver couldn't admit it.

"I am sorry if I wasn't," Orlif said, shaken by this.

Then Weaver de Speck said that he remembered being left alone in a room in Halifax when his parents were out. He was only four or five. He remembered that his mother had told him she would be right back but was gone a long time. There was nothing in the room but a metal crib and a washbasin—and he was scared. His parents had had an argument about who was to care for him and who was to go to their meetings. And he had kept saying, "You stay, Daddy," and "You stay, Mommy."

And he grabbed his small game of pinball and ran to them, saying, "You play with me, Daddy."

And they both had left him.

Orlif remembered that cold autumn day and it all came back—how Weaver was huddled up in the corner under the crib when Orlif got home. He thought he'd only be gone five minutes but, as always, absent-mindedly, he had lost track of time. He started talking about Immanuel Kant to someone, and became very engaged, and soon two hours had gone by where he thought he was being very forthright in his knowledge.

"Oh—my son is at home," he remembered.

"I will do better," Orlif said now. "I promise—I will do as best I can!"

"It's too late," Weaver said, almost with poignancy. "It is too late."

And for the first time, he touched his father's face.

Now, after all these years, the money had been dribbled away. The inheritance that his son's birth obtained was all but gone.

They might mock him—at work they certainly would—but Orlif began to carry an old rosary on him. Sometimes just to reach down and touch it when things seemed to be going wrong. They had begun to notice him at work once more—as a person they should really and truly try to get rid of—and the one who wanted him gone the most was a former friend, twenty years his junior, a man whom he had supported, whom he had paid out of his own pocket to find a publisher.

This was the putty-faced fellow who now said that Orlif's day had come and gone, and that he was a jingoist, and maybe a racist.

"I am not a jingoist," Orlif said, and then he asked, "Am I—a jingoist? No, I am not! Racist? Well, you can bet your bottom dollar I don't cozy up to that."

But he did not go into the common room. He did not eat his muffin with them anymore. That is, his 10 a.m. muffin.

There was something so duplicitous about Catholics that it was all bound to come splashing out among the progressives at St. Michael's university. His former friend told people Orlif had betrayed him and was a charlatan. He had somehow forgotten that Orlif had gotten him the job—and Orlif was too shy to remind him.

"Look here," he said one day, going into the hall, "look here."

But then he only nodded and patted the putty-faced fellow on the shoulder and said, "Good job—you'll go far—far-reaching—you will go." Then he became confused. "You are a reacher—for far-off things—far things, so yes, there you go—you will fairly go—far."

So, in these fantastically new times, where girls became boys and boys became girls, and all was new and strange, Orlif, in falling back into old ways in order to find comfort and faith, would soon be gone. His former friend, the ordained darling of so many women, with his putty-like face, only smirked when Orlif said that tampons in the men's washroom seemed a tad presumptuous.

"You would think so," Ms. Ellen Shaver said. "Yes—you would think so."

"Well, I don't mean to be presumptuous—but it seems a tad presumptuous."

"It's comforting to men of the right mindset," Professor Shaver said. She herself was transitioning to become Eddy Shaver, and Orlif, as usual, was the very last in the department to know.

"Yes—well then," Orlif said. Then he muttered, "Well then."

But he did say once, “She removed those gorgeous, wondrous knockers—I noticed that right away.”

And people heard he had said this, too.

Each day he went to the office, each day he taught his class, each day he walked home and made himself a bacon sandwich and ate alone.

*I will leave Vivian*, he often thought, *and I will run away—to Canada, yes, I will run away to Canada.*

But he suddenly realized that he was already in Canada, and had been for years, and winter would soon be here. And there was nowhere else in the world to go. And he couldn’t leave Vivian. Who would take care of her if he did?

GERTIE'S PLANS HAD BEEN PUT ON HOLD. HER WEDDING dress hanging in the closet, her shoes beneath it, was, if you looked across the room, as if a ghost was now ready to step down the aisle. Twice Shamus asked her to take it away—but she left it where it was, and he could not look at it. She told him it was bad luck to move it to Musselman's house, so until she was married, it would remain in the upstairs closet.

"But it's four years, girl. What if he doesn't come back for four years? Are you prepared to wait for four years? You are a young, healthy woman—a real beauty—do you know what I mean?"

"Of course I know what you mean. But I am prepared to wait four years!" she answered, not looking at him.

"That's impossible—impractical—and inadvisable—besides being inadmissible," he shouted. Then he told her of the prosecutor who had, as he said, "an eye or two on you during the trial," knowing Musselman wouldn't be around to "marry you."

"Then I will leave and marry him in the place where he is."

"You mean in the prison?"

She wouldn't answer.

"In the place of hell—odious is what it is," he stammered. "Don't do it—find someone else—someone nice and polite—someone who doesn't murder and then write up poems."

She did not speak.

“Please, Gertie—you can’t—please.”

She turned and walked away, and he could say no more. He even said, “I will say no more.”

And he cried, just a little—a few sniffs.

But worse, the guilt itself was worse—the guilt of non-disclosure.

Then—the money itself—he had run right out—not right away, but within two days—and spent the money—the two hundred, something he had said he would never ever do. He had promised he wouldn’t spend it—said it was blood money—and said he would spit on it. He even did spit on it—a little.

And what had he spent it on? Bingo. The tavern where he bought a round for everyone. Yes. He had spent it on bingo, at a restaurant and the tavern—and brought popcorn home for Pruty and an Oh Henry! bar, guilt-ridden over it all.

“You’re not eating your bar. When are you going to eat your Oh Henry!?”

And to go back a bit, for days just after the murder (some years ago now, before Gertie and Jamie became, as they say, *an item*), he spoke to Gertie about young Musselman:

“What is he like?” he would ask her fifteen times a day.

Until, in the end, young Gertie, studying for her exams, shouted: “Papa—you asked me that a hundred and two times! I don’t know!”

“But does anyone like him—I mean, now he is a murderer and everything?”

And she said a very strange thing at that moment: “I don’t think anyone likes him but me—but he doesn’t talk to me! And no one knows if he is a murderer!”

Then one day she told Shamus that Jamie’s uncle had taken him to Nova Scotia. And she said, “And no one will miss him ” and then whispered, “Except me.”

He was relieved after that. The boy had gone away. Good riddance, too. Yes, best to get rid of murderers. So he sighed, stretched, made fun of Pruty a bit, and went and lay down.

Now Gertie and Jamie Musselman were engaged, and he had been taken to jail. If there was such a thing as eternal retribution, this must be it! Hell had no boundaries at all. It came to him in the middle of the night.

Now seven years had passed since that murder. And Beal now blamed him: "Why did you tell me about it? I had a job to go to, I was trying to straighten my life out—I really was—and then this. Why did I meet you on Jane Street—why?"

But Shamus couldn't answer. He only hung his head. And then he said, "We are all rushing toward some kind of confession, and we don't even know."

And then, leaving Pruty, who had been saying the rosary (which bothered him), he went for a walk.

"Too many Hail Marys, Pruty. A few are okay—but don't go to hell with the joke."

And, "I would never have bought you the rosary if I thought you were going to act like that!"

In the last two weeks, she had to see Dr. Heatherington because of pain. She knew the doctor was getting sick of her visits and finding her phone calls very annoying. But still, she so hoped in the solution he said he had for her. Pruty knew Heatherington had something up his sleeve, the way he looked at her with bold eyes and his immaculate beard. His cheeks flushed when he spoke, and he looked at her in a peculiar way, as if he wanted her to understand something delicate. Something extraordinary he was planning for her.

She just wasn't sure what.

On another note, Shamus felt his world crumbling. He remembered those men who had murdered a family, and had put the safe in the back seat of their car and drove around town. Secretly, they had to show what they had done; they wanted to prove to everyone and especially to each other what it was they had done, that they could be as unthinking and as foolish.

Shamus was terrified now they would all head in that direction too. Beal and Weaver and—himself.

He went for a walk that afternoon with a walking stick he found on the pathway to Pattern Cliff, and he just kept going.

Gertie came home from work. She had gone to Musselman's house but had a strange feeling she must now visit her father's home. It was just after dark, and as she came out of Musselman's, of course people stared at her. It was a very extraordinary thing, a woman like her in Musselman's house alone. A gold digger—which is what her few friends now called her.

"That's what a pretty snatch can do—" some of the men who drank at Stothart's said as they saw her walk by, said it loudly enough for her to hear.

Oh, how moral immorality can be!

The grand house was dark, save for the light in the upstairs back hallway and in the tiled bathroom at the back on the first floor. Each day, she went there—to sit, to stare at the paintings, look into the great rooms and contemplate her life together with him.

After which, she drove downriver.

It was very dark in the kitchen, and Shamus was lying across two chairs. For some reason, the little cactus plant had tipped over and lay sideways on the windowsill. There was a harsh wind blowing down across the roof, and the trees waved in the mad hills behind them. Pruty was back in the corner, sitting in her chair, with her pink rosary.

"So anyways, don't turn on the light," he said.

"Why not?" she said.

She turned on the light and saw him—his left eye swollen. His lip too was fat and looked as if he had been blowing a trumpet. He had a Band-Aid across his nose, and his left pant leg was torn. There was another Band-Aid on his left big toe.

Pruty told her he had tried to kill himself.

Pruty said that the neighbour, Mr. Taylor, had phoned. Mr. Taylor said he had been walking along with his fishing rod in hand, a few nice fall trout in his basket, and saw Shamus on the end of Pattern Cliff that overlooked Glidden Pool.

"Oh, hello, Shamus," Mr. Taylor said, waving to him.

"Why hello, Wilbur," Shamus answered. "How are you?"

"I am fine—yes, I am fine."

"That's nice—I mean, that you are fine—I'm fine too."

And then he took a swan dive—or some such dive—off the cliff. He spread out his arms and then suddenly brought them in, and fell in a heap like a folded umbrella.

Mr. Taylor and another man who had been fishing just up beyond Glidden Pool crossed the heaviest part of Arron Brook in the rapids and found him lying on a bed of grass. The only grass there was. To the right or the left was rocks, beyond that the falls. But he had managed to fall into the soft grass and, though hurt, had lived.

He swore he did not need an ambulance, or that it was any more than an accident.

"I don't think it was an accident," Mr. Taylor told little Pruty, "but I have no way of proving it one way or the other."

Pruty was in the corner, shaking like a leaf, her hair that Gertie had washed and cut the night before shining under the one light bulb, her feet in small woollen slippers, with leather bottoms black and shiny, for they had never been walked upon. Only the heels were marked, where she sometimes dug into the floor to stop. She had a T-shirt on that said, *For the love of God, press these buttons.* The two red buttons were positioned over the nipples of her breasts.

That day, once again, Shamus had looked for the envelope.

But it was not in the drawer—where it had been.

Pruty, however, knew where it was—and Pruty was silent, trying to decide things that nobody should have to decide. How often she had wanted to tell Gertie, and how often she started to, and how often she did not.

All of them were damned—by him.

Gertie went to the phone to telephone an ambulance. But Shamus stopped her.

"No, that will involve the police—so don't phone anyone or—or—"

"Or what?"

"Or I won't let you see Pruty again—I will lock Pruty up every time you come here—pon my soul—pon my soul!"

Ashamed, she went into the small TV room and slumped in a chair, holding her cellphone in her hand.

Pruty wheeled up and sat beside her.

"Oh, Pruty, what will we do?" she said. "Our world has crumbled—a few years ago it was fine—everything was okay—and then Mommie took sick and now—things have gone downhill—downhill. How will we prove my love is innocent?"

Gertie laid her head on Pruty's shoulder, and Pruty put her arm around her and looked tentatively at her father.

After a while the house was absolutely silent. Then his voice came in a broken whisper: "I have a sore toe too." Then: "Sore toe, Pruty."

"Why—why, why!" Gertie asked.

There was a pause as if he was trying to think clearly. "I just found out my brother is an alcoholic, if you want to know."

"But everyone knows he is an alcoholic—everyone—you are an alcoholic yourself."

"Yes, but he is my younger brother—"

"But you haven't seen him in ten years, and the last time he was here, you threw him out of the house."

"I did?"

"Yes."

"Well, there you go."

Pruty, however, knew where the letter was. She had it under the seat where she sat her bum. The day she had upset her wheelchair and lay on the floor, she managed to reach the drawer and had hauled it out so she could get up.

It was at that moment that the letter fell on top of her—some old fishing flies had fallen on her as well—that is, the acceptance of the resignation by the Department of Defence, and on the back of this envelope the list of monies saved.

SAVINGS FOR JAMIE'S CAR

| Dad | Jamie |
|---|---|
| 1425 | 275 |

She stared at the letter for an hour. It was a dignified letter. Very—what was the word she heard at the environmental meeting?—very elitist, top quality.

"Oh Jesus," she said. And then, "Oh Jesus."

What might happen if she told Gertie—and what would happen if she did not?

She had placed the envelope along with her books—*Ethics* by Aristotle, which she was determined to read, and two romance novels—under her seat.

It was about this time she began to say the rosary. As if, by saying it, she could somehow stop the tide.

It was growing cold. It was now the last of November, and the wood beyond their house had the intermittent sound of rifle shots from those hunting deer. They bled away in the white skies of afternoon, and sometimes the old house shook.

Every few days Pruty would put on her mittens and hat and would wheel herself down to the church to see her mother's grave, and then see Father Benjamin. Always between two and three in the afternoon.

The little priest, Father Benjamin Yorsa—whom most called Father Benjamin—had been here over seven years now, and had almost frozen. He walked about his small home in huge slippers and four sweaters. He sat in the vestry with an electric heater on near his legs, and he wore a woollen scarf about his neck. And he wore gloves and earmuffs to bed, and he said prayers. And sometimes the prayers said: "Get me out of here."

All of this was a new world to Father Benjamin, who, along with his brothers and sister, had been left on the side of the road, four of them in one huge cardboard box, with their eyes peering out at the world like lost kittens.

Mother Teresa in the few times he had met her had called him little Benjamin, and he had always been tiny. A tiny little man who had travelled first to Rome, and then to Frankfurt, where he sat in an airport for almost the entire day. And then, because of a lack of priests in the New World, on to New York, Boston and finally Montreal. There he went to Notre-Dame and met a huge priest—well over six feet tall, white, with huge feet and hands, who gave him a hug and almost crushed him.

They packed him some peanut butter sandwiches and some juice and gave him a new rosary and sent him, by train, on his way to New Brunswick.

"My little Benjamin," Mother had said to him, "God's messenger, go and serve the Lord."

A few altar boys blew up French safes and told him they were balloons.

It was Pruty who told him the difference, when she came one cold morning in the fall and saw them taped to his ceiling, believing it was a tribute on his birthday. This was some years ago—after her mother's funeral.

"They are not balloons, Father—"

"No?"

"Not on your life, and if you wanted a life with them things on, it would be harder to get one—no matter how hard the lad is."

"Well, I am not sure what you mean. What are they?"

"Well, to be blunt—when a lad squirts, he has nowhere to go."

"Oh—so you say—?"

"Yes," Pruty said, "the squirt, Father—well even if it is a generous squirt, a noble squirt—a very decent squirt—it has no place to go."

"I see—yes, of course—yes."

Then, getting upset, she said, "I brought you a card for your birthday—but get them effing things off your wall. You gotta learn these things, Father, or you will be taken advantage of. You have to realize here you are nothing more than a babe in the woods.

You are a child in the bulrushes, a small fry in the stream of life, with a goddamn striped bass eyeing you up—is what I think."

She wheeled down to the church, and took communion, and taught catechism to the grade four students, and tried to take piano lessons, and started a fund to help the graveyard, and went to a party far down off Load Road with the Dugan boys.

Then she went to confession and confessed to Father Benjamin that while attending that party she had three glasses of rum and sang a song called "Too Drunk to Fuck" and had everyone laughing—and then threw up.

"What do you think of that, Father?"

"I'm not sure—"

"Well—it's a mystery. I acted some crazy."

"Yes—I dare say it is a mystery."

She wanted to get married. She knew she was not supposed to think marriage was so important, but still, she thought that perhaps someday she could be like others. No, she was more independent than a host of young women because she had no choice but to be. Many would think of her, if they did at all, as being frivolous, but her eyes shone at moments of the day with grand wisdom.

She mentioned Weaver a dozen times. But she thought Dr. Heatherington liked her better—he was divorced, and had given her an antidepressant which he said should help, and came to her house three times—and as she said, "I even made him hot chocolate."

"Are you sure, Pruty? One should be sure."

"Not about the antidepressant, Father. I tossed those lads."

"I mean about his intentions."

"I think he is very honourable, and he is very kind. He said to me I am the one case he is most concerned about—so what do you think of that—the one case!"

"Well, I see," Father Benjamin said.

Oh, she knew it was all fantasy, but even if it was, it was fun to pretend.

"And he also said he can relieve my problems." And she smiled delightedly.

"What are your problems?" Father Benjamin asked.

"Oh, dear me, Father—dear me—dear me—so many of you silly, naive priests don't know nothing. I am often in terrible pain."

WE WILL REVEAL WHAT HAPPENED.

One day Jamie was no longer in protective custody but had been allowed into the general population and was sorting books at the prison library. The warden had brought him in and asked him if he knew books.

"Yes," he said, "I do know books."

"What do you think—you think you might be able to help straighten and put our shelves in order?"

"Of course."

And so he went from the basement holding cells and up the green metal stairs, and along the hall and up another stairs and then a side stairs, and through a doorway into the library. He too had such a vague memory of that night, he often thought that maybe everyone else was right. He had told Gertie to find someone else.

She didn't tell him the very prosecutor who had prosecuted him had twice asked her on a date. That he had met her in the hallway of the courthouse, during the trial—that he took her aside and commiserated with her. That he had smiled and rubbed her shoulder, saying all would be well. That she had blushed and had ran down the hall. That it seemed he wished her to be a conspirator against her own fiancé.

Everyone in his family was now gone, and the only person who believed he wasn't guilty, it seemed, was Gertie.

"Hell, I am marrying you—so get used to it," she told him.

He worked in the library for over a week before it happened.

It was reported at first just as an incident—and then that an unnamed inmate—and then finally that Jamie Musselman had been stabbed by someone while trying to intercede in a dispute over a comic book. It was so absurd—the people involved did not know who he was, and he who stabbed him did not care about the comic book.

But no one was more guilt-ridden than Father Benjamin. He drove to town and saw Mrs. Winnifred White, who went to mass regularly. He asked her what he should do. Who were Nin's parents, did she have anyone in the world to take care of her?

No, she did not—she was a little waif and perhaps a felon—a "felony waif," Winnifred said.

"Then there is nowhere she can go? So, I will have to keep her until she decides to tell what she has to tell."

"What in heaven's name does she have to tell?"

But he simply shook his head and said nothing more.

"But Father," the woman said, "you cannot keep her there—what will people think?"

"But does it matter what people think? What they already think of me they think—what they already say about the Catholic Church they will say again. And my concern is her."

"But I think it matters a great deal what people think, and people will always think the worst—and what if they do. They will look at you as being—well, you know . . ."

He queried her with his look—moved in his chair and picked up a small doughnut, placed it on the saucer that held his teacup, rubbed his tiny fingers to get rid of the sugar and looked at her questioningly. Then he looked at the little doughnut again. The questioning look was, it seemed, as much about the doughnut as anything else.

"Well, you know—a really black little foreigner living with a really little white woman."

"Ah," Father Benjamin said.

That night, however, Father Benjamin had to go to the reserve. There he had to give last rites to Mr. Samuel, who had been a trapper and a woodcarver, and who had served in Korea. And they had gathered about the bed as Father Benjamin did so. One of the women had made him tea, and there was a plate of tea biscuits—and others sat in the small parlour—some of the men were playing crib at a table.

Little Nin was left alone. She was pacing back and forth. She had been in hiding almost two months, and today she had contacted a friend. Finally, she got up enough gumption to turn on her phone—a pink phone with the picture of a rabbit on it—and had phoned her one friend, the friend she felt she could tell all of this to. Well, it wasn't the only one she told something to—she had told the priest. But now, thinking of Jamie Musselman in jail, where he had been stabbed, she decided to phone her friend—the most completely sympathetic person she knew.

That person was Marsha—the young woman who dressed in black and held seances in her garage.

"Come to me," Marsha said in a strange voice with sudden authority. "I knew you would call."

"You knew?"

"Of course, Ninny poo—I knew—I always know—I know what is happening. I can tell you have something you wish to reveal to me—so come now."

"I will. I will come now—I don't know how I will come—but I will come now. I have to get it off my chest and see to it that things are straightened out."

"Yes," Marsha said, "I will solve many crimes—many, many crimes will be solved under my jurisdiction—"

"Your jurisdiction?"

"Yes—I am the one—the chosen one to solve these crimes. I will send someone to pick you up—and you will come to me."

Little Nin left by the side door—by the back way, around to the front of the church. She paused a moment by the headstone of one of her first ancestors, buried after a boating accident in May of 1794. He was one of the pioneers that Mickey Bowels had once delighted in talking about at the Miramichi Historical Society. He spoke to Little Nin about him as well—when she came into his store to get warm.

It was the first time Little Nin had left the church basement since she went into hiding, and she hadn't realized the air had turned so very cold. She put on the knitted hat that Beal had bought her, with her name, Little Nin, stitched inside.

The next afternoon it rained and then turned to snow. Orlif Speck had been depressed all day. It was horrible enough when they had asked Weaver—before he had gone away the first time—what he had put into the toilet to plug it so, and he had said that he had put in one of his father's essays because it was silly.

But as we now know, the day after Weaver left, Orlif, in clearing the line (Orlif couldn't begin to think anyone else would do such a job, so he dug up the septic tank by himself—he wore his corduroy jacket and his hands were filthy as he dug), found money—the bills that had in terror or convenience been thrown into the toilet some days before. Orlif put the money in the back room where he carved his figurines.

Then, after all this time, Weaver had come back. So had Mr. Beal.

The boy in the prison had been stabbed.

Little Nin had gone away.

And none of this should have happened. Orlif believed it was a design against him because he had never raised his voice to his son. Or ever disagreed with Vivian and her intolerance—an intolerance which was completely acceptable in this age and allowed Weaver to be solitary and alone. An intolerance so accepted against the male world that those who did not show intolerance were considered in some grand way unworthy. An intolerance that filled the university corridors and the cryptic novels of young boys and girls. And an intolerance that allowed darkness to come into the hearts of cruel men and use it to their benefit.

A few days before (that is, a few days after he heard about the stabbing) he came very close to getting into a shoving match with one student who came late and disrupted his talk, and when Orlif asked him to be quiet, the student continued to speak as if Orlif was nothing. Everyone had heard the rumour, the rumour that he was about to lose his position, and the more titillating rumour about Vivian and the German professor.

The boy came in late, sat down beside two other boys and, pretending to whisper, said loud enough for others to hear, "Had a good night last night—hey, got dead drunk, all hungover—good night—a married woman, too—she was out at the bar, tiny little skirt—her husband is away—but I'll be hard pressed today to keep up with the nonsense in this course."

Orlif asked the boy to please be quiet, he was trying to discuss the second philippic by Cicero and needed people to pay attention.

"Cicero, Cicero, where you going to go—ey oh," the boy said.

Orlif was only a part-time lecturer now and had no influence over anything anymore. He had fumbled away any chance at tenure at two universities. And if his wife hadn't had some money left, they would be lost. His wife had married him expecting such a grand career—and now disappointment had enclosed her, and their small house proved it. So, when she demanded to sit beside the German intellectual, he knew why.

He slammed his book on the desk and that got their attention. But then he looked so nervous at all the dust rising around him after he had slammed his book that they began to laugh. He went to the boy, the boy stood and pushed him, and walked out, slamming the door, and poor Orlif had tears in his eyes.

Today, he was home in the stone house, thinking of that callow boy and what he had said. He remembered the German Hegelian whom he had invited to give a very special talk, about rice paddies. But this German Hegelian environmentalist, who spoke German, didn't seem to think Orlif knew anything—and besides, he wanted to see a buffalo. He was very angry they didn't have a few dozen buffalo out in the yard. He was a professor from the University of Cologne, and poor Orlif had once visited that city and wanted then, of course, to speak of Nero's mother. But the environmentalist had no knowledge of mothers of Nero. He had not much knowledge of the lost legions of Varus, or the Germanic war of 9 AD—and so Orlif was pushed to the side, and Orlif's wife, Vivian Speck, took over and waltzed with him and held his hand and drove the German environmentalist, who was very German, with a German accent, and was upset about rice paddies in Taiwan, to all his appointments and then back to the airport. But she did not come home until late the next morning. She had simply not come home.

And how at the dinner the night before the German left, she had said, "Orlif, you go sit over there somewhere—I want to sit by our visiting professor."

Orlif had planned the visit for over a year. A year of planning and hoping and wishing that things would go well; that the specialist—this German specialist who specialized—would think Orlif was the real deal as well. A real environmentalist. With very liberal environmentally accepted credentials. (For all liberals seeking liberal credentials wish for two things: 1. to be thought of as extremely radical; and 2. to be instantly accepted as profound.)

The thing about saying one was very progressive, as Orlif well knew, was always to look mischievous when it was said, as if you had just done something slightly underhanded that others of your ilk would smile at.

Especially, it seemed, if you were a professor and were talking to a fairly receptive woman like Vivian Speck. And this is exactly what this Hegelian had done when speaking to Vivian. And Vivian had done it back—as if they were both sharing a secret.

"Oh, yes," he had said, conspiratorially. "I am the most progressive man in all of Germany." And he swiped the hair out of his eyes and glanced quickly at Orlif.

And Vivian was charmed by this Hegelian. And Vivian kept saying, "Oh, I could tell you were, professor—I could tell you were."

This is what Orlif Speck had seared into his memory: his wife rushing over to sit with the environmentalist, and volunteering to take him to the airport.

The Hegelian said he lived in a remote village in the mountains just to breathe the fresh air, and to get rid of the smell of mankind. And he hiked with a pole, too. This is what he told Vivian, and

Vivian had said, "Yes, the smell of mankind—how I do the same, professor—the smell of mankind—how I do the same!"

A few days later, she made Orlif his favourite lemon pie.

But he only fussed and muttered to himself and could say nothing more. Except: "Ha—he doesn't even know who Cologne was named after."

It was shortly after that when they heard of the death of Dr. Musselman.

Hell has no boundaries; it can be anywhere at all. He wanted not to confront his son, but to hug him and tell him he was loved.

And now, today, all these years later, the memories came back and scalded him.

He knew now what Dr. Heatherington was going to suggest to Pruty. Euthanasia. Dr. Heatherington thought of it in a most clinical, non-emotional way—nothing morbid, dear me—and nothing religious either—but just a simple concoction of drugs, and she would sleep, her breathing would become slow and then at a certain point cease. And Heatherington would be beside her. He would monitor her pulse, check her eyes, then he would check her heart with a stethoscope and finally, placing it down in his medicine bag, he would say: "Yes, her suffering has ended."

And he would nod as if he had just completed an experiment that ended in victory.

She would just go to sleep—maybe in a field of buttercups.

"A field of buttercups?" Orlif, who had phoned the doctor, had asked because he was worried.

"Well, I don't know why you are phoning me—but yes—her final moment will be blissful."

"Blissful—yes, of course—but you see—what I am meaning to say is—"

But the doctor said impatiently that there was someone else on the other line and hung up.

Now today sleet and snow came against the kitchen window. A strange morbidity clung over all things, and Orlif decided to go for a walk.

Going for a walk in the sleet and snow, the cold coming in out of the bay water, the fresh smell of naked earth, debilitating to all who didn't know the strange beauty manifested upon us because of it—that would take his mind off things.

One of the Canadian professors, in order to ingratiate himself with the American professors at their little university here, told them, "Goddamnit, in this hellhole, moose roam the roads."

And they all had a great laugh. Orlif had laughed as well, ho de ho. But he had never seen a moose and would long to see one.

He put on his coat and ankle-high insulated boots and big blue mittens and a scarf and out he trudged down over the small bank to the road, along the road to the sign, past the sign to the highway and along the highway toward—where was he going?—toward the church lane. How did he find himself there? He would always be bewildered by "why" and at the same time know that he could go no other way; the sleet and snow that came down against his face, so he had to turn his back to it, made him finally go in that direction, so the trees on the church lane would shield him. And he felt in his pocket for his pipe—because Vivian was dead against pipes—pipes were passé, just as Weaver said *he* was.

This pipe was taped with electrical tape because he had broken it during an argument with her. She did not believe what he said one afternoon, and he said, "But it did happen, Vivian—it did."

"NO—you are telling a lie—"

"I am not."

"And your lies are transparent—everyone knows."

And he got so angry, he broke his pipe and had to tape it together.

So, he had to find a quiet place to light it, and smoke in solitude.

*Germans,* he thought. *Yes—she was enamoured by a German? Germans—they are always at your feet or at your throat.*

He went to the little stream that flowed out from Little Hackett Brook, such as it was—it was hardly a brook except in the rain, and then it swelled to high level, perhaps four or five feet, which it was today. Soon, though, it would drain away and freeze for winter. Winter would come—song of the snow.

So he went to the little stream and was trying to light his pipe, and thinking of the Roman Empire—a kind of hideous empire it was, too, filled with people like Tiberius, Caligula (Little Boots) and Nero—and then he thought, why was Nero so bad? And it came to him: Just as Salome danced to acquire the head of John, Nero beheaded Saint Paul to show his power. Then, seeing a moose-bird nearby, he remembered the little budgie that his dad had, a long time ago. He sat on a wet stump and the drizzle of rain mixed with snow fell through the desolate-looking pine trees.

He hauled from his pocket the note that he had hidden from everyone and opened it.

> Come and see me please—if you please would—sometime when my dad is away—please I need to talk to you. I can't tell anyone yet. I feel frightened. I am some worried about our Weaver—Weaver is up against some trouble! I feel as if—something terrible is about to happen. I have big information, and I am unsure who to tell, Pruty.

(She had wheeled down to his little house, and had put it in his mailbox, and was seen determinedly wheeling home through the mud and sleet.)

He would have to visit her, but he was filled with trepidation as to why.

And then he blinked, rubbed his running nose and saw the suitcase floating toward him from Little Hackett.

A suitcase that said: *From Mother Teresa to Benjamin. Toward your life's great journey.*

From Mother Teresa herself—given some years before, so one of the snaps was broken, in travels around the world, with pictures on it of the Eiffel Tower, Big Ben, the Statue of Liberty—and inside, when Orlif managed to pull it toward himself with a branch and hauled it up on the bank and opened it, there was Little Nin, naked, with her legs tucked up and her head resting on her hands as if she was asleep. There wasn't a bruise on her body, just a sad, contemplative little look, as if she was about to be loaded on a plane and travel to Paris on her own. The little piercings stuck out of her face as if they, good, bad or indifferent, didn't matter anymore. Still, they shone out in the brisk, bleak day.

How did she die? How was she in a suitcase floating along without a care in the world around tree branches and windfalls, to where poor Orlif Speck was smoking his pipe?

In fact, for a moment, he thought she was asleep and drifting along. So he poked her with a little stick. And then he decided, just for a second, that Mother Teresa must have put her in the suitcase—and then it seemed that he came to his senses and began to yell for help. No help came.

So he closed the suitcase, put his pipe in his pocket, picked up the suitcase and carried it as best he could along the road, with Little Nin tucked up inside, and a picture of the Eiffel Tower and

Big Ben shining in the rain, and his pocket smouldering from the lit tobacco in his pipe.

There was no one who knew who might have killed Little Nin. For sure they checked her phone, which they discovered just beyond the graveyard, and Marsha was questioned. And as Marsha left the station, she said she was by far the most important person in the case—that people wanted to know about what she knew, but she was sworn to secrecy because of Scotland Yard.

"Scotland Yard?" someone asked.

But Marsha, her face impervious to questioning, just stared off into the distance. She had known Little Nin had something to tell her—and she would solve this case, "for the betterment of all mankind." Her picture was in the paper. But Marsha said they had gotten her in a bad light, and she was very upset.

That was all that was known about it. The police were very quiet. But so were others. Especially the parishioners of our little Catholic parish. The very worst things about the Catholics were dredged up at the university. In the common room the most egregious hatreds that often spilled over whenever Catholics were mentioned were now exacerbated.

Orlif's former protege was the worst, decrying Catholics at every turn and looking about with pontifical sanctity and getting up and leaving the room whenever Orlif entered.

But Orlif, who had just started after an absence of forty-two years to go back to church, felt he had learned something from the mass and from Father Benjamin—he had learned that things like sanctimony and arrogance were signs of a tyrant, were signs of Satan the accuser, and that Christ would set him free.

Still, such professors who spoke against Catholics were those Orlif had once trusted enough to confide in—but he now felt alienated from them. So it didn't matter how they spoke or what they said or how they said it or when, during this dark time they did say it, but he would nod and say nothing.

For days Vivian and he never spoke. And then she took to phoning certain people. She said she would kill Father Benjamin as an act of justice.

"No, no, no," Orlif kept muttering when she was on the phone to her comrades—mostly women younger than her, who believed in her desperate mentorship. "I beg you. No, NO, NO."

And then she said to him: "The Church murdered Nin. I will burn the Church. I will prove myself to the world—to the entire world—do you understand—I will prove myself to the entire world!!" And her eyes did sparkle.

"If you do—" he said.

"What will you do—if I do?" She smiled.

"I'm not sure—but if you start burning churches—I might—I just might—go away."

Vivian did tell him that she was doing it for him—that at a time when it was proven that Catholics were horrid, if she did something, the university might start to look kinder upon him—and maybe tenure would be granted after all.

"But you are blaming without proof," he said.

"Who cares about proof when the child is dead—who cares who I blame!"

Still, sometimes, in the middle of the day, she would cough until there were traces of blood on her lips and her heart would pound in her chest.

Nin's coffin was placed in the smallest of all slumber rooms, with one candle burning in the corner, and the picture of Little Nin as a child staring out at you from the polished table where a few cards were placed. There was a picture of her when she was eleven, with the four little chickens she had raised.

The coffin, brown and small, seemed distant when one entered the room, and as one approached, they saw Little Nin with her cold hands folded around a pink rosary. She wore a dress with a white collar that seemed slightly starched, as if it might itch her cheek. The decorative face piercings were gone, where they had been covered by cake makeup; and two elderly ladies, one her gram and the other her great-aunt, sat on chairs to the left of the coffin and a few distant cousins stood in line.

A few others were in the opposite room drinking tea, and date squares sat upon a flowered plate. The Dugan brothers were there—having grown up beside what was left of her family.

People did line up to view the coffin and stood in silence when they witnessed her tiny little hands folded over the rosary.

Marsha sat beside the coffin as if protecting it from all others and looking urgently at the visitors as if awaiting some request.

Such was the visitation and wake, for Little Nin.

Beal sat in the car at the end of the parking lot, looking at the light in the slumber room window, and the candle burning down. In all his life she was the one he actually had loved, and the only one who had loved him, and now, in spite of all his bravado, this had happened. Everyone said that Beal had gone down and kicked the door of the little chapel behind the church and found Father Benjamin hiding behind a picture of one of our various outmoded popes and dragged him to the holy water font, and was about to drown him, when the police came.

That was not true. He hadn't even thought of Father Benjamin doing such a thing. He only thought it was retribution for what he himself had done.

For he remembered she never got to the movie with the hobbits, never enrolled in the courses she wanted to take, never took viola lessons so she could become—as she said one night when they were all alone—"a better human being."

All his life he wanted to become famous in our town, do brave, dangerous and outrageous things—and for what?

Father Benjamin for his part didn't know how the suitcase got used—had no idea the suitcase was even there—had forgotten about it, because it had been delivered that day long ago—the day of the picnic, and Mrs. Samuel from the reserve had unpacked it and put it away because Father Benjamin was walking around the picnic grounds, smiling at all the white people, wearing a black sweater and a silver cross.

So, he told the police that he didn't even remember the suitcase, really. And this did not bode well for little Father Benjamin. He was brought into the station to talk—he was asked about his growing up—what did he think of women—why was Little Nin at the house—how long had she been at the house—did he do anything to her when she was at the house—so then what did he do to her?

He went home. He went to the church in the middle of the night and sat in the pew and stared at the Virgin and wept. He wanted to say the funeral mass, but they did not allow it—they sent for Father Leo to do so. And Father Leo took Benjamin aside and asked him to please not attend. In deference, the bishop himself attended wearing one of those cone-like hats.

The little coffin sat in the centre of the middle aisle. The church was full, and there were reporters present.

MURDERED WOMAN LAID TO REST AT SAINT PETER AND PAUL, the newspaper read.

PROTEST THAT HER FUNERAL MASS WAS CELEBRATED IN THE PLACE SHE WAS MURDERED!

PRIME MINISTER MAKES A STATEMENT.

WOMEN OUTRAGED.

ANOTHER DISGRACE.

All of this seemed true.

Orlif was present and looked very distraught—almost unable to stand. The only thing he remembered about Little Nin in all the time he was here was that one day he bought her an ice cream when she was about twelve years old. She was filthy and her shorts were too small for her, and she had a free-ride bracelet from the circus, which had been here a week before, still on her wrist.

Her face had lit up. "Oh sir," she had said, "an ice cream!"

That memory came to him so forcefully he had to sit down. Orlif Speck was sitting down on the side of the ditch, along the main highway, in his worn suit pants after church because he thought of such a thing.

Benjamin went back to the rectory and sat in the small inner chapel that he had. He stared at the icon of the Black Madonna, who had taken him far and wide in this terrible world.

"You were supposed to protect me—you said you would," he lamented.

Poor Benjamin knew horrid things had happened within the sanctuary of the Church. He knew of the terrible treatment of boys and girls. He once thought people would see in him the face of kindness and hope. But now, Satan the accuser seemed to rise high above them all. Lucifer the proud angel had fallen, become Satan the accuser of all mankind. So that each self-righteous act was the act of Satan. And each act of Satan was one of terror.

He began to get calls from people saying they would do him in.

He had seen the world of terror for too long, he did not know if he could see it anymore. He walked with a limp because of a snakebite when he was a child, and he missed his brothers and his sister. They were put in a cardboard box and left on the side of the highway. And what had become of them all? He didn't really know.

He thought, our little Benjamin, of running away—and then he thought of taking his life—and then he thought that it had to be that man Beal.

But he could not say, for Nin had gone to confession, and he had prayed with her, holding her hand. But then something did come over him as he stared at all the candles lit in tribute and hope to the Virgin: "Beal loved Little Nin."

It came as if from an actual voice.

That was all he heard. "Beal loved Little Nin."

When gossip stated that it was Father Benjamin who had murdered her because she was pregnant with his child and the Church would frown on that, Marsha said this is what Nin had wanted to tell her. And she knew it—and had a secret message, too—and an important secret message that she wouldn't divulge yet—but the FBI wanted to fly her to Washington.

"All the way—the entire way to Washington."

That is, Marsha did not know that Ottawa was the capital of Canada, and believed it was Washington. Well, what matter—more than one of our professors and political gurus did as well.

And so she sat in her chair in the den and the doorbell would ring and her mother would say: "No—she is too distraught—you shouldn't bother her today."

"Who is it, Mother—pray tell—who is it?"

"It's the lady from the Moncton *Times*."

"Ah, then—I have a moment. I am tired, but—do let her in."

---

Vivian's life changed again—her activism was renewed.

"DISGUSTING," she told Orlif.

She phoned her young proteges. They said they would join her—would all be there.

But that did not happen when the time came.

BOWELS WALKED IN THE EARLY SNOW, THE LATE NOVEMBER streets and the leaves having fallen down. And the park was barren, yet it would be wonderful when the lights of Christmas went on—and it would be wonderful when the snow came, so thought Mickey Bowels.

But it was dreadful, this memory of Little Nin. She had come to him, before she had gone away—he had no idea that for the past two months or more she was living in the basement of the church down in Bartibogue. The last time he had seen her, she had sat on a chair in his store and said, "He didn't do so. I have to tell someone."

It was late in the summer. She wore a big pair of billowy white shorts and a halter top. He had given her some money a few days before this visit. He remembered her painted nails, the nails bitten and the little bra strap falling off her shoulder.

"Jamie Musselman," she said. She whispered it to him, as if she was in some way afraid of the truth or the very name.

He turned to her—a peculiar look on his face. He had been placing shoes on a rack, with school about to start and the smell of cooling air and new shoe leather, and just then a man came into the store. The man wanted a pair of Dockers, but was not sure what size or colour.

It took a while. When this was done, Little Nin was no longer there. He opened the door, but it was a quiet, empty day, and no one sat in the park.

He looked down toward the Blackhorse, and no one was on the sidewalk. He shrugged. Went back inside. And he never saw her again.

Now, he tried to put it out of his mind, but he couldn't. He was angry with himself as good men are when they have done something wrong, even by omission.

But why hadn't he taken Little Nin's look seriously?

Was it because he still loved Gertie and wanted the boy guilty?

Yet all of this had made Gertie more determined, and more resilient and more serious—and *older.* He, Mickey, had even run for town council hoping to impress her. But he did not do well. He sat all night by the radio, listening to the results, but he himself attained fewer than three hundred votes. He knew Pruty had followed his campaign and cheered him on.

The day after he lost, he had heard of Jamie's injury. He heard of it as he was taking his posters down from the poles around the square.

Now Gertie left in a daze to go see her fiancé in the hospital, carrying her suitcase, and almost in self-mockery her wedding dress just in case they might marry.

Before she left for Dorchester, she went back to Mother Church and took communion.

And as she left for Dorchester, Shamus and Pruty watched her go—Pruty wheeled after her all the way out the drive—waving and shouting:

"Good luck—say hi—for me—good luck, Gertie—and all my love!"

However, Marsha said she had secret knowledge that the police wanted to acquire.

"Oh yes, Gertie was involved—Jamie wouldn't have done it except for Gertie. How he ever got mixed up with the likes of her—down off Load Road—my oh my."

Then she looked at her fingers and adjusted the brooch on her bosom.

Dannielle, who spread many rumours herself, said she didn't know why Gertie took the train. She could have driven the Mercedes—that was Jamie Musselman's as well.

Orlif could think only of his son.

How Weaver used to wrap presents for them near Christmas—even if it was only a peanut butter bar. He had suffered terribly for his parents' own new way of things. No tree had adorned their house, no mass gone to, no presents bought.

Orlif sent notes to Pruty asking her how Jamie Musselman was. And Orlif thought, *If he dies, I will tell.*

Or, *If he gets even a speck worse, I will tell.*

Or, *I will tell tomorrow afternoon by three o'clock—by three I will tell.*

At home, Vivian was more than sure there was a devil, and it was Father Benjamin—and had been on the phone to people who agreed with her leadership.

But sometimes poor Vivian would be too weak to call. She would sit by the phone and stare into nothing. Still, she had meetings, once a week, and even though ill, she would prepare for them with diligence, putting out pamphlets and snacks, and making sure with great diligence that her certificates were in view.

Pruty wheeled in the wind and rain to attend one of these meetings the night after a visit from Dr. Heatherington. She looked heartsick over something—at least, this is what certain women said, who helped her navigate her wheelchair through the door and helped her get a cup of tea.

Pruty sat and listened quietly to what was being said and finally, her body shaking, spoke up. "Excuse me, but I think the way you talk, you are the ones who are deceived."

"Well—what are you saying?"

"Well, excuse me all to hell and everything, but maybe this is where we are going on the wrong track of life—the wrong signal to the train or whatever. Dr. Heatherington—do you know Dr. Heatherington?—how many here have heard of Dr. Heatherington? Put up your hands? Well, he come to visit last night—so many days I went to doctors trying to find relief—and the medicine cost too much, and the pills they gave me didn't work. Then Dr. Heatherington came to rescue me. He was my hero—I never met a hero like him—as big a hero as John Wayne, and he told me jokes, too—and bought me a milkshake, so there you go—but yesterday—was it yesterday—yes, yesterday—about seven o'clock in the evening, after I had done with supper, he just said that I should be put to sleep.

"I was somewhat—at least a little—I think, anyways—in love with him, and he sat close up to me, and said he wanted to be the one to take care of me, so I thought, that's probably a marriage proposal right there. Oh yes, I am as naive as a goat—I know that. And it's all a game with me, and really, I am wiser than you think. Still, I closed my eyes and waited for the big French kiss. There I was with my lips puckered up, waiting for the smack. You see, he said he wanted to be the one to take care of me forever.

"But alas—he wasn't going to marry me—he was hoping I would off myself. I mean, it came as a bit of a surprise. Besides, he is so clean—absolutely spotless and smelling antiseptic—so I thought it would be a date." Here she shuddered, and all her bones seemed to shudder.

"'I will make sure it is painless,' he said to me.

"What the fuck? Well, that was quite a revelation, let me tell you. Dr. Heatherington said that if I was in pain, and the pills did not work, and my bladder was a problem—and the suffering was such that they couldn't help me—I could consider it. And he would be my angel of death."

She smiled and then smoothed her skirt and looked up at all of them with a face almost beatific in its sorrow.

They simply stared at her, without speaking, and tears ran down her face as she spoke.

There was almost two minutes of silence, and she didn't wipe her tears away, and then she said: "I want you to know, I want you all to know—I have had a terrible life. But what would happen to Gertie—so tell me, who is suffering more than Gertie? For nine years I have been going to one doctor and another—but he is the first one to say that he could put me to sleep—like a toad or a hamster. So here I am waiting for how he said he could help me, and maybe take me on the date of a lifetime, and he tells me to take a needle and go the fuck to sleep."

None of them spoke. They weren't sure if they were supposed to. Vivian didn't quite know what to say, except that she would agree with Dr. Heatherington—but she did not say so.

Pruty smiled bravely as the tears came to the corner of her mouth, as if the tears found a place to rest.

"Yes," Pruty said, "I am not at all stupid—but it's okay to daydream, isn't it—and pretend you can walk—and have dreams of flying through the air. I don't think Weaver meant to burn the Book of Revelations—I think he is struggling with its wisdom.

So, I just thought I'd tell you all of this, so you'd come to your own conclusions. And I am trying to figure out what tenure is—Weaver told me his dad Orlif never got tenure—what the fuck is that?"

They were silent.

And Pruty was exhausted, and closed her eyes for a long, long while.

Then she said, with her eyes still closed, "Well—maybe that's what you all think I should do?"

No one spoke.

So Pruty left, and she wheeled up this rocky, dark path—a path made for murder. She felt no one in the world cared for her anymore, even people she had relied on when she wrote them trying to get a new motorized wheelchair.

She went home, back to that small little house, the only place she knew.

She tried to understand what people wanted from her, and wondered if her father wanted it too.

"I'm afraid you won't get a motorized wheelchair," Dr. Heatherington had said to her a few days before.

He was taking her blood pressure as he spoke and did not look at her. He was very impersonal. He didn't smile. She waited for a smile, but he seemed preoccupied. So she smiled for both of them, and then looked out the window when he asked her to breathe and hold her breath.

Then he said that she would lose muscle mass—he said this while being remote and non-specific in a very detached way. That was after he had told her all about Paris. And she said, "Oh my—Paris, would I ever like to someday go there—"

But before she finished her reverie, he interjected with: "I'm afraid things will become more uncomfortable for you, so I am wondering if you ever thought of the other option. I did speak to Shamus about it."

"What other option, doctor—what other option, please tell me if you have another option?"

"Oh, I have a wonderful—option for all concerned—a very brave one," he said, giving her a needle in her little behind that, in fact, was quite magnificent-looking (which is what he thought). She could feel his hands on her behind.

"You could, with your dad's help—just go to sleep."

"Go to sleep—"

"Yes, my pet—go to sleep," he said, reading the thermometer and looking at her as he held it up and shook it, and then nodded.

"Go to sleep—for how long?"

He grimaced just a bit, putting the thermometer aside, and, looking very dapper in his white medical shirt, said with his pretty eyes looking down at her—but something was wrong, because there was something else, she didn't quite catch it:

"Well—you'd go to sleep forever—it would be very blissful." Then he said, "I've mentioned this to your dad, so you speak to him about it."

And she said, "You mean like just go to sleep in a coma—or something—"

"No, my dear—I mean go to sleep—a painless death."

For many, many moments she stared at him—so that even he, the imperturbable Dr. Heatherington, became uncomfortable. Her eyes blazed with a kind of fierce bravery seen only in those who have suffered too much. And in a way, her eyes deeply frightened him. Then she whispered, "I gather you asking me to marry you wasn't your first fuckin intention?"

He gave a terrible start and looked away in confusion. He picked up the stethoscope and placed it in his bag. That was the only sound for a moment.

But Pruty kept looking at him, trying to understand. And her look was one men know that only a woman can give—a look of dazzling, inaccessible intuition.

No matter the pain she had been in—the days of almost but not quite agony—she had believed Dr. Heatherington was trying to help her, so she could be there for Gertie. Because that is all she had talked to him about—Gertie.

It was Gertie this and Gertie that, and Gertie once again.

Didn't he know how she loved Gertie? Didn't he even know!

Oh, she knew she would never marry—but the scenarios she set up were sometimes fun.

But now she knew—she knew now, no one cared.

Heatherington drove home.

He went back to his house, in through the garage that entered into the kitchen. His house was bigger than Dr. Penny's. Not that Dr. Penny's house wasn't fine, with its huge back patio.

"I have to help Gertie," she said. "I have to help Gertie before I die—I will help Gertie first."

Gertie spoke to Pruty on the phone every day, sometimes twice a day, and sent her text messages, and one day, bursting out crying, she said, "Oh, why did this happen, Pruty—tell me? Was I so wrong that God is getting back at us—am I lost, Pruty? Am I lost?"

"No, Gertie—you are not lost—but I am dreadfully afraid others are." Then she added, "But Mickey told me things would change, and pretty soon."

"Mickey?"

"Yes, Mickey—he is trying to help you—he is trying his best. So don't worry." Then she added, "He lost the election too."

And Gertie was ashamed that she didn't vote. She was ashamed at how she had treated him even though she knew nothing else could be done.

That night, Pruty could feel the cold through the window and hear the wind; it did not stop, and the bushes outside were twisted by a flurry.

Pruty wheeled into the kitchen and told their father that she would go to the police. She had to, there was no other way to prove the boy innocent.

"Little Nin is dead—dead—and I did nothing—but I cannot stay silent now."

It was up to her, and it seemed no one else. A grand weight had now been lifted from her. She told him she knew he had something to do with the murder of the Colonel—and even if it was something minor, she still was determined to confess.

"What did I have to do with it?"

"Oh Shamus! You took money—and it was in an envelope—and for a long time I didn't know the connection—but I do now know—I do! You told them where to go!!"

She opened up the seat and hauled the envelope out—showing him what it was. There was even a look of surprise on her face—as her hand moved eagerly toward him—and she said, "Okay then—here—"

"Put that away," he said, "put it away—for God's sake put it away."

And so, without speaking, she did—put it away.

Later, she fell asleep in the chair looking out the window at the glow of lights from the house down the lane, the reindeer on the roof and the Santa in the yard. And, as many times when she was a child, he carried her to bed. He closed his eyes as he put her in her nightgown. All the little bottles of medication were on her dresser, beside a picture of Gertie and a picture of her mom. There had been a picture of him, of Shamus, but she had hidden it.

Dr. Heatherington had mentioned it all to him—it was legal now—if they wanted to dispose of her like a little lamb.

"To free her from herself!" Heatherington said. It made his appetite for cleanliness and decorum, propriety and efficacy understandable.

Heatherington was interested in Pruty for several months, thinking it would be the best way. He hoped she would lead the way for others much like her. In that way—in that one way he was a visionary to others who believed in what he did. And he was commended at many moments for his justice and propriety.

Finally, Pruty said today, after all of this had been discussed with her in meticulosity, "What do you want me to do, Papa? You want me to go to sleep like a hamster. If you do—if you are sick and tired of me—maybe it's all for the best. I know I am in pain—and maybe I am a pain—you have to change my clothes and wash them and keep me clean—and you are getting old," and she smiled at him as if to comfort him in his decision—and to help him forward if he needed nudging. "But first we have to free Gertie's love. It is the only thing I wish to do."

When Shamus carried her to bed that night—and laid her down—the wind had not diminished, and he saw her empty wheelchair, the stickers she had placed on it, the lights on it, and burst into tears—and when he went to fold it and put it away, the seat unlatched, and he opened it up.

There were now two inspirational books that she had sent away for: *How to Find God in Your Life* and *When the Pain Comes.*

And underneath those books, and the little New Testament, and two romance novels, he found the letter. The letter accepting the resignation from the Department of Defence, and the scrawl on the back of the pages of the money Colonel Musselman and his son, Jamie, had collected for a car that was never bought all those years ago.

He took a match to light it, lit the match in the dark and watched the match burn down, and just beyond the match—just beyond that—little Pruty slept.

So, the match burned his finger, and he tossed it aside.

"What have I done?" he whispered. "What have I done to my children?"

He put the letter back, turned out the light and went upstairs.

AFTER LITTLE NIN DIED, MANY IN OUR TOWN HAD A terrible crisis of conscience. They remembered the little waif in the park. And others, like Pruty and Shamus, had unbearable secrets—and so too did Orlif Speck. Vivian wanted to take some kind of action against this Benjamin.

For days Orlif had said, "I hope you are not planning to do something," and "Leave it go—until the police decide who it might be," and "Please, I beg you—I won't ask you anything again—but leave him be."

But she couldn't. She simply couldn't leave it be.

And one of the reasons was that Orlif pleaded with her not to. The other reason, more personal, was that her article on seventies feminism had been rejected by *Canadian Feminist Magazine.*

So, one afternoon she went out in a determined way, and smelled the smoke from chimneys along the highway. She drew things on the door of Father Benjamin's little house and wrote certain foul words on his windows as if proclaiming a victory. Then, coughing and cold, she walked down to the church.

Everything looked desolate there. Only one car in the parking lot, belonging to the First Nation band member Mrs. Samuel.

She tried to light matches, but the strong wind off Sheldrake blew them out.

There was a pile of stones acting as a marker for the grave of Little Nin's ancestor. So she grabbed five of them. No one else had answered her call, and she was alone, a forlorn figure standing against the wind.

She threw a stone—and then another. Then she turned and ran across the graveyard, trampling the place where Little Nin had died. She yelled a curse word, but she didn't even know why. She tramped up along Little Hackett. One of Little Nin's mittens had been caught on a branch and, soaking and frozen, hung there still.

But Vivian made it home, exhausted by all she had done. Yet already the groundskeeper had phoned both Orlif and the police.

"A crazy woman just smashed the biggest window of our church."

When the window broke—when it shattered—there were four people inside the church. No one moved, for there was a sacrament being performed. The priest, Father Leo (Father Benjamin was in protective custody at this moment), did not even look sideways. Neither did the two witnesses, Pruty and Mrs. Samuel, the First Nation woman who Beal had at one time thought was his mother.

Neither did the person being baptized: Mr. Weaver de Speck.

You see, an article had come out the month before: THE TWENTY-FIVE MOST IMPORTANT CANADIAN FEMINISTS AT WORK FOR EQUALITY AND CHANGE!

Vivian was not mentioned in this article.

For days she had said nothing, and then Little Nin was murdered.

After it came out that Father Benjamin was not the murderer—was not, and in fact had tried to protect the child—Vivian ran back to Orlif.

She had to pay for the stained glass window or be charged and face jail.

As always, when he was needed, she came to him. When she was younger, she would leave, and then, when academic work piled up, she would come to him, beseeching at the door of his apartment.

So when it was said she would have to pay for the window, some twelve thousand dollars, or the police would lay a charge against her, she came to his room at the back of the house.

She spoke of how he, Orlif, had kept them poor. He was going to say, "That is not true, Vivian—it is not." But he didn't.

She tried to get him to speak, but he would not. Instead, he pretended to be absorbed in reading Ovid.

So she left him with this: "Well then—yes, sit there—sit there, Orlif, for you are impotent and cannot help anyone—that's why the German you invited here preferred me—yes, preferred me—and let me tell you how he preferred me—for an entire night and day—he preferred me in every way."

He looked up at her with dull, sore eyes and took off his reading glasses.

Orlif was some years older than she was and was once irrational enough to be a father figure to her. He had stayed with her for many years trying to live up to his promise of fidelity. He had long heard of her notorious uncle too, whom she had supposedly carried on with in the mid-sixties, causing something of a scandal.

When he first saw this uncle, he sat silently in the garden outside their house in Rothesay. That was the day Vivian was told she must have a child to get her inheritance. The uncle thought this all hilarious.

"Are you sure you're up to the task?" he said to Orlif.

Orlif never knew how to answer defamation, because of personal honour. "If I see him again," Orlif often said about the uncle, "yes, if I see him again, I'll give him a real piece of my mind."

The uncle was dead now, years ago. Terrible things had come out about a certain scandal involving the whole family. The entire family.

Now he read in the paper that Vivian had to pay for the stained glass, and he, Orlif, was to be dismissed as a lecturer at the end of the year. The paper knew the situation even before he did.

And later that same night, Vivian once again asked him for help.

He couldn't stand—couldn't stand—to see her cry.

"I don't have any more money," she said, and tears ran down her cheeks. "I thought my friends would help me—but none of them know me, it seems. I'm sorry, okay—I'm sorry—you know I'm sorry."

"I know," he said. "Please don't cry. I know."

It was the end of his career. And he had so loved to teach. He could not let her down. He could not abandon her.

He went to the bank and cashed in the last of his private bonds for her, the funds he was planning for ten years to use to go to Rome and Athens (he always felt guilty he had not told her about this), and that cold night he gave her the money in a huge white envelope. She was to give it to the parish council. That was terribly embarrassing—those old women and their dull sons, and to stand there and apologize to them.

"You have to come with me," she said. "Please—I can't go alone—you have to."

"Yes," he said, "of course—I won't let you go alone."

She wiped tears from her eyes as he looked up at her.

"It is no matter." His lips trembled. "No matter."

He remembered the smell of diesel buses in Switzerland as they pulled away from the cold station where they had sat awaiting a late bus to Zurich. And it was night, and she was angry at him, and his beer was flat.

Why couldn't her life have been unbroken? Why couldn't it have been great? Why was so much wasted?

In Zurich he had met the German, who impressed him—though he was only an eighteen-year-old student at that time. Over the years, the German had become well-known, and Orlif had planned his invitation to come and speak, which all seemed so glamorous. It was a way for the department to be grateful to him, to honour him.

He had planned it for so long.

"Yes, I met him as a student," Orlif would tell people. "Yes, as a student, mind you. We kept in contact, you see—over the years—both very interested in many of the same things."

That was what he had planned, at any rate.

Tonight, he slept in the spare room, folded his trousers to make sure the press held, hung his shirt on a hanger and, sitting alone on the cot, thought of her naked beauty even now.

Yes, the German he had planned to meet and to celebrate all those wonderful things about Hegel with must have preferred her, in every way.

PRUTY WHEELED TO THE WINDOW IN THE THIRD WEEK of Advent and looked at the clumps of grass, only slightly covered.

She said she would wait for Gertie to come home—and they would take the letter to the police together—but she wanted Shamus to face the fulsomeness of his participation in the destruction of his future son-in-law, and in the abysmal way he had behaved to Gertie, a daughter he had promised his wife he would care for.

"Did you tell Gertie yet?" he said, his voice scared.

"No, Papa, I want you to tell—for I don't know what I even know—so I want you to tell what you know so Jamie can come home. That is, if he can come home, which I think he might be able to—but you know better than I—and if you wish me to drug myself to death—I will. But first you have to tell Gertrude."

"Of course, my little Ruby Tuesday, of course."

"And no more stealing my pension cheque, okay? You promise."

"Yes, Love Whistle, I promise."

She seemed happy now, more happy than ever, and she said, "Bend down, Papa, so I can kiss your cheek."

In the letter accepting the Colonel's resignation, the Head of Command had written and Pruty read it aloud to him: "'You took care of your wife, and child, and we marvelled at your love for them, when every day you were suffering as well from the shrapnel wound you never spoke about.'"

And Pruty said, "Papa—that was in the letter you were going to burn!!"

He began to weep. He was in grand part weeping, weeping for his wife. The whole misery he caused others overcame him with a heaviness he could not bear.

Now and again Pruty's little body shook in pain, and he noticed that. She was in pain now every day. And she went to prayer sessions at the church. She held the rosary for hours and would grimace, and when he looked at her, she would try to smile.

He had no idea in the world what he could do. *Where does my love come in?* he thought. And the answer came, *It has never gone.*

"My little glow bug," he used to call her. He looked at her, and everything about her showed her pocket-sized, sweet humanity.

Shamus went and sat in Gertie's room. The picture of Jamie Musselman looked at him from the corner, near a curtain that was blowing.

How the boys had all made fun of little Pruty. Oh, not the most of them, just some. Did he remember so? Yes. But he was a better man then. A greater man. He carried her on his back, he took her to doctors here and in Halifax, he held her close to him. He made sure—because she couldn't go to Brownies—that she took a correspondence course in Brownies. He sewed the badges on her uniform himself. He made sure she was never left out. The Brownie uniform was still hanging on a wire hanger in her closet. When the Brownies went to camp, he would drive her there during the day, and Gertie and some other girls would help take care of her. Then he would bring her home at night.

Yes, he did. And he remembered the time—oh yes, did he remember—when one of the cottage boys asked her to go to the drive-in in Bushville, one night long ago, and she dressed up in Gertie's new slacks, and the boy took her in his car. She had come home dishevelled and wouldn't speak about what the boy said or tried to do, and when Gertie asked her, she started to cry and said she didn't like the movie anyway. (The boy had asked Gertie first to go and said that Pruty was second best, but if she gave it to him, showed him her little bush, he would know what Gertie's bush was like. This came out later.)

She turned her wheelchair to the corner and stared at the wall all day. Then, a night later, the car drove by in the heat and awful dust, and three boys started taunting her and yelling mean things. Did Shamus remember? When the car turned in a drive and came back?

He jumped up and ran to the road, flung the door open as they went by, grabbed the boy out of the Volkswagen car as the car zigzagged to a stop, and shook him. And didn't he say, "You dare treat my daughter with disrespect—a child in a wheelchair—how dare you!!"

Here he was in an old pair of jeans and half-torn boots, a shirt with the two bottom buttons missing, and he was a man. And he grabbed that boy by the collar and walked him down to the cottage by the bay—and stood in defiance of them, and he spoke in such eloquent terms of how a young man should conduct himself with a disabled child. And he said he was ashamed of them. And his face was red, and his hair was thinning.

Did Shamus remember? And did that boy later write an apology and say, "I want Pruty, I beg Pruty, to forgive me," and send her a basket of fruit?

"I will not eat it—I will not," Pruty said. But later that night, when darkness came, she was seen nibbling on a grape.

In fact, at one point, they both thought of that long-ago incident at the same time. How brave he was then!

Many a boy came to visit Pruty so they could see Gertie, and they all knew this, but Shamus deflected it and told Pruty to never mind.

"Your beauty is in your heart, my girl—like a big bowl of apple sauce—all that grace is in your heart."

That was when Shamus was still a man.

And then, little by little, drink and the days of infamy passed over him, like a giant blowing wind, without him even knowing it would. He became a sot and a liar and a perjurer in a trial—that was the worst—it sent an innocent man away. He became worse than a reprobate.

How horrible without anything being intended. Or was something about it—intended? Was it, in fact, all, in some way, intended by a motive he didn't control?

There was a man some years back, before the Specks had arrived—yes, a long time ago—when the world was filled with white snow in the winter, and Hackett Brook was where he hunted, and he had a small barn where he trained his horse—there was a minister of the cloth they had compromised for money with a boy in a room, he and a few others. The boy was a derelict, some said he was Mallory's grandson—no one knew. They had started out at a community picnic and got the minister, with his pudgy frame and his heavy black coat, to come with them. They were all drinking, and the minister said, "Okay, I will, just this once." And he had a drink with them. "I hope Momma doesn't find out," he said.

After a while, he kept eyeing that young boy.

"You can have him—he's willing," they whispered. "Lots of people have him—he's willing." So they didn't mind getting the boy to do what he did.

The minister awoke with this boy early the next morning. He was horrified that this urge he had had from the time he was fourteen had now played out and surfaced upon the world. He thought of his mother.

He trembled before them, he tried to explain, he even sank to his knees. They all commiserated with him, told him they would keep the secret. They had looked at him with tenderness. But beneath that were half-mischievous, half-hidden and contemptuous smiles.

"Go preach and teach and we will be silent—no worries, what are friends for."

And Shamus was the man who went every month to the Baptist church to collect the money. Always dignified, always wearing a yellowed white shirt and old vest and a tie—and smelling of aftershave and horse manure—did Shamus appear. And the minister frightened, always so terrified. That terror was looked upon as just—and no one seemed to care—so Shamus pretended he did not care either, even though he was bothered by it all.

"Please," the minister beseeched him, "please—it's just my mother, you—see—mother."

But Shamus must continue. He must prove to those friends he was worthy. He would go back to the others and say, "I told him we must continue."

So the minister began to take funds from the parishioners in the church to pay for what he did. He did it after a service on Easter Sunday.

Then one day the minister looked at Shamus, startled, in a strange way, and said, "It is you—I didn't know until now it was you."

"Who?" Shamus asked. "Who am I?"

What did he ever mean by that? There were wood chips on the ground beneath Shamus's feet, and Shamus's eyes were yellowed from drink, and he smelled of wine, and his hands were dark from dirt and his white shirt was yellowed with age.

"I did not know it was you," the poor minister said.

The minister committed suicide. There was an investigation, and Shamus hid—he hid as always. They all ran and hid and met a few weeks later at the horse haul in Barnaby. The minister had hanged himself with a coarse rope from a rafter in his uncle's barn.

"It was not me," Shamus said. "I didn't do nothing."

And at that time the little girls still looked up to him as their hero—they still believed in him.

He was bound to meet Beal sooner or later. He had met so many others.

So his whole life came flooding back—from the first time he stole, to the time he met Beal on the sidewalk—the very robin which fell from the nest to cause it all. That small beating heart of that small bird.

*It must have died by now*, he thought, *it must have gone the way of all robins—and fallen from the sky on some trip southward carrying its feathery burden on its journey into the night.*

It was so very cold in the house. So very cold now. There was almost no heat. The wood was depleted, and he couldn't pay for oil. Pruty's little cheque didn't cover it no matter how many letters she wrote. They told Pruty they would put her in a home. She said no. They tried to give her morphine. She said no. She took Ativan and other painkillers, and pills for bone density. Some days she smoked a joint or two. She had some money in a jar that sat in her basket that was pinned to her chair. He had often stolen that.

She had been given so little in her life that if she sang "Too Drunk to Fuck" and wheeled back home in the wind and rain, what would it ever matter?

And what had actually happened to her savings?

Did he remember when, a few years before, Pruty said that she had a boyfriend—a boy from England? She had become his internet pal because her mother had been from England too.

She sent that boy money, every penny that she had saved—she had sent him every cent she had, transferred it on the internet—some twenty-three hundred dollars. This was going to be her boyfriend, and he was going to fly from England and meet her—and she had met him on the internet, and he said he loved her.

"I love you, my dear sweet girl," is what he wrote. "I wish I could come to see you, but I take care of me mum who is ill. But I might come if I could get some money together."

And she was ecstatic that she had someone to love.

Did poor Shamus remember how Gertie and he had tried to talk her out of it all—that the boy would not be there, that perhaps it wasn't even a boy—perhaps it was just a computer used by scammers to say what she wanted to hear—but Shamus took her down to Halifax anyway, didn't he, to meet the boy he knew wouldn't come. Just having gotten his licence back, he rented a car—though it cost him most of what he had—and fussed over his shave and the aftershave he wore and dressed Pruty in her white dress with white leggings.

She sat eagerly in the back seat, speaking of wonderful things so outlandish that he knew she didn't even believe them herself. They would go to Mexico on their honeymoon and he would carry her so she wouldn't have to take her wheelchair, but perhaps she'd rent one down there—and Shamus could visit, and maybe they would go to Florida instead.

Then she was quiet, and her face grew pensive.

"Oh, he will come, I am sure, Pruty," he said, and they kept waiting for the plane in that empty airport along an empty row of plastic seats with the hot sun beating through the windows. And even when Pruty started to cry, even when she admitted that she had sent Gertie's picture to this intended beau, even when she was humiliated, he kept saying, "There is a late plane coming in, Pruty—we will wait for it—he probably is on it."

She had sent him all her money. He was to be her beau. And didn't Shamus wait, wait long into the night. And Pruty could tell he was praying for that boy to arrive. Then there was the sweet smell of summer flowers and summer rain when they went outside.

And didn't Shamus comfort her—and hold her in his arms—and when one of the security guards said, "Why is she crying?" didn't Shamus say, "It is no concern of yours why my daughter is crying—you do not love her—I do!"

Then, just a while ago, the doctor phoned and revealed to Shamus his solution. "She is in pain—every day—so I can help her—help you relieve it. I am hoping you might convince her. The way she is living with you is not an appropriate situation. You know you haven't been the best father, and there are things society can do at the moment to make things right. Especially if the father has failed in support of seriously disabled offspring."

"Well, what do you intend?" Shamus asked.

"Well, I have an answer far more efficient than praying to the Virgin Mary."

"How do you mean?"

"There is a fine cocktail of drugs."

"A cocktail—what does that mean?"

"It means she will be relieved of her pain forever—we can do it at Christmas—I have long advocated it as a solution to military men who are suffering from PTSD—and to the mentally disabled. And to pensioners who live alone. I could come to the house and do it in a familiar setting beside your Christmas tree on Christmas Day. She told me in a phone call that it is up to you—if you wish her to do so."

"So—let me ask—do what in a familiar setting?" Shamus asked.

"Relieve her of her pain—forever. I think that is the best solution."

"In what way—?"

"She will just go to sleep—forever."

He shuddered, and did not answer.

But Pruty had told him what he must do.

"Papa, you can go and speak to the police, and I will be with you." And she added, "I will hold your hand. Keep me alive and I will hold your hand, and then, if you want me to take a double dose of something and go to sleep, I will. But I have to stay alive until then."

That was two days ago when she spoke those words, "I will hold your hand."

And very strange—well, Shamus did not know himself how strange—he was holding in his hand an ancient book that Jamie had given Gertie to read—to prove, when they were in high school and Gertie had gone alone to his birthday party, that he had actually read it: *Iphigenia in Aulis*.

Wind came up in gale force—as it came over his shed with only a few sticks of wood left, and his house that wasn't insulated, and his chair with the stuffing gone, and his brass cup he won at a horse haul, and his picture of his wife.

Yes, how Pruty and he had watched *Star Trek* together in that little house, with the wind blowing down, and all the wood they used, and the TV blurry when Captain Kirk was travelling to the stars! And how she delighted in Captain Kirk and said, "Beam me up, Scotty," when her father carried her to her room and she was falling asleep. Many nights there was just the two of them.

How he had tried to take care of her, even if he had failed. But he would not fail anymore.

He finally said, "Pruty, no one will hurt you. No one will hurt you again!" He felt very glad he had said that. Then, with a resolute voice, he continued: "I told Beal where the money was—Weaver was with them—I told where the money was. It was we who killed Colonel Musselman and not unfortunate Jamie. Little Nin wanted us to confess. She was the real hero. Not anyone else. I have been struggling with this for a long time, my love. For over six years."

And poor Pruty, whose ears were bad and who hated to wear a hearing aid because she said it ruined the look of her ears, well, Pruty did not hear. She did not hear, she was thankfully fast asleep, and the gale blew, and the door had opened—and Gertie had come in. So it was Gertie, newly married, with a gold wedding ring on her finger, who had heard all her father had said.

Now she stood inside the door with some flowers she had brought home for Pruty and listened as if to a queer sound coming from some other dimension she wasn't yet aware of. It was so shocking, it hung in the cold air for an indescribable moment—as if she was trying to decipher whose voice it was as a thousand little dancing imps sang in the dark.

Shamus could hear her coming up the stairs, and for a moment, when she entered the room, he thought Pruty had suffered a miracle.

He sat with Gertie all night. Neither spoke. But when dawn was breaking, when light finally came to their little house, Gertie said: "Oh, my soul, Papa—oh, my soul."

The next afternoon he telephoned Heatherington, who said yes—of course he was expecting his call. It would simply be a matter of filing the right papers, and having the right mix of drugs available—

But Shamus said, "Don't ever come near her again—never look her way again—never offer your services again, or you will have to deal with me." Then, remembering his manners, he added, "Sir."

Then he ironed his shirt and mended his pants, and shined his shoes, and got ready to go to the police. Still, he was too upset to go that day. He sat by the Christmas tree with his head down, with his hat in his hand, staring at the floor.

"Papa, we can't wait any longer. We will go tomorrow," Gertie said.

"Yes—tomorrow—Pruty will come with us—from now on I will not leave her side."

"Papa," Pruty said, "I know you are sorry—and new days will follow the old."

That night, as Pruty slept, she had the last dream she would ever have of Dr. Heatherington. She looked at him as he took her temperature, and she told him to go away—that she was going out—for a moment she flew somewhere—and then it was a boy with her, and she ate a cookie—and sat on a fence. Then another boy whom she had once seen at the exhibition was walking a draft horse. She remembered him, and he came over to her. He seemed to fly toward her at will.

She looked at his strong, naked chest, the hair on his belly down near his leather belt, and in her dream his hands were on her bum, feeling it. She went to take his hand away, but he said, "It is time. Yes, it's time—"

And in her dream the young, strong boy took off her top, felt her breasts, and she felt her panties coming down, and she had an orgasm. In fact, as strange as it seemed, she had never had an orgasm before. And it was prolonged. It went on, and it lasted and lasted, until she gave a soft, grateful moan. Then he disappeared, and a woman said, "Did you have a ticket to ride?"

"I most certainly did," she said.

When she woke, it was just turning light. A new snow was falling across the barren field.

She lay still and reflected upon all of this. That never before had God given her such a deep moment of pleasure. Besides, today there was no pain.

No, she would not go to sleep. Not yet. She would save Jamie Musselman.

Life would be worth it after all.

IT WAS THE NIGHT VIVIAN HAD TO DELIVER THE MONEY. Who would come with her? All day she was frightened of having to meet and speak to this priest. What would he say? He would be angry. He would hate her.

Someone had to come with her.

Yes, her husband would. She had relied on him for years. She asked Weaver too. She asked him humbly—and with hope in her eyes. It was the hope that he looked at, and then at the tablecloth, and he picked at it with his index finger.

"Of course—I won't allow you to go alone," he said. "Dad and I wouldn't allow you to go alone. You understand, Mom, we would never allow you to go alone."

"That is good, Weaver, because we never know how those kinds of people might react—you know, I was always concerned about people like that—and how they might react—how do people like that—you know, react to people like me."

"Why?"

"Because—people like me are out to change the world."

He was startled by this and smiled at it.

"Yes—change the world—we all want to."

He finally told her that he believed it was women who would

save the world. That he had thought that—not because of anything else but because of Pruty. And Little Nin.

He looked up at her quickly, and his eyes suddenly showed all his years of sorrow.

"Little Nin in fact changed the world," Weaver said, "—and Pruty too. The little crippled girl changed the world. Little Nin with her last breath changed the world."

"I don't understand you," she said. "I never understood my son—I never understood my own son. There are a thousand Little Nins. If one aborted a thousand Little Nins, there would always be a thousand more."

"But don't you see—that is not at all true—she had the gift that is given to the children of God," he said, for the first time expressing himself. "All people everywhere are born to be singular and precious, and none of your theories will ever change that—and neither will the theories I once believed in."

He opened the paper bag he had his lunch in when he was in his room and saw the cucumber he had not eaten. He looked into the paper bag like she remembered he did as a little boy. Then, after a bite of a cucumber, he continued. "Pruty struggles. She really does. Yes—I was at her place for my walk. Pruty told me she is going to the police with her father and Gertie. Her father spoke about a robin—and how the robin changed his life—or in fact how his life was changed when he first hyped a horse up on gunpowder during a horse haul. He told me that things are going to be revealed—and he cannot stop them. I am sorry, but it involves me. Yes, Mother—it involves me. They will go to the police, and I will have to go away."

"Why? In what way would it ever involve you?"

"Because I am human—and nothing human is alien to me—and I took a chance—I one night took a chance—a stupid chance, and I failed—and nothing can be put back. Dad knows—yes, Orlif knows, and he must be in agony."

She gave a start. "I do not know Pruty very well—"

"But you see, Mom—if you did, your life too might have been changed by a girl who has hardly ever read a book—and I have read everyone from Hesse to Vonnegut and found no answer better than hers."

Weaver had once, not long ago, told Pruty of being left alone, and sometimes, on summer afternoons on the streets of Halifax, he wanted to die, and Pruty had said, "But I knew, Weaver—I knew—I knew the first night I met you—I knew when we went that long-ago day to the park. But Weaver, come to me whenever you wish—for I am someone who suffers too."

"Perhaps it is too late?" Weaver had said.

"Oh, my soul." Pruty had laughed. "Oh, my soul—it is never too late—ask our Virgin Mary and see what she says about it all—and if she didn't know this moment would come. That everything we do and all that is done is known in the universe."

"What if I don't believe in her—"

"But Weaver de Speck—Weaver de Speck—what if she believes in you?"

And that was when he was baptized.

Later that night, the three of them, all noted for their learning, their attributes and understanding—their neighbours looking at them from afar as superior in so many ways—left the house to pay the money to the little church. Orlif wore his long coat and his big yellow mittens. Vivian her long coat and long grey skirt. Weaver his short winter coat and black leather gloves.

The apology had to come from Vivian herself, though she was scared. And at this moment, as they got into the car, Weaver realized she had always been scared—of being found out. He didn't know why.

But Pruty had told him, after the death of Little Nin, that in the whole world a person was only frightened of one thing. "In all the world, people are only frightened of one thing, Weaver."

"And what is that, Pruty?" he had asked.

"Why, Weaver—don't you know? Of not loving enough."

So, when they arrived at the little parish centre, it took a long time to convince Vivian to get out of the car, because she was terribly frightened.

And since this family was always hers, they simply waited in silence on her to open the car door. She had been for years the representative, the bold and radical symbol, of them all.

They heard the wind blowing, and the car rocked slightly. She lighted a cigarette and waited. Then she butted it in the ashtray and looked behind her to where Weaver sat. There was another moment of silence.

Finally, they heard the door open, and she stepped out.

They followed her over the small snow ruts of other cars and entered the parish hall. The place was half-full of children doing reconciliation for their communion. Small booklets had been placed upon tables, lights flickered from the tree.

There was Mrs. Samuel and her son, and Father Leo and a nun, and eight or nine parents. A group of children all sitting or standing or running.

Everyone was surprised when the three arrived—that strange young man who had so much education, and his father a professor at the college, and Vivian—that stern, imposing woman who knew so much about life that people were frightened to talk to her because she had always seemed to insult them. Who was so imposing that once, Winnifred White got so flustered, she curtsied when she saw her. Vivian didn't know of the enormous impression she had made on these humble people, who had only wanted her to like them.

They had no idea Vivian was coming this night—this cold night—to pay a debt. Some didn't know that she was the one who had broken the stained glass window of Christ on the Cross. Nor would most ever know why she had broken it. And more startling, hardly anyone held it against her.

All that Mrs. Samuel had said was that the woman "was upset."

And they all said, "Come in—we are having tea—and the children are about to sing."

The three of them stood at the door, still huddled together—three lost people, all hoping in some way to be saved. Perhaps not even knowing, until now, that they wished to be.

And when the parents asked her to sit, and have tea, and listen to the children, and one of the men stood to pull out a chair for her, she blushed such a deep crimson, her face was almost purple, and none there chose to notice. A little girl's mother ran to get them tea and shortcakes, and all of them pretended they hadn't seen the white envelope with the money inside.

HOWEVER, THERE IS ALWAYS A REAL INVESTIGATION, AND it goes on underneath—subliminally or otherwise—and sometimes is never considered until it comes in full force or form to the surface.

Phyliss Matters, who had been taken off as lead in the investigation years before and had never been taken seriously, told her new dear friend Mickey Bowels that she was not done with anything.

So she and Bowels began to collect bits of information—bit by bit—and Bowels discovered that Weaver de Speck and Beal knew each other, and left shortly after the murder. Enough people at the Blackhorse had seen Weaver there and had seen them together in the park with Little Nin.

Phyliss discovered that everyone was wrong about almost everything. Dannielle, who was now engaged to a spineless man from her work and delighted by how many had turned against Gertie, might have been the weather vane of all error as she strode along the sidewalk, enthralled at all that had occurred, ready to gossip and tell and tattle at all turns.

The stabbing of Jamie Musselman exposed much of the worry. At his trial, the prosecutor had said that there was motive and opportunity, and boldly had turned to Gertie herself (yes, she was beautiful, and no man could simply say he was not interested).

Then he walked back to his chair looking both unapologetic and distraught. Now, however, with the stabbing, it became of some importance whether or not he and the court was right.

The strange death of Little Nin also began to bring it all home to Phyliss, especially after what her new friend Bowels told her.

That is, he had told Phyliss about what Little Nin had said to him that day in his store.

So when she drove down on that cold day to the roadway where Orlif had dragged the suitcase, she walked all the way back to the churchyard along Little Hackett Brook—and there near the trees by the graveyard she found Little Nin's phone. Someone had tried to throw it into the water, but it had landed in the mud on the side of the bank.

She roped the area off—closed the gate to the graveyard itself and asked for impressions to be made of anything—footprints, handprints—that might be found from the back of Arron Brook all the way to Little Hackett.

She then had a tech expert at the RCMP's forensic department in Fredericton clean the phone, and ten days later (for it took time to get the phone to work) dialed the last number Nin had called, and Marsha—the girl who said she had hidden messages under a rock, the girl she had interviewed in school long ago, when all of this had first happened—answered.

So, Phyliss drove up to see Marsha. Marsha welcomed her, again spoke of these events she was involved in, her eyes half-closed as if in slumber and her left hand tapping the armrest of the chair. She said she had premonitions, and the secret service had asked not only for her services but her presence.

Detective Matters listened patiently to this hour-long regale and nodded and shook her head at all the wondrous things Marsha said; and then had one question—and this question had to be answered.

And the question was: "Who was with you when you received that phone call? Who went to pick Little Nin up and came back to you and said they couldn't find her anywhere?"

"What do you mean?" Marsha asked.

"I mean, I want you to tell me who was with you—and who went to collect Little Nin at the church."

Phyliss Matters, of course, already suspected.

The same fellow whose boot prints were in the wet soil, though he had gone to great lengths to eradicate them, who had thrown her phone thinking it would not be found, and who put Little Nin naked into the stolen suitcase. The man who, by indicating how the suitcase had been dragged, had been hoping to place the body in the church vestry to implicate Father Benjamin—but who couldn't because Father Benjamin was, at that moment, returning from giving last rites on the reserve, his car lights now shining on the very door within which the man was hoping to hide his crime.

So, the man had to think of somewhere else. And he took the suitcase across the road to Hackett Brook, threw the phone away, and the suitcase managed to make its journey toward Arron Brook that next afternoon.

That this had brought disgrace to Father Benjamin, who was left high and dry in a cardboard box when he was a child of four—found with his other siblings with a cup of water, and a stale piece of bread, and a rat for luck, which was placed in the box with them but had eaten the bread and nibbled on one of the children—and, Phyliss continued, "You in your folly wish to make disgrace of him—who came here to a land of snowdrifts and blind whiteouts to give comfort to parishioners because Mother Teresa told him to go and serve the Lord? And he listened to their complaints about poverty from people who had never gone a day without food? Is that who you wish to destroy? No, I am not a Catholic and do not pretend to be—and had not been in a Catholic church until investigating this crime—but I know that he is no killer!

"So, who was with you? For some have already declared the church should be burned—and in fact have broken a stained glass window worth twelve thousand dollars!"

The actual murderer dragged the suitcase into the woods and deposited it into Little Hackett Brook. Then, as his boot marks did suggest, he ran to his car parked by Chase's Hollow, just down the road from the little place where Vivian and Orlif had their dark and foreboding house.

Who was that man? Phyliss Matters asked. She had discovered all of this without much trouble and within a few days of the phone being returned.

The case of Jamie Musselman had almost cost her her sanity, and did cost her her marriage. And Bowels was the first man she had become close to since then.

So, she was more than angry about it all. It was something that had torn the River apart.

And she said perhaps the soothsayer Marsha would tell her who was with her when the phone call came, so she would not be charged as an accomplice to murder, herself.

Marsha looked flabbergasted and started to cry and called for her mother, who said: "You leave that poor child, who has done nothing to anyone, alone."

So let us go back a little way. Just a few afternoons, to the last part of the interview with Marsha.

Who was with Marsha when the phone call came—that is what Detective Matters demanded to know. She had spoken to Mickey Bowels about it, and for the first time they both realized both cases could be linked, and all of this might have happened in a different way. In fact, the dislike of young Musselman could be traced back to high school. For Jamie was a target—alone in a strange town.

As we know, Marsha was terribly ecstatic in her long dress, her white face bodacious and her hands bedecked with rings. She looked at her purple-painted fingernails and sighed, as if this was a tremendous bother for someone who had already been interviewed by the Moncton *Times*.

"I knew you'd come," she said to Phyliss Matters when Phyliss had first arrived.

"You did?"

"Yes—sit down, please—I only have a moment."

"You only have a moment?"

"Usually at this time of day I am meditating—"

"Of course—I will only keep you a moment."

So Marsha did talk on and on, and finally, with grand imperiousness, asked, "Well then—what is it you wish?"

"I have one question—who was that man who was with you when you received the phone call?"

As we now know, after Marsha became upset, her mother came into the room to protect her, but Phyliss Matters said quite emphatically, "These questions will be answered here or down at the station. Who was with you?"

By this time, Phyliss Matters already knew.

It was the man who had come to the house and had arrested Jamie Musselman—someone who, with Marsha, had once used this crime to make a name for himself in our school, and who had become a police officer.

Cappy Manse—the boy who bullied Jamie Musselman for weeks after the death of his father, who had driven his scooter by the boy as he walked to school and shouted, "How's the murderer this morning?"

And also bullied him in the washroom, and broke one of Musselman's fingers in the altercation. And sat behind him in class and whispered that Jamie had no right to be here, and spoke about his mother in foul terms, *Ho di ho ho.*

Cappy or Capshaw (as was his name) went to Holland College after the boy had gone away to Nova Scotia—and Cappy couldn't stand learning and hated people who thought they knew, and became a policeman and drove his squad car through the bleak streets and stopped at the curling club and visited Gertie—and spoke to her of love; he was sure she wanted him with his uniform and his cap.

But before that happened, oh, some nights when Little Nin was alone and had nowhere to go, he put her in a cell—and there, at two in the morning when all was quiet, he did what he wanted with her—because it was only Little Nin, and he could do so. And he did it so many times, too—and at first he believed it would never be known.

"Take off your clothes, I am going to search you," he said to Little Nin one night when she was asleep in the third cell. "Come on, now—I don't have all night—yes, the panties too—I don't have all night."

He was at Marsha's when the phone call came.

"I have something to tell you—and no one else knows—I have to tell," Nin said. "And I want to talk to the police."

"Come and tell me," Marsha said.

Cappy believed she would tell about those long-ago nights.

So he drove downriver to see her—to ask her to be calm—to tell her she couldn't speak of those moments in the jail cell.

He told her he was Constable Capshaw Manse and she had better be smart.

He drove the last hundred yards with his lights out, walked the last three hundred yards, and saw her on the side of the lane.

Her sneakers glowed as she walked, and she had been to confession.

He took his flashlight and shone it in her face.

"What are you doing?" he asked her. He said he would give her a drive to the station and she could tell him what it was she knew.

"No, thank you," she said.

He told her he would arrest her if she didn't smarten up.

She tried to back up. She backed up all the way to the gravestone of her ancestor she didn't know about.

And she put her arm up to deflect the glow of the flashlight—but he grabbed her arm, and then he grabbed the beads Father Benjamin had given her—because she was foolish enough to hold the beads up to him, saying, "Go away, Mr. Monster."

Mr. Monster is what she had called him those nights he told her to take down her panties and lie on the cot.

She struggled, holding up the beads, and he hit her with his flashlight. He didn't mean to—but from the moment he had taunted Jamie Musselman, from that moment, this must happen.

And he had worn his police-issue boots to the crime. And he had dropped the police-issue flashlight when he put her naked body in the suitcase.

So, how long did it take Detective Phyliss Matters to know it was a policeman and not Father Benjamin, and to take Father Benjamin, whom the crowd was railing against, into protective custody?

Two hours.

But things had to proceed, and as they did, it took time. It took more than a week for the phone to come back; another week to get her ducks in order.

And this was when Vivian took it upon herself to throw the stones.

"A statement will be made," Phyliss Matters said a day before Shamus and his daughters drove to the police station, buffeted by the great sky and blasts of wind. She had placed Father Benjamin in protective custody days before.

She took her statement from Marsha and left the house without saying goodbye.

She telephoned Capshaw Manse and told him that though it was confidential, she had vital information about the case.

Capshaw Manse came to work at ten the next morning, ready to be of assistance, and said the suitcase proved the priest's involvement in the crime.

He went into the lock-up and stared at the little priest and said, "Boy I'd love to get into that cell with you, Father Benjamin—you know she wasn't much, was she—but she was still a human being."

He was freshly shaved, his hair was brushed back, his fingernails had been washed and clipped, he smelled of strong aftershave, and the only thing one might notice was the scratch mark on his chin.

For a few hours nothing happened in that police station. The computers were on, the phone rang, police officers spoke to one another of various things.

Then, at two that afternoon, Detective Matters asked to see Constable Capshaw Manse.

At first, she was very conciliatory about Little Nin, and how he knew her—how he must be himself grieving—and then she spoke of Marsha and how she had made a name for herself all about town over the years because of this case. And Cappy Manse said: "How so, Phyliss my love—how so?" And he was smiling—his teeth were so very white, and he wore too much aftershave. He loved to flirt with her, and he had said to his fellow officers, "Someday I'll have her stripped off and put the blocks to her."

As he was smiling and flirting with her now, she said, "So, when you went to pick up Little Nin—where did you meet her?"

"Me?" he said. "I wasn't there."

"But we have Marsha's statement that you went to pick up Little Nin."

"But I couldn't find her, Phyliss dear."

Then Detective Matters showed him his flashlight, confiscated his boots and had a junior officer, Felica Maltby, swab his mouth for DNA.

She herself didn't bother to stay in the room.

Later that day, when the priest Father Benjamin was let go, Beal went to him and asked if Little Nin was happy.

"Yes, she was happy, at least in one way—she loved you."

It became known that she had said, "Go away, Mr. Monster," and held up her beads to protect herself.

"Go away, Mr. Monster."

And Beal was not there to protect her.

He could not get that plea, "Go away, Mr. Monster," out of his mind. He put his hands over his ears and sat in his room—he was back in one room.

When he thought of Little Nin, he thought of her coming home and shouting, "He said you could have the job—he did! And I told him—I did, I did—I told him I loved you—okay, is that okay to tell people that?"

He thought of his mother waiting on the bank overlooking the ships, and the sailor from long ago who paid her five dollars and went back to Liverpool. That is what his birth was worth—five dollars. While Weaver's birth was worth 2.7 million.

It wasn't until the death of Little Nin that he began to realize it. That they weren't much different after all—and perhaps not even loved, but by Little Nin and Pruty.

"Go away, Mr. Monster" haunted him, troubled him, and he finally did what Father Benjamin suggested he do: In order to honour Little Nin and free Jamie Musselman, he turned himself in. He didn't even mean to do that—he just went to the police station to pick up Nin's belongings. They were in a plastic bag—some lipstick, six dollars, a small red hairbrush. They were taken out and put on the counter. With them was the old red coat and knitted hat.

Looking at the hat, he saw Nin's name that he had stitched into it so she wouldn't lose it.

He asked to see Phyliss Matters. Nin's cellphone would be kept as evidence.

"I am sorry for Little Nin—I am very sorry for it all," Detective Matters told him, holding his hand, as she often did with men she interviewed.

Those were the kindest things said to him since Little Nin had died.

When he was sent to prison, Beal never wore the cross given to him by Father Benjamin. It wasn't because he didn't believe; he didn't feel worthy enough to do so, now he knew about those nights in the jail cell when he wasn't there to protect her.

In prison he was sent the book Little Nin had of Dylan Thomas's poems. And as he read "And death shall have no dominion," he came across a note Nin had written in the margin: "Oh, I wish my love could have known Jamie Musselman, who wanted to read these poems to me—think if that day Jamie wasn't kept in after school. Think if Mr. Beal had met him. It may have changed all our lives."

SHAMUS NEVER SPOKE ABOUT WEAVER—ONLY ABOUT himself.

"I am a plague upon humanity," was how he started off, and then it got worse—until finally Pruty and Gertie were bawling, both hugging him desperately and telling him to stop calling himself a plague.

It was all over the news then. Gavin was interviewed on national TV.

"Was your friend Weaver de Speck involved?"

"Oh, I doubt it very much," Gavin said, though having come to town three times over the last two years, having tracked it, back and back, in secret, he knew he was lying.

Vivian came to Weaver de Speck. She was both sick and old. Her breath was raspy, and she smiled kindly, hopefully.

"I don't care about anything now—I want to take care of you." And she smiled as if saying that she wanted to make everything up to him.

"Oh, I know," he said. "Don't say any more—nothing matters about it now. Only—"

"Only what?"

He paused. "Only I wish you were happy."

He had attended her meetings when young—she took him to too many—and he remembered them all.

Yes, he had looked at Gertie through the window, but he had never in his life been with a girl. He had confessed that to Pruty not long ago: "I looked at your sister through a window."

"You did?"

"Yes, Pruty—I did, when she was naked—I looked at her."

"Well," Pruty said, "what man wouldn't, Weaver? What man in their right mind wouldn't?"

"But I hate myself—why do I?"

"Because you don't know yourself as well as I know you."

"I don't understand?"

"Well, I love you. So there you go."

All his life, it seemed his mother had wanted him to hate the right person—and that person turned out to be himself.

He now looked at her. Orlif had given up his chance at tenure, and they went to many places in Europe. Weaver de Speck hardly remembered it—he was too young—except he remembered sitting on their trunk in a train station at night, wearing a cap.

Weaver sat in his room listening to the reports on the radio coming from CBC, and later in the day on television, where they showed a picture of Jamie Musselman as a boy and a picture of Colonel Musselman's wife, Teresa. Then a picture of Mr. Leonard Beal, a picture of Shamus McDow, and suddenly—suddenly—a picture of himself, Weaver de Speck.

Then he got a call—it was from Pruty—she had been calling him for over an hour, but his phone had been turned off.

"I seen your picture," she said. "Come to see me. I will be with you."

"Why?"

"You were left alone, and I don't want you to be left alone anymore. Either does Gertie and either does Papa. They kept Papa, and Gertie is with him. So, I am alone."

He told her he had a present for her—and she would certainly be surprised.

He was planning to cross through Arron by the pathways Pruty had once shown him. His present for her was the only present he had bought in a long time. He had picked it up at the bookstore in town. He had only gone in there because it was freezing cold one snowy afternoon. But it was a book called *Studies on the Book of Revelation* by some priest over a century before.

So, he had wrapped it in white ribbon for Pruty. And he waited until dark to leave.

Weaver left on Christmas Eve. No one knew where. Both his parents begged him not to go out into the freezing night.

"You will be okay. I will be by your side," Orlif said.

Vivian told him they would get a good firm to represent him—people she knew who had defended her long ago.

"I don't want to be defended," he said.

Orlif tried to hold him, but he tossed Orlif aside. Then he picked his father up and kissed him and held him for a long time.

He turned and smiled and kissed his mother as well.

Weaver was quite strong. He could have been a mason, which is what he had wanted to be when a boy and he watched an old man laying brick across the street from his house. But his mother had never allowed for a boy—and it seemed less and less that Canada wanted a boy. This is now what Orlif understood as they watched him vanish.

"I am sorry," Orlif called, "I am sorry."

But the sound of the wind interrupted his call.

That is, the fog and gale seemed to cover Weaver as if he never existed, as if all the love he had for them they had squandered. Just as they had squandered the 2.7 million they had charged for his life.

It had started to snow hours before—and now the snow was deep.

They searched the wood all along Arron Brook; they followed his tracks in the snow until they disappeared.

Weaver remembered Little Nin smiling at him when he went to the apartment.

"Oh, hello," she said. "It's Mr. De Speck. We're safe."

And now he was running away in the snow.

Vivian did not understand how her son loved and listened to her, in quiet agony, those years past. And believed in her like some Rock of Gibraltar that couldn't be washed away.

And now he was leaving with a book to give to Pruty because he was the one who was lost. He had told Pruty he would take her to midnight mass.

"Really?"

"Sure—I've done worse," he had said.

The snow was deep, and the wind was harsh and grated the tops of trees. And soon he was disoriented. He didn't know how many twists and turns the greater Arron Brook had. He had not known the woods or streams at all. Pruty knew them and took him there one summer day, him pushing her along, and showed him the pathway to the blueberry field and the stream where she caught a trout.

"One trout, Weaver, that's all I ever got—but still, it was a trout."

"Thank you so much," he had said. He told her that day that once, long ago, he had a fishing rod he had saved up for, and waited all summer for his dad to take him to a stream.

Little Pruty—how terrible her suffering—and yet, he had made her suffer more.

Tonight, the gale wind caused a moose to walk beside him and then pass on. He looked at its great hide as it swept by, and he was frightened of some enormity of circumstance he didn't understand.

He had been at Pruty's the night they had put up the tree. Shamus had lifted her up to put on the four bulbs and the star, and Pruty had said, "Oh, Weaver, would you like to put on the star?"

And the lights came on and the tree was lit. And he realized now this was Pruty's answer. It was the only way she could answer anyone about medically assisted suicide. Or as she said to him, "They want me to cash in my chips."

And then she said, her hands shaking, "Oh, Weaver, would you like to put on the star?"

And now, through the wind and snow, the blistering gale, there was a lone star above him.

"Come and see me," Pruty had said. "We will go to midnight mass, you will take communion, and you'll never be alone no more."

Dannielle was now no longer talking. This Christmas Eve, a grand guilt had come over her when she heard what actually had happened. The news had come on, and she was silent.

All Dannielle's actions, from the moment she met Gertie, the moment Shamus came for money—the moment she tormented the girl and Bowels—the moment she said Jamie had murdered, the moment she got screwed by her boss—all of this was the flotsam of the town.

Father Benjamin was preparing for midnight mass and he would not comment. He would not say anything, but he would welcome the birth of Christ.

And some seven miles away, Weaver ran in the dark, with the filthy bills now stuffed in his coat pocket and his scarf blowing behind him. He had meant to get to Load Road and see Pruty, but he was far away from that. He needed to see Pruty—because—why? Because he was going to tell her he didn't mean it—he did not mean it at all. He was going to ask forgiveness. Yes, he was determined to give her the present he bought.

From overhead, when he came into the last field before Toomey's quarry, he could be seen walking in the opposite direction.

It was now minus fourteen and the wind scattered the snow, and his boots were filled. If he could see Pruty, then he would go to the police. He hadn't taken the money to run away, as poor Orlif thought. He had taken the money to give to Detective Matters.

Of course, it was simple—he wanted to be held by Pruty—he wanted her to hold him and forgive him.

He should have known that she already had.

He picked up snow and put it in his mouth. He came to the crossroads. Two paths did diverge. He went to the right; it was overgrown. He walked on, and branches slashed his face. He stopped and listened to the swish in the wind. Far away—far away he could hear something—he did not know what.

*So, this is the woods,* he thought. *It's a shame I know so little about it.*

He turned and crossed the upper stretch of Little Hackett and followed along a way—until he saw an opening in the trees. There was a light of the church across the way. He didn't know there was a deep gorge between.

And as he moved into the clearing, there was a gentle slope, then a slight uphill struggle. It seemed very familiar, so he believed he was on the right path.

And then, with a sudden humility filling him, he softly, very softly, called Pruty's name, whispered he loved her more than he ever loved anyone, and took another step.

He fell from the very place Shamus did. He fell, however, at the most dangerous angle.

If he had taken the path to the left, he would have been on the Load Road in behind Pruty's little house in ten minutes. The path where he had chanced to see Gertie in the window those nights.

Vivian was out looking for him about this time, her nose running, her eyes filled with tears, her boots filled with snow, her pants soaking wet, her hat pulled down. When she stared at Orlif, she saw a sad, elderly man wearing his checked cap with its earflaps and decided to love him more. And now she walked from one pathway to the other and, ending up at Pruty's, she said, "Pruty, do you know where he is?"

"I am sorry," little Pruty said. "I am not sure."

"He said he was going to go to mass—with you," Orlif said.

"Yes, but—he never came."

"Pruty, I will give you anything if you help us find him. We will help him—he needs our help—he always needed our help."

"Bring the toboggan around, I will go. I have to leave a note for Gertie—she is on her way home. So I will leave a big note and then away we go."

"But maybe you are in too much pain," Vivian said, and she was startled and crying and her jacket was covered in snow.

"No—I am not—and it is no matter—I will go."

They helped her dress and then they left into the night—travelling along Load Road, Orlif pulling her in the toboggan, the wind blowing down across her small pink gloves, her shouting, "To the right, Sir Orlif," "To the left, Sir Orlif," toward the direction of Pattern Cliff.

Then Pruty said, quite eagerly, "He wanted to come to me to be safe—but in the darkness he might have turned the wrong way."

WHEN JAMIE WAS RELEASED FROM HOSPITAL, HE DID NOT go back to prison. He went home. But he had lost a kidney and had to convalesce for some time. Gertie moved Pruty in with them.

It was startling to see most of their names on television.

Jamie took a job stocking shelves at Sobeys grocery store. He gave advice to professors who wrote him. He studied on his own and supply-taught at the high school. He studied marine biology and made model airplanes and gave lectures at the university. He walked with a cane. He remained an agnostic.

Sometimes, he would go away—to Iceland or Greenland, doing research—and Gertie would go with him.

He was good friends with Orlif Speck. Orlif tried to write, but didn't seem able to put down on paper what had happened to him. Often, he was seen sitting on the veranda of the great house waiting for his friend Jamie Musselman.

When Vivian took sick with fourth stage lung cancer, Gertie and Pruty demanded she be moved into the big house in town, where they took care of her—where Dr. Penny visited when she could. Jamie took her for rides that last summer in his canoe, and they would travel down past Toomey's quarry in the twilight, the sound of Jamie's paddle in the soft, dark currents, and Vivian would say, "Oh, this is so delicious—I wish I had done this many times before. But you see, I got so busy and life got in the way. Yes, I got busy and life got in the way."

There was a famous Supreme Court judge in the United States Vivian had always admired, and lo and behold, Gertie and Pruty worked and wrote and made phone calls until this woman sent Vivian a card, and Vivian held it for hours.

And Pruty sat with her and listened to her explain how she followed this great woman's career, and Pruty kept saying, "Oh, Ms. Speck—a card from that woman judge—you should be so very proud."

"Yes, I am a little bit," Vivian said, smiling slightly, but she hardly had the energy to open her eyes.

Orlif wept like a child when she died.

JAMIE HAD A SAILBOAT AND THEY TRAVELLED DOWN TO Boston and New York, where in the summer afternoons they visited the museums and galleries, Jamie carrying Pruty on his back.

Orlif and he spoke of Cicero and Seneca, of Hemingway and Fitzgerald, and got in arguments about ethics.

"If Seneca was a great man, he wouldn't have sued Boudica," Jamie maintained.

They never mentioned the murder of his father. But sometimes, on seeing something special, Orlif would take a picture and, forgetting, say, "Oh, I want to show this to Weaver—he would be so pleased."

Gertie organized many family outings and her and Jamie's travel, helped with charities and curled in the winter. So, it was a life in a small town. So it was with that they were gifted with their child, Nin, in 2019.

In July of 2019, Pruty and Orlif were married. Shamus was released from jail.

Many a day Shamus did not realize where he was. His most common comment was "I'm flabbergasted."

No one knew why he was flabbergasted. Once, Orlif asked him and he said, "Because I'm forgiven."

On other days, he would walk behind Jamie, asking him if he wanted a kidney.

Pruty struggled with pain, but many days were much better than others. And a few days a week she had no pain at all. Her orgasms when she had them were prolonged ecstasy, as if God was giving her a small treasure to keep as her own.

In fact, she gave up most doctors and became in a way her own doctor, and every night she had a large marijuana cookie and a solid drink of gin. Sometimes you could hear her sing.

She doted on her niece and spent most of her pension buying the child clothes, and had Orlif read to her Euripides and other "old fellows." She got in arguments with the government and city council, and travelled on her motorized wheelchair up one street and down the other, so you might see her anywhere. She kept a garden and placed flowers on Weaver's grave and had Orlif drive her there three or four times a year. She had the book on Revelation that Weaver had bought for her and quoted at the grave the passage where Christ said if one knocked, he would dine with them. She often read from Revelation 21:4—from one of the pages Weaver had burned:

> *And God shall wipe away all tears from their eyes; and there shall be no more death, neither sorrow, nor crying, neither shall there be any more pain; for the former things are passed away.*

FATHER BENJAMIN WAS TRANSFERRED TO NOVA SCOTIA. Many of our Catholic churches had closed because of vile scandal and sin that priests were actually responsible for and our bishops had tried to hide. The churches out west began to be burned, and our government seemed to be delighted by this, as were many of our most forward-thinking writers.

Gavin himself wrote a book that would be published in May of 2020. In that book, the prosecutor denied he had made any mistake at all. In fact, he said he believed Jamie could easily have been involved. But Gavin did say that the prosecutor had in fact coveted the fiancée of Jamie Musselman.

Mr. Beal died quite suddenly, in his cell, in his sleep. It was a stroke, and he was only forty-three.

Bowels and Phyliss Matters married. Sometimes they played bridge with Gertie and Orlif—Jamie did not play. Gertie became a fine bridge player and went on tournaments to various parts of the province.

"A master," Pruty said, "at knowing who holds the cards!"

Bowels became a long-term member of our city council.

Dannielle is divorced and no longer works at Lounsbury's.

## ACKNOWLEDGEMENTS

I would like to thank my editor, Ward Hawkes, and my copyeditor, John Sweet. There are many others, most importantly my wife, Peggy, who was with me when no one else was, stayed with me when no one else would, cared for me when no one else did, believed in me when the world turned its back, bore the burden of my life when she didn't need to do so. I bring you lilacs from our field, I kneel before you.